MR MONK ON PATROL

Please return on or before the latest date above.
You can renew online at *www.kent.gov.uk/libs*
or by telephone 08458 247 200

CUSTOMER SERVICE EXCELLENCE

Libraries & Archives

00884\DTP\RN\07.07   LIB 7

MR MONK ON
PATROL

Lee Goldberg

CHIVERS

British Library Cataloguing in Publication Data available

This Large Print edition published by AudioGO Ltd, Bath, 2012.
Published by arrangement with The Berkley Publishing Group, a division of Penguin Group (USA) Inc.

U.K.   Hardcover   ISBN   978 1 4713 0678 5
U.K.   Softcover   ISBN   978 1 4713 0679 2

Printed and bound in Great Britain by
MPG Books Group Limited

To Valerie and Madison

AUTHOR'S NOTE AND ACKNOWLEDGMENTS

The TV series *Monk* was set in San Francisco, shot in Los Angeles, and written in Summit, New Jersey, where my friend Andy Breckman, the creator of the show, actually lives. I also spent some time there over the years, plotting the stories for my *Monk* episodes with Andy and his incredibly talented writing staff.

A significant portion of *Mr. Monk on Patrol* is set in a place called Summit, New Jersey . . . but the town that I've depicted, while it bears some passing resemblance to the real place, is entirely fictional. I did this because I'm a lazy writer and wanted to take enormous creative liberties with Summit's geography and political structure.

And I did.

Any parallels between what I've written and any real people, places, or institutions in Summit are entirely unintentional, accidental, and coincidental. I really like Summit and would like to be able to go back and visit Andy without being tarred and feathered.

I'd like to thank Andy and his brother, David, as well as the usual suspects — Kerry Donovan, Gina Maccoby, and Dr. D. P. Lyle — for their support and enthusiasm during the writing of this book.

I look forward to hearing from you at www .leegoldberg.com.

CHAPTER ONE:
MR. MONK
AND THE OPEN HOUSE

The Victorian house at the corner of Cole and Hayes streets was listed for sale at two million dollars, which was a fair price considering it was newly remodeled, immaculately maintained, and only a short walk from the University of San Francisco, Golden Gate Park, and Haight-Ashbury. However, it was going to sell for a lot less than the asking price, if it ever sold at all. I wasn't a real estate expert, like the dead woman on the entry hall floor, but I knew that murder always brought down property values.

The dead Realtor's name was Rebecca Baylin. She was twenty-seven years old, shirtless, and her head was caved in. Ordinarily, Adrian Monk wouldn't be able to look at a topless woman, but there he was, framing the scene between his hands and tipping his head from side to side to examine her from different angles.

Monk would be repulsed by someone with a bit of lettuce stuck between his teeth, or a missing button on her shirt, or a single pierced ear, or a zit on someone's chin, and yet he had no qualms about staring at all manner of horrific violence perpetrated on the human body.

It made no sense to me, but then again, there was a lot I didn't understand about my obsessive-compulsive boss, even after all my years as his underpaid and overworked assistant, agent, driver, shopper, researcher, publicist, and all-around emotional punching bag.

I'll make a guess, though. Maybe the reason he could look at Rebecca Baylin was that her nakedness was negated by her lifelessness. He didn't see her as a woman anymore, or even as a person. She'd become something that was out of place, a disorder that had to be made orderly, a mess that had to be cleaned up, a question that had to be answered. He wouldn't be able to rest — and by extension neither would I — until he'd figured out what had happened to her, caught her killer, and restored the balance that had been disrupted by her murder.

And I knew that Monk would. He always did.

This was a fact that Captain Leland

Stottlemeyer had come to rely upon. It was why Stottlemeyer fought countless political battles to employ Monk as a consultant. It was why he found the patience to tolerate and forgive all of Monk's aggravating eccentricities. And it was why he called us down to that open house on that foggy Saturday morning to meet with him and Lieutenant Amy Devlin.

"This home was Baylin's listing," Devlin said. "She was supposed to host an open house here this morning. A couple came by at ten a.m. to see the place, found the door unlocked, and walked in on this."

Devlin gestured to the body on the floor.

"We've got the couple sitting in the back-seat of a black-and-white if you'd like to ask them a few questions," the captain said, standing beside me and chewing on a toothpick, the tip tickling the hairs of his bushy mustache as he watched Monk work. Stottlemeyer wore a wrinkled off-the-rack suit and a tie that had gone out of style with disco.

"That's not necessary," Monk said. "You can send them home. They didn't do it."

"How do you know?" Devlin stood across from us. She had short black hair that looked like she'd had her gardener trim it with a weed whacker, and she wore faded

11

jeans and a gray hoodie under a leather jacket.

"It's obvious from the rigor mortis and other physical indications that she's been dead for at least eight hours."

"That doesn't mean they didn't kill her last night and then come back this morning so they could discover the body and rule themselves out as suspects," Devlin said.

She watched Monk with obvious impatience, her hands on her hips, parting her jacket to reveal the badge and gun that were clipped on her belt, not that there was anyone around at the moment who'd be impressed by them. She'd transferred to homicide recently after a long string of undercover assignments, and I think on some level she enjoyed advertising that she was a cop instead of working so hard to hide it.

Or maybe she just wanted easy access to her gun so she could shoot Monk if he continued to irritate her.

"That sounds awfully convoluted to me," Stottlemeyer said. "Almost Disher-esque."

"Disher-esque?" she said.

The captain was referring affectionately to Randy Disher, the cop she'd been brought into homicide to replace after he took a job as the police chief of Summit, New Jersey.

"Never mind," Stottlemeyer said. "Were you serious with that theory about the couple who found the body?"

"Of course not," Devlin said. "But it's exactly the kind of ridiculous conclusion that Monk usually comes to."

"Except that when he comes to a conclusion," I said, "he's always right."

Stottlemeyer gave me a cold look. He hated it when I brought up Monk's perfect record in front of people. It only stoked Monk's ego and Devlin's animosity toward him. But defending Monk was a reflex for me.

If Monk heard the compliment, he didn't acknowledge it. He turned his back on us, walked around the body one more time, then drifted off into the adjacent living room.

Devlin sighed with frustration. "I don't see what the big mystery is here."

"How about who killed her?" Stottlemeyer said.

"Beyond who the actual perpetrator is," Devlin said, "the circumstances of her death don't strike me as a mind-boggling puzzle requiring outside assistance."

She had a point, not that I would give her the satisfaction of hearing me admit it.

It used to be that Stottlemeyer called

Monk in on only the most difficult, unusual, or high-profile murder cases. But ever since the captain remarried, he'd begun bringing Monk in on more and more of the routine homicides, particularly if they happened on weekends, just so he could get home sooner. That's because Monk often solved cases on the spot that would take an average detective a day or two to sort out.

Monk's amazing eye for detail used to rile the captain. But nowadays, Stottlemeyer didn't have as much ego invested in proving that he and his detectives were capable of doing the job without Monk's help.

The same couldn't be said for Amy Devlin. She never denied Monk's abilities, but she found him enormously irritating and wanted to do her job herself, even if it took a little while longer for her to close the case.

Since Monk was busy wandering around the living room, Stottlemeyer focused his attention on Devlin. "So, what do you think happened, Lieutenant?"

"Baylin stopped by last night to prep the house for today's showing and either she left the door unlocked or someone came by pretending to be interested in the house. Whoever it was tried to sexually assault her. When she resisted, he brained her with a heavy object and fled."

Monk turned around, nodding to himself as he drifted back in our direction.

"You agree with her, Monk?" Stottlemeyer asked.

"No," Monk said. "I need to meet the owners of this house right away."

Nobody had mentioned them at all, so it was a surprise to me that something about the crime had led Monk to them. "You think they might have something to do with this?"

"Of course not," Monk said. "They are people of class, distinction, and impeccable moral character. They would have nothing to do with a murder."

"You don't know their names and you've never met them," Devlin said. "So how can you possibly make any assumptions about their character?"

"Look at how they live, Lieutenant. Everything is clean, orderly, and tastefully organized. They are a remarkable family and I want them in my life." Monk picked up a framed family photo from the coffee table. It showed a young couple on the beach, standing behind their two children and their two golden retrievers. The whole family was dressed in jeans and white shirts. "Look at them, so balanced and symmetrical. If more families followed their example, we'd have fewer divorces, a lower crime rate, and far less gum on the sidewalks."

"It's not going to happen," I said.

"I don't see why not," he said.

Monk had an incredible eye for detail, but because he was clueless about the nuances of basic human interaction, there was still a lot that he missed, which was why he was lucky to have me around.

"Because those people are models," I said.

"For all of us," Monk said. "Everybody should follow their extraordinary example. They are true Americans."

"What I mean, Mr. Monk, is that the family does not exist. They are professional models who were hired to pose for those pictures. This whole house is staged."

Monk looked around, seeing everything anew. "You're saying that this Realtor was perpetrating a massive fraud? How do you know?"

I started to reply, but Devlin cut me off, eager to take the opportunity to trump Monk.

"Because it's too orderly, too clean. Everything is perfect," she said. "It's an idealized version of a home. Nobody actually lives like this."

"I do," Monk said.

"This was a spec home," Stottlemeyer

16

explained. "The owner bought it, remodeled it, then hired a company to dress it like a movie set to maximize its features, hide its shortcomings, and make it more attractive to buyers."

Monk regarded the picture again, this time with sadness. "I wish they were my family."

"That's the point," I said. "To make this house, and the idea of living in it, as alluring as possible on every level. What we buy is often based more on emotion than practical considerations anyway."

"No wonder she was murdered," Monk said. "Think of all the people she's tricked with this elaborate ruse."

"You're the only one," Devlin said. "Nobody is fooled by this. It's like a commercial. We all know it's fake."

"But it could be real," Monk said, "if everybody made just a little effort."

"The only thing that's real in this house is the dead body on the floor," Devlin said.

"Speaking of which, could we please focus on the murder?" Stottlemeyer said. "Tell me you have something, Monk."

Monk set the photo down on the coffee table. "Someone wants us to think that the murder happened exactly the way Lieutenant Devlin thinks it did, but it didn't."

17

"What makes you say that?" Devlin said.

"The murder weapon, a heavy object of some kind, is missing. And because everything is orderly and in place, it's clearly not an object that was already here, within immediate reach, that was grabbed in the heat of the moment. Everything is where it is supposed to be."

"Because he brought the weapon with him," Devlin said. "And left with it, too."

"Wouldn't it be more likely that an assailant would bring a knife or a gun rather than a brick or a bat?"

"Yeah, but I wouldn't rule it out," Devlin said. "Maybe clubbing women over the head and then molesting them when they are unconscious is his thing."

"Then why was she bashed multiple times?" Monk asked. "And why didn't the assailant complete the assault?"

"Maybe he didn't mean to kill her and walked away because he's not into necrophilia," Devlin said. "Or maybe this is exactly how he gets his jollies, but he doesn't complete the act with the victim."

"Yuck," I said.

"Perhaps you're right," Monk said to Devlin. "But where's the blood? Her hair is thick with dried blood but there is only a little on the floor. Scalp wounds bleed a lot.

There should be a large puddle of blood, not to mention some spatter on the walls from the force of those blows. But there isn't any. The place is immaculate."

"Because he's seen *CSI* and cleaned up after himself," Devlin said.

"I don't smell any cleansers," Monk said.

"Your nose could be wrong," Devlin said.

Stottlemeyer shook his head. "There are bloodhounds that could take lessons from Monk."

"She was definitely killed somewhere else and dumped here," Monk said. "The murder is as staged as everything else in this house of lies."

"Then we'd better go get ourselves some facts," Stottlemeyer said.

CHAPTER TWO:
MR. MONK
AND THE FIVE STARS

Five Star Realty occupied a storefront unit on the ground floor of a new, four-story office building on Geary, just west of Divisadero.

Inside, there was a curved reception desk in front of a wood-paneled partition adorned with a picture of the San Francisco skyline. The receptionist sitting there looked like she was anchoring the eleven o'clock news.

Behind the partition was a warren of about two dozen cubicles bordered by a half circle of five glass-windowed offices and a conference room, which was filled with a dozen shell-shocked Realtors who were comforting one another as we came in.

On one wall of the reception area were dozens of photos of various homes being offered for sale, including the one Baylin was killed in.

On the opposite wall were five framed

photographs, each showing one of the Five Star partners sitting at his desk and holding his chin in one of those businesslike poses that photographers love but that nobody ever strikes on their own.

While Stottlemeyer and Devlin badged the receptionist and made their introductions, Monk drifted over to the row of photographs of the partners. He cocked his head from side to side, then began straightening each photo, until he got to the fifth, which he took off the wall and gave to the receptionist, a twentysomething woman in a too-tight minidress with hair so blond you needed sunglasses to look at her.

"Hold on to this," Monk said.

She looked it over. "Is it broken?"

"It's fifth," Monk said.

"I don't understand," she said.

Devlin was about to speak up, but Stottlemeyer silenced her with a stern glance. He'd been through this kind of situation before, and so had I, and we'd both learned the hard way that it was better just to leave Monk alone.

"Five is an odd number," Monk said. "One of the worst."

"But we have five partners," she said. "That's why we're called Five Star Realty."

"You'll want to change that, too. You can

21

put that picture back up when you have a sixth partner and a new name."

"The partners aren't going to like this," she said. "Those pictures have been up there since the day they opened this office two years ago."

"They'll thank me later," he said.

A man strode out of the conference room and approached us. Women can get away with coloring their hair, but for some reason men just can't seem to pull it off. This guy's hair was a shade of brown not found in nature, much worse than the gray he was undoubtedly trying to hide. He had tasseled loafers, crisp slacks, and a tailored, monogrammed shirt. He'd cut his chiseled jaw shaving, which meant Monk wouldn't be able to look at him.

"I'm Cameron Griswold, one of the partners here," he said, offering Stottlemeyer his hand. "To be honest, we're all in a state of shock. We can't believe what's happened to Becky."

"I take it she was well liked," Stottlemeyer said.

"Enormously. You can't be a success in residential real estate if you aren't a natural people person." He looked past Stottlemeyer to the wall. "Why have you taken down my picture?"

22

"You're fifth," Monk said.

"Never mind him," Devlin said to Griswold. "You can hang the picture up again when we leave. Was there any reason why someone would have wanted to do Rebecca any harm?"

"Not that I can think of," he said. "Becky was a power seller, and not to belabor the point, but you don't reach that level without making both buyers and sellers happy."

"You can't hang the photo back up," Monk said, looking in Griswold's general direction but not at him. "What you can do is bring in another partner and change the name of your company."

"Monk, please," Stottlemeyer said, then turned to Griswold. "What about the owners of the house? Was there any reason somebody would want to send them a threatening message?"

"The home was bought as an investment by a contractor who is highly respected in the community for his loving restoration of Victorian homes. He not only doesn't have enemies, he has a fan club."

"But that's not the case with you, is it?" Monk said. "You've been getting angry letters, nasty phone calls, and countless visits from outraged individuals since the day you opened two years ago."

23

"No, of course not," Griswold said. "Where did you hear that?"

"I saw your sign," Monk said, stepping up to him, but looking past him. "Five Star Realty. It's an affront to the decency of all the people in this neighborhood and everyone who drives by. Why don't you just spray obscenities all over the building?"

The Realtors in the conference room were all staring at us with bewilderment, probably because even though Monk was talking to Griswold, he was looking at them.

"Monk," Stottlemeyer said sternly. "Mr. Griswold just learned that one of his associates was brutally murdered. This is not the time or the place to argue with him about his company's name."

"I beg to differ," Monk said. "It vividly illustrates the evil and moral rot that permeates this office and that led directly to Rebecca Baylin's horrible death."

"That's enough, Monk," Stottlemeyer said.

But then Monk did something astonishing. He cocked his head, rolled his shoulders, and smiled. It was his tell. I knew what it meant and so did Stottlemeyer, who squinted hard, as if he wasn't sure that he'd actually seen it.

"You should have hired a sixth partner,"

Monk said to Griswold while gazing at the conference room. "Was that what Rebecca wanted to be? Was that what got her killed?"

Four men emerged from the conference room and marched out to join Griswold. I recognized them as the other partners whose pictures were on the wall.

"Is there a problem, Cam?" one of the men asked. His hair was peppered with gray and he wasn't trying to hide it.

"There was a huge one, but he's just solved it for you." Monk turned around and picked up the photo of Griswold that he'd given to the receptionist. "You can change your name to Four Star Realty now."

Griswold looked at Devlin and Stottlemeyer. "What the hell is this lunatic talking about?"

"I have no idea," Devlin said.

"This." Monk handed her the photograph. "Read him his rights."

"You can't arrest a man for having five pictures on his wall," Devlin said. "Or having an odd number in the name of his business."

"Someday that will change," Monk said. "But in the meantime, you can arrest him for murder."

Devlin faced Stottlemeyer. "Captain, you tell him. He might listen to reason if it comes from you."

"Monk's right," Stottlemeyer said.

She stared at him. "You can't be serious."

"If Monk says this man killed Rebecca Baylin, then he did," Stottlemeyer said.

Griswold's eyes went wide, but he wasn't nearly as shocked as his partners.

"You think Cameron killed Becky because his picture was the fifth one on the wall?" asked the gray-haired man.

"Yes," Monk said.

"Did you hear that, Captain?" Devlin said.

"I did," Stottlemeyer said.

"And you still want me to arrest Griswold?"

"I do," Stottlemeyer said.

"Well, I'm not going to do it," Devlin said. "Not until I hear something rational that remotely resembles grounds for arrest."

"Finally, a voice of reason," Griswold said.

"The picture of you at your desk has been the fifth one on the wall for two years," Monk said.

"That's right, since the day we opened," Griswold said. "And as far as I know, that's not a crime."

"You cut your chin shaving this morning," Monk said.

"Are you going to tell me that's a crime, too?"

26

"It's disgusting and it proves you replaced the photo on the wall today. Your chin is cut in that picture, too."

Stottlemeyer and I moved closer to Devlin and looked at the photo in her hand. It was hard to see, but it was there. Griswold's chin was cut in the same place.

Devlin looked up at Monk. "How did he see that?"

"It's a gaping wound," Monk said.

"It's a speck," she said.

"It's a gaping speck," he said.

"I have a prominent chin. I often cut it shaving," Griswold said. "That's true now and it was true two years ago, not that it makes any difference."

"But it must, otherwise you wouldn't have gone to the trouble of re-creating the scene, clothes and all, and taking a new picture, which you swapped with the old one this morning before anyone else came in," Monk said. "You didn't want us to see that there was something in your office that isn't there anymore."

"It's been two years," Griswold said. "A lot of things aren't in my office that were back then."

"Except the murder weapon." Monk gestured to the four photos of the partners on the wall. "You all have matching desk sets.

But in your picture, Mr. Griswold, the marble pen stand is missing."

Stottlemeyer shook his head. "I'll be damned."

The gray-haired partner came over to us and squinted at the picture. "Not only that, Cameron, but two years ago your hair didn't look like you were coloring it with horse crap."

"The sun has yellowed the photo, Merle," Griswold said. "It's the same picture that's always been there."

"Your office will prove otherwise. Bloodstains are notoriously difficult to clean up," Monk said. "Just because you can't see them doesn't mean they aren't still there. I have no doubt that a forensics team will find stains all over your office from the fight you had with Rebecca Baylin last night."

"You'll need a search warrant for that," Griswold said. "And no judge anywhere in this country would give you one based on that photograph. You should be out there looking for the rapist who killed Becky, not wasting time rummaging through our office."

"We don't need the photo to get a warrant," I said. "We have your voluntary confession."

"Now you're trying to put words in my

28

mouth, but it won't work," Griswold said. "Look around. There are a dozen witnesses here who have heard every word."

I smiled. "That's great. They can corroborate that you said Rebecca Baylin's killer was a rapist."

"So what?" Griswold said.

Devlin spoke up, taking out her handcuffs. "We never mentioned that the killer staged the scene to make it appear that she'd been sexually assaulted. So how did you know about it?"

Griswold was nailed and he knew it.

"Put your hands behind your back." She read him his rights as she cuffed him. When she was done, Monk wagged a finger in his face, though he looked at the stunned Realtors in the room as he spoke.

"Let this be a lesson to you. This is what happens when you willfully ignore odd numbers," Monk said. "Everything goes to hell."

CHAPTER THREE:
MR. MONK
AND THE BIG FAVOR

The way I see it, the top motives for murder
are usually money or sex, and in Rebecca
Baylin's case, it was a combination of the
two.

We found that out because Stottlemeyer
was able to crack Cameron Griswold after
only thirty minutes of questioning in one of
the interrogation rooms at the police station.

Baylin was Five Star's biggest seller, and
Griswold's occasional lover. The previous
night, she'd threatened to leave the business
and take all of its best clients with her unless she was made a partner and received a
substantial retroactive payment reflecting a
higher percentage of what she'd already
earned for the company. Not only that, she
told Griswold that he could forget about
any more after-hours hanky-panky with her
at the office or anywhere else. She'd found
a new, much younger lover.

They argued, Griswold's temper got out of hand, and he walloped her with his marble pen stand.

To cover up his crime, he took her body to the house that she intended to show on Saturday and made it appear as if she'd been sexually assaulted. Then he tossed the pen stand into a gutter and went back to clean up his office. He was on his way out again when he saw the photograph on the wall, which, to his guilty conscience, seemed to highlight the murder weapon in neon.

So he ran home, hurriedly shaved off his stubble, dressed himself in the same clothes he wore in the photograph, grabbed his digital camera, and went back to the office to restage the photo on the wall.

Griswold took a picture of himself, printed it out on glossy paper, and replaced the old photograph, which he shredded. He got only a couple of hours' sleep before returning to the office the next morning.

He thought that he'd committed the perfect crime, a pretty spectacular achievement, considering he'd done it entirely on the fly.

But then the police showed up, and Adrian Monk went straight to the photographs like a laser-guided missile. Griswold couldn't believe what he was seeing. In fact, he still couldn't understand how he'd been caught so quickly.

Devlin was having a hard time adjusting to it, too.

She sat at her desk, glowering at us as she pounded out her report on the case on her computer. It looked like she was typing with her fists.

Stottlemeyer had asked Monk and me to stick around, so we were waiting in his office while he was off doing some business or other. Monk was busy organizing the files on the captain's desk and I sat on his couch, reading back issues of *American Police Beat*.

Ordinarily, the police trade paper wouldn't have attracted my interest, but the last few issues had had our friend Randy Disher's face all over the front page.

That's because Randy was the police chief of Summit, New Jersey, a town in the midst of a major corruption scandal. A low-level accountant for the city spotted what he thought were mathematical errors in the salaries paid to city council members for their work on various commissions. But the more the accountant dug, the more irregularities he found, and he took his discoveries to Randy.

It turned out that the mayor and the city council had been pillaging the city treasury, secretly paying themselves outrageously high salaries for serving on commissions that never even met.

But the corruption went deeper than that, involving loans to the councilmen from the city, kickbacks from developers, and scores of other swindles.

So Randy notified the state attorney general, who swooped in and arrested just about everyone in city government — except for that lowly accountant and Randy Disher.

"I see you've been reading up on the mess that Randy has found himself in," Stottlemeyer said as he came in.

"Poor Randy," I said. "It must be hard enough coming into a town as the new police chief without having to deal with a local government that's crippled by a corruption scandal."

"That's nothing compared to living with Sharona," Monk said.

"You think living with her is harder than being the police chief of a town where all the city leaders are in jail?" I asked.

"Hell yes," Monk said, stepping aside to allow Stottlemeyer to take his seat behind the desk.

Sharona Fleming was the nurse who preceded me in my job as Monk's assistant. She left Monk to remarry her ex-husband

— but that didn't work out. When she came back to San Francisco for a visit, she hooked up with Randy, and now they were living together in Summit.

She was opinionated, strong-willed, and didn't take crap from anyone, least of all Monk. We didn't always get along, but I liked her.

"She's not so bad," I said.

"That's because you've only seen her around me," Monk said. "I was a calming influence."

Stottlemeyer coughed. "You were?"

"She's a hard woman to keep under control," he said. "I don't think Randy is capable of dealing with her as effectively as I can."

"I think he's got some leverage that you don't," I said.

"You mean he's armed," Monk said.

"They love each other, Mr. Monk. Love is a powerful influence."

"Love is the leading cause of murder," he said.

"Randy's got bigger problems than either of you realize," Stottlemeyer said. "That's actually why I asked you to stick around, so I could have a word with you about him. He called me last night. He's not Summit's police chief anymore."

34

"He's been fired?" I asked. "After what he's done for that city?"

"Worse," Stottlemeyer said. "He's the acting mayor."

"You're kidding," I said.

"Nope. According to the city charter, with everyone in authority behind bars, he's the next in line of succession until new elections can be held. And that's months away," Stottlemeyer said. "So now it's just him, that accountant, and a skeleton staff running the city."

"Who is the police chief?" Monk asked.

"Randy is juggling both jobs. He's completely overwhelmed. It's a small town, and although there's not much major crime to speak of, he still needs someone he can depend on to handle the detective work while his six officers roll on the emergency calls."

Monk nodded. "So you want us to keep an eye on Lieutenant Devlin and make sure things run smoothly here while you're away."

I glanced at Devlin, who may have been a great actress when she was an undercover cop, but was doing a lousy job at hiding her alarm at Monk's suggestion.

"Not exactly," Stottlemeyer said. "Randy wanted me to go out there for a week or so, but I can't. I used up all my vacation and sick days on my honeymoon."

Devlin sighed with relief and turned back to her report, but now I was the one who was alarmed. I had a very bad feeling about where this conversation was headed.

"So what's he going to do?" Monk asked.

Stottlemeyer turned to him. "He's going to call you, Monk."

That's what I was afraid of.

"What for?" Monk asked.

"To go out there for a while and solve crimes," Stottlemeyer said. "You're the best detective he's ever known. He's not going to find anyone he trusts more or who can do a better job."

Monk shook his head. "I can't."

"Why not?" Stottlemeyer asked.

"I have commitments here," Monk said.

"Like what?"

"Consulting for you," he said.

"We'll get by without you for a week or two," Stottlemeyer said and glanced out the door at Devlin, who was working on her report but already seemed to be in a much better mood. "I can think of at least one detective who'd appreciate the extra work."

"I have two appointments a week with Dr. Bell," Monk said, referring to his psychiatrist.

"He'll survive without you, too."

"You don't know how much he needs me," Monk said. "Not just financially, but emotionally. He thrives on routine."

"You can keep your appointments over the phone," he said. "Problem solved."

Monk shifted his weight between his feet.

"I have to dust every morning," he said. "I can't do that over the phone."

"Dust when you get back," Stottlemeyer said.

"Dust accumulates," Monk said.

"Great. That will give you something to clean when you get back. We both know how much you love cleaning, so the dust thing is actually a perk."

Monk rolled his shoulders and shifted his weight between his feet again. The idea of jetting off to New Jersey had knocked him off balance and he was trying to even things out in his mind.

I could imagine the issue that Monk was wrestling with.

If he went, it would mean taking enough food, water, linens, dishes, silverware, and cleansers to last for weeks.

He'd need a moving van.

And once he got there, he'd find himself in unfamiliar surroundings, which meant he'd feel lost and unbalanced, which made him panic.

It was already starting. He was shifting his weight more often now, like he was standing barefoot on hot coals.

"What about Natalie?" Monk said. "She depends on me for her livelihood."

"She'll go with you," Stottlemeyer said.

"I will?" I said. "Don't I have a say in this?"

"Of course you do," Stottlemeyer said.

It didn't sound like it to me.

But I had even fewer commitments than Monk. His life of shrink appointments and dusting seemed busy compared to mine lately. Even so, I didn't appreciate that Stottlemeyer assumed that I would drop everything — not that there was anything to drop — and run off to New Jersey simply because he thought I should.

The phone rang. Captain Stottlemeyer snatched the receiver, identified himself, then listened. "How's it going?" He listened some more. "I see." He glanced at Monk, then at me. "As a matter of fact, they are both right here. Let me put you on speaker." He clicked a button on his phone and placed the receiver on the cradle. "Go ahead, Chief."

"Hey, Monk, Natalie, it's me, Police Chief Randy Disher." Despite the pressure he was under, Disher still had that happy-go-lucky cheer in his voice.

"Shouldn't we be calling you Mr. Mayor?" I said.

"So you've heard about what's happened out here."

"Captain Stottlemeyer was just filling us in," I said.

"They've got me running the city, which is an enormous honor, but to be honest, I don't really know what I'm doing. I'm a cop, not a politician."

"You've got to be both when you're chief," Stottlemeyer said. "Or a lowly captain."

"The thing is, city business is taking up so much of my time, it's hard for me to stay on top of police work, and that's really what I was hired to do. I'm afraid the criminal element is taking advantage of the situation."

"What do you mean?" Stottlemeyer asked.

"We've had a string of residential robberies lately. I don't have the manpower for extra patrols and I don't have anybody with the investigative skills to figure out who the bad guys are. I need help."

Stottlemeyer looked pointedly at Monk, who avoided his gaze.

"Can't you ask the state police to step in?" Monk asked.

"Sure I could," Disher said. "But then when things settle down here politically, everyone in town will remember that I couldn't do the job I was hired for and I'll be booted. I really need this to work, Monk. Not just for me, but for Sharona, too. Our life is good here and I want it to last."

"It will," Monk said.

"Only if you'll do me a big favor and come out here for a week or two and be my consultant," Disher said. "This is a small town. You could solve the cases we get here in five minutes. We'll pay your expenses, provide you with a car and all the disinfectant wipes you need. It would almost be a vacation for you."

But it sure as hell wouldn't be for me.

Monk rolled his shoulders. "I'll think about it."

"I appreciate that, Monk," Disher said. "I'll talk to you soon."

He hung up. Monk turned to me. "I can't go to New Jersey."

"Why not?"

"Because it's not here," he said.

"You've traveled before," Stottlemeyer said. "You went all the way to Germany a couple of years ago."

The captain had a good point.

"That was an emergency situation," Monk

said. "My psychiatrist was over there and the man who took his place here was missing an arm. I had no choice."

"You don't have one now, either," said someone with a distinctly New Jersey accent.

The three of us turned to see a woman standing in the doorway wearing a cheetah-pattern V-neck, a tight denim miniskirt, knee-high boots, and hoop earrings large enough to throw tennis balls through.

"You're coming, Adrian, if I have to tie you up, throw you in a crate, and ship you there by FedEx."

Chapter Four:
Mr. Monk
Goes Through Security

Amy Devlin got up from her desk with a big grin on her face and approached the woman in the doorway. "I don't know who you are, lady, but I like you already. I'm Lieutenant Amy Devlin."

They shook hands, the woman's charm bracelets rattling.

"I'm Sharona Fleming. I'm the reason you and Natalie both have your jobs."

"She's Randy Disher's girlfriend," Stottlemeyer explained.

"I'm the love of his life," Sharona said.

"I stand corrected," he said. "She was also Monk's first assistant."

"I'm the nurse who saw him through a total mental breakdown, made him face his fear of everything, get out of the house, and start solving murders again."

"Right, that's what I meant," Stottlemeyer said.

Devlin's grin got even bigger. She was getting a kick out of seeing Stottlemeyer and Monk thrown by a woman.

"What are you doing here?" Monk asked Sharona.

"I flew here on the red-eye to remind you, in person, of how much you owe me."

Monk rolled his shoulders. "I still have all the accounting ledgers for the years that you worked for me. I can prove that I paid you every cent that you were due."

"I am not talking about my salary," Sharona said.

"Then what are you talking about?"

"Everything I did for you, Adrian!"

"You mean your job. For which you were handsomely paid."

"It was a pittance and I went above and beyond what I signed on for."

"Oh really? As I recall, whenever I asked you to do a little light cleaning, you always said, and I quote, 'I am your nurse, not your maid.'"

"When Captain Stottlemeyer proposed hiring you as a consultant, I was the one who convinced the department that you could do it, because I would be at your side at all times to guarantee you wouldn't have another breakdown. I told them they had a moral obligation to you after you'd dedicated your life to them. You have that same obligation to me. So you are going to get on a plane back to New Jersey with me tonight."

"I'd rather not," Monk said.

"I'm not asking, Adrian," she said, and turned to me. "I've got a ticket for you, too, Natalie, and we hope you'll come along. We've heard from Captain Stottlemeyer that you've got real chops as a detective yourself."

I was floored. I looked over at the captain. "I do?"

"You do," he said.

The frown on Amy Devlin's face, however, indicated that she didn't think I had chops, not that I particularly sought her validation. I'm not even sure what chops are, unless we're talking about lamb or pork. But no one had ever told me I had chops in anything before, so I was pretty flattered.

"Randy has been my friend for a long time," I said. "If Mr. Monk goes to New Jersey, I'll go with him."

"Then you better go home and start packing," she said. "You, too, Adrian. We don't have much time. The flight leaves at six."

Sharona turned on her heels, rather high ones at that, and marched out of the office. I got up from the couch and looked at Monk, whose face was ashen.

"You're right, you really are a calming influence on her," I said and followed Sharona out.

Since I didn't know how long we'd be gone, I stuffed a week's worth of clothes and toiletries into a suitcase, locked up my house, and drove over to Monk's apartment, calling Julie on my way to let her know that I was leaving town for a while. Her response surprised me.

"You're an adult, Mom. You don't have to clear your travel arrangements with me."

"I thought you might be worried if you didn't hear from me," I said.

"It would be a relief," she said.

"Why? It's not like I pester you all the time with phone calls."

"No, of course you don't," she said. "You'd prefer to characterize it as 'responsible mothering.' "

I felt this sudden, powerful sensation of déjà vu. That's because I'd actually had the same conversation once before.

But not with Julie. I had it with my own mother. I was about Julie's age, and off at school, when my mom called to inform me that she and my dad were going on a short vacation.

My nightmare had finally come true. I'd

45

become my mother. She would be thrilled, assuming I ever told her, which I never would.

At least now I didn't have to worry about Julie missing me. I could worry instead about why she wouldn't.

With that out of the way, I started to think about the trip ahead. I wasn't wild about the way everybody had ganged up on Monk, shaming and threatening him into going on a trip he didn't want to take. I would have preferred that they'd been nicer about it and at least pretended that he had a choice in the matter.

On the other hand, there was no question that he owed it to Randy and Sharona to help them out, and there was nothing keeping him in San Francisco except his love of routine, his discomfort with change, and his crippling fears about traveling.

So I was glad that Sharona would be going with us. I'd flown with Monk a few times before and it was always difficult. He's got phobias about germs, recirculated air, seats other people have sat in, confined spaces, not to mention the whole concept of flying, and that's just for starters.

There was an experimental drug called Dioxynl that he took before our flights to Hawaii and Germany. The drug relieved his obsessive-compulsive disorder and nullified his phobias, but the flip side was that it ruined him as a detective and transformed him into an overly energetic, self-centered party boy with no internal censor between his thoughts and his mouth.

The alternative was to endure Monk on phobic overdrive, whining and complaining constantly and obsessing about everything and everyone around him. And that was assuming that we could even get him on the plane.

Either way, it would be a long, stressful trip for us, the cabin crew, and the passengers.

When I got to Monk's place, Monk and Sharona were still arguing over what he should pack. He wanted to bring almost everything he owned, including the furniture. But she talked him into bringing just two suitcases — one for his twelve sets of identical clothes, the other for his linens — on the promise that she would arrange to have the rest packed up and shipped.

It was a lie, of course, but she was so good at it that she almost had me convinced.

I got us to the airport three hours before our flight was scheduled to depart to compensate for the increased security and for Monk's being, well, Monk.

Check-in went smoothly enough but I knew we were in trouble when I saw the long lines that snaked in front of the security checkpoint. There were lots of people crammed very close together in narrow, roped-off lanes that curled around and around and Monk didn't like that. He drew into himself as much as he could for fear of brushing against someone else.

We were all so close together that we could smell the deodorant, the aftershave, the perfume, and the body odor of the people around us. I tried to deduce things about their lives from those smells, their clothes, and their interactions with their fellow travelers.

For instance, there was one guy in the row beside ours who had a nasty sunburn, smelled of turpentine, and had some tiny flecks of red paint in his hair and on his neck. I immediately deduced from those keen observations that he was a housepainter who worked outdoors.

I had no way of knowing if I was right about the guy, short of asking him, but it was a game I played with myself all the time. It was a way to keep myself sharp to assist Monk in his investigations.

Lately, I'd become more involved in his cases, not only to keep myself interested but also because I enjoyed it, which is why I was so flattered to hear that Stottlemeyer had praised my skills to Disher.

The captain was probably just buttering me up so I'd go with Monk to New Jersey without putting up a fight. And if he was, well, kudos to him for manipulating me so well.

We reached the conveyor that led into the X-ray machine. Sharona dropped her purse in one of the plastic baskets and began shedding her jewelry, her jacket, her belt, and her shoes.

"That's enough," Monk said, grabbing her by the arm. "This isn't a strip club."

"You're required to remove this stuff, Adrian."

"You expect me to believe they're going to let you run naked through the airport?"

"Relax, I'm done. This is all I'm taking off."

"Thank God, because otherwise you'd need a pole and some music."

"Now it's your turn, Adrian," she said. "Take it off."

"Are you insane?" Monk looked around. "You expect me to disrobe in front of everyone?"

"It's the law," she said. "You, of all people, should respect that."

It was so nice having her around to handle him for a change. It was an enormous relief to need to carry only half the load of managing Monk. It dawned on me that this trip to New Jersey could turn out to be a relaxing little vacation for me.

"It's only your jacket, your belt, and your shoes," she said. "You don't even have to unbutton your collar."

"Okay." He rolled his shoulders. "I'll do it. Where's my privacy curtain?"

"They don't have curtains," I said.

"That's indecent," he said.

Sharona noticed the TSA guards were beginning to eye Monk suspiciously and she whispered to him, "Adrian, if you don't stop making a scene and move along, the guards are going to give you a full-body and cavity search. Is that really what you want?"

That was all the incentive to comply that he needed. He motioned urgently to me for a disinfectant wipe, which I carry by the ton in my huge purse. I gave him one.

Monk thoroughly wiped the plastic basket before he took off his coat, carefully folded it, and laid it down inside. The whole process must have taken five minutes.

The people around us in line began to fidget with frustration, especially the house-painter in the next line. I smiled at him to show that I sympathized.

"Hurry up, Adrian," Sharona said. "We have a plane to catch and so do all the people behind us."

"Forgive me, Sharona. Unlike you, I'm not used to stripping in public." Monk handed me the used wipe, which I placed in a Ziploc bag while he removed his belt, rolled it up carefully, and laid it on his jacket.

"You have to take off your shoes, too," I said.

"How am I supposed to walk without my shoes? The floor is filthy."

I'd come prepared for this. I reached into my purse, took out two shower caps, and held them out to him. "You can put these on your feet like booties."

"Wipe," he said.

I gave him one. He slowly and thoroughly wiped down another basket, then set his shoes inside it after putting the shower caps over his socks.

By this time, all of the security personnel and everyone in line were watching him, the guards with wariness and the travelers with impatience. I began to fear that a cavity search was in store, not just for him but for me and Sharona as well. That was assuming the crowd didn't beat us up first.

The other line was moving twice as fast as ours. The turpentine guy was nearly at the metal detector himself. I smiled at him again.

"How's the house painting business?" I asked him.

He gave me a look. "Excuse me?"

"The sunburn, the flecks of paint in your hair, the smell of turpentine — it's a dead giveaway that you're a painter who works outdoors."

He seemed suddenly very self-conscious and ran his hands through his hair, checking for flecks of paint.

"Really, you can see all of that?"

"It's a gift," I said. "And a curse."

"That's amazing," he said

I nodded, pleased with myself. "So I've been told."

Actually, that was the very first time, and I turned to Monk, hoping he'd overheard, but he was staring at the metal detector as if it were a vicious dog as Sharona walked through. I was disappointed, but at least I had my deductive skills confirmed.

Sharona didn't set off any alarms and moved on to the other end of the X-ray machine to retrieve her stuff from the baskets.

Now it was Monk's turn to go through.

He took a deep breath, let it out slowly, then leaped through the detector and almost right into the arms of the TSA guard on the other side, a heavyset African-American woman.

"You can't be jumping through the scanner like that," the guard said. "You have to go back and walk through slowly."

"But that will expose me to more radiation," he said.

"You have to do it, Adrian," Sharona said as she hurriedly put on her jewelry. "It won't hurt."

"Not now," Monk said. "But it will in ten years when my skin is falling off, I glow in the dark, and you're tormented by the unrelenting guilt."

Monk took a deep breath, leaped through the scanner to the other side, then turned to face the guard again.

"Come along now, sir," the guard said, beckoning him forward with a wave of her hand. "Slowly this time."

He took another deep breath, closed his eyes, and stepped through the scanner, wincing as if he were being stuck with needles, then came through to the other side. He opened his eyes and exhaled as he stood in front of her.

"Whew, thank God that's over," he said

and started toward Sharona, but the guard blocked his path.

"Step over here, please," the guard said, motioning him to a glass-walled cubicle.

"What for?"

"I need to pat you down," she said.

"No, you don't," he said.

"Yes, I do," she said.

"But no bells went off," he said. "I'm clean. Very, very clean."

"We select people at random for pat-downs," she said. "I am selecting you."

"Why?"

"Because you're behaving strangely," she said.

"There's nothing strange about not wanting to be irradiated."

"I can pat you down or you can step into the full-body scanner." She gestured to a large machine that looked like a bigger, meaner version of the metal detector. "Your choice."

"What does that machine do?"

"It shows me what's underneath your clothes."

"I am underneath my clothes," he said.

"I want to be sure that's all you've got under there," she said.

"Just do it, Mr. Monk, and stop arguing," I said, aware that all the guards were tensing up now, and it was making everyone else tense, too, including my new admirer the housepainter, who'd just come through the other metal detector.

"I don't understand why you are doing this to me, a clean and upstanding citizen," Monk said, "while you let bank robbers sail through security unmolested."

"I don't see any bank robbers," the guard said.

Monk pointed at the housepainter. "You don't see him?"

The man jerked as if poked with a cattle prod and bolted back through the metal detector again, plowing through the crowd of waiting travelers like a linebacker, hellbent on reaching the escalator that led down to the terminal exit.

An alarm bell went off somewhere and a bunch of TSA agents scrambled after the guy, tackling him and taking the rope line down with them. The taut rope ensnared a line of travelers as it was pulled down and swept them off their feet, too, creating pandemonium.

The guard looked at Monk and waved him through. "Have a nice trip."

CHAPTER FIVE:
MR. MONK IN THE AIR

"How did you know he was a bank robber?"

I finally asked Monk the question after we'd gone to the gift shop and purchased some Fiji water and Wheat Thins for him and some candy for Sharona and me. We were sitting at the gate, waiting to board our flight.

"You would have known he was, too, if you'd seen him," Monk said. "And smelled him."

"Actually, I did both," I said. "But I deduced from the scent of turpentine, his sunburned face and neck, and the flecks of paint on his skin that he was a housepainter who worked outdoors. I asked him and he confirmed it."

"And you believed him?"

"Why wouldn't I?"

"Because he's a bank robber," Monk said, cleaning the rim of his water bottle with a disinfectant wipe before opening it and tak-

56

ing a sip. "You saw all the signs."

"I did?"

"He robbed a bank but the money was booby-trapped with a red dye pack that exploded in his face. He was wearing a Halloween mask, but the dye still got in his hair, on his ears, and on his neck. His skin wasn't red from sunburn, but from the irritation caused by the turpentine and abrasive rubbing he did to get the dye off."

Sharona shook her head. "This is exactly why Randy needs you, Adrian. You're a one-man police force. You don't even have to be investigating something to solve a crime."

I wasn't finished with this yet. I didn't see where I'd gone wrong.

"It was a lucky guess," I said. "You made one set of assumptions based on the evidence and I made another. Mine were just as valid. I could have been right."

"No, you couldn't. You didn't look closely enough at him," Monk said and set his water bottle down. Sharona picked it up.

"Fiji water?" she said. "This isn't your usual brand."

"They went out of business," Monk said. "This is nearly as good and as uncontaminated. That's rainwater that fell on mountains of Viti Levu island in 1515 and percolated through layers of silica, basalt, and sandstone, where it remained sealed and pure until it was drawn out in the bottle you now hold in your hands."

"Wow," she said. "So it's like you're drinking really old wine, only without the kick."

"Oh, there's a kick," Monk said. "I could tell you stories."

"Okay, tell me."

But I wasn't finished with Monk yet. "Wait a minute, he's got some explaining to do. What didn't I see that you saw?"

He turned to me. "His face and arms weren't red, just his neck and ears. That suggested he was wearing a mask and long sleeves."

"Still consistent with painting," I said.

"His eyes were bloodshot, too, from the tear gas that's also released with the dye pack."

"Still consistent with my theory. They could have been bloodshot from not wearing sunglasses or from allergies or from getting paint in them. Tear gas from an exploding dye pack is not the only explanation."

"You're forgetting that red dye has a substantially different composition than latex paint."

"And you could see that chemical difference just by glancing at the flecks?"

"I'm not blind," he said as he grabbed the

58

water bottle back from Sharona and took another sip. "Paint flecks and dye flecks also have markedly different textures."

"Markedly," Sharona said, nodding with agreement. "You didn't know that, Natalie?"

She was just teasing me but I was in no mood for it. I didn't like being reminded that my deductive skills were still lacking.

Then again, Monk might know the chemical and textural differences between dye and paint, but he didn't know Facebook from the phone book, couldn't win a taste test between Diet Coke and Diet Pepsi, and wouldn't recognize Lady Gaga if she showed up at his front door and belted out a song.

So what if I didn't know all the arcane stuff that he did. That didn't make me inept. It just meant I would miss some things that he wouldn't.

And vice versa. Let's see how he'd do on a murder case where the solution depended on knowing what Diet Pepsi tastes like, knowing the entire Lady Gaga songbook by heart, and being able to navigate Facebook.

I couldn't wait for that case to come along.

I glanced at the flat-screen monitor behind the counter at the gate. We had only a few minutes before boarding. It was time to raise the issue that I'd been avoiding.

"We'll be boarding soon, Mr. Monk. Have

59

you thought about how you want to deal with the flight?"

"I've already prepared my last will and testament," Monk said. "If that's what you're concerned about."

"What I meant was, do you want Dioxynl? Or maybe a tranquilizer?"

"I am not taking any drugs," he said.

"It will make the flight less stressful for you," I said, "and everybody else on the plane."

"I don't want to die a junkie," he said.

"One pill won't make you a junkie, Adrian," Sharona said.

"It's how it starts," Monk said. "Today you have an aspirin, tomorrow you're a crack whore."

"But if you're going to die today, it won't come to that," she said, "so what's the difference?"

"I don't want my senses to be impaired. I may need them."

"For what?" she asked.

"Using the parachute," he said.

"Passengers aren't given parachutes," I said.

"Still?" he said, exasperated. "It's been years since I notified the FAA about that issue."

"You really expect airlines to give each

passenger a parachute?" Sharona said.

"It makes more sense than equipping every seat with a life vest for flotation," he said. "That's like giving people parachutes on boats."

I had to admit that his argument made a certain amount of sense to me, which was frightening. I'd clearly been working for him too long.

They started boarding our flight a few minutes later and Monk seemed a bit weak-kneed as he got to his feet and surprisingly subdued as we walked down the Jetway to the plane.

I'd prepared myself for the arguments to come. For instance, I was ready to tell him that he shouldn't think of the three-seat rows in the plane as odd-numbered, but rather as six-seat rows cut in half, and since six is an even number, it all balanced out in the end. Besides, at least the plane was divided symmetrically.

But I didn't have to make that argument or any others, because by the time we got to our seats, Monk could barely stand, and he was out cold after we got him buckled into his window seat.

I took the seat beside him and Sharona took the aisle. She was smiling with smug satisfaction.

"While I was talking to Mr. Monk, you put something in his bottle of water, didn't you?"

She nodded. "Adrian will sleep all the way to Newark."

"He'll be angry," I said.

She waved off my concern. "He'll thank me later."

While Monk slept, Sharona told me about life in Summit, which was only a thirty-minute train ride from midtown Manhattan, so while it felt like a small town, it was essentially an upscale bedroom community for people who worked in New York City.

It was a great place to live.

The main drag was Springfield Avenue and appeared much the same today as it had for decades, a picture-perfect example of small-town USA. But if you looked a bit closer, you'd see that the coffee shops and mom-and-pop stores were being squeezed out by fancy cafés, art galleries, and boutiques selling designer clothing and home décor.

The town's roots as a pastoral farming community were still evident in the rolling hills, tree-lined streets, and lush landscaping around the homes, many of which dated back to the early 1900s and had been impeccably restored and maintained.

That takes big bucks and there was plenty of that in Summit. The residents tended to be highly educated, well paid, and totally self-absorbed professionals with busy lives.

So as long as the schools were good, the streets were clean, the crime rate was low, and no demands were made on their time or money, the citizens didn't pay any attention to what was happening in local government.

And why should they? Everything was orderly, smooth, and peaceful, requiring nothing from them except prompt payment of their property taxes.

So thanks to the apathetic citizenry, the politicians were able to pillage the treasury without anyone noticing or caring until a clerical error and an overzealous new police chief stripped away the facade to reveal the corruption under the surface.

"But enough about the town," Sharona said. "Let me tell you about Randy Disher."

"You're forgetting that I know him," I said. "We worked together for years."

She shook her head. "I thought I knew him, too, when I was working for Adrian. But I really didn't. What you saw was this eager-to-please, goofy guy totally wrapped up in being a cop and proud of it."

"And he isn't that guy?"

"Oh, he was. But I didn't know then where it was all coming from. He's this incredibly sincere, warm, passionately loyal man who had nothing else to focus those qualities on except the job and his boss, so they became a substitute for what was missing in his life."

"The love of a good woman," I said.

"It seems so clear now, but it took me ten years, and remarrying a guy I divorced, moving away, and divorcing him a second time, to discover that my Prince Charming was right in front of me all the time. I can't believe I blew him off for so long."

"Why did you?"

"Mainly because he was a cop. Until I started working with Adrian, they were people I was brought up to avoid. It was a hard habit to break. Besides, he had that ridiculous cop swagger, which was laughable because he was so sweet. I couldn't take him seriously."

I knew what she meant. It was often hard for me to see Randy as anything but comical. But she was right, part of it was how hard he tried to be tough, only to be undone by his boyish good nature. Oddly enough, it was his likability, not his toughness, that made him such a good cop.

64

Captain Stottlemeyer often said that people opened up to Disher in ways they never would to any other cop, perhaps because they sensed, on some level, his inherent decency.

"He's the sweetest, most attentive and honest man I have ever known," Sharona said. "But his good nature gets him into trouble."

"He's too trusting," I said.

"He always wants to see the best in people, which is strange for a cop. Most of the cops I know assume everyone is a dirtbag, and they are usually right."

"So how has Randy changed now that he has you?"

"He's calmed down. He's less eager to please, more willing to take charge, even if that means alienating people."

"What about you?" I asked. "Have you changed?"

"I used to come on strong. I'd get into people's faces before they could get into mine. But I'm a pussycat now."

"So I've noticed," I said.

"Don't judge me by how I handle Adrian," she said. "That's different. Now that I'm with Randy, I'm trying really hard to be more aware of other people's feelings and work not to piss everybody off. We're living in a small town, Randy has a high-profile job, and I know what I do reflects on him."

"Is that the only reason?"

"Well, now that I'm with him, I've got a lot less to be angry about."

"So he wasn't the only one acting out because he didn't have somebody to love."

She gave me a look. "When did you become a junior shrink?"

"About the same time I became a junior detective," I said. "It's required when you're working with Mr. Monk, but I don't need to tell you that. How does Randy like being the chief?"

"He loves it. It's a small force, only six officers, so he's really been able to make it his own. There isn't much crime in Summit, nothing compared to what he dealt with in San Francisco, so he's been able to relax a little but still wow everybody with what a good cop he is. Then the scandal hit and changed everything. Now I'm afraid everyone is expecting way too much from him. And that he's expecting too much from himself."

"Enough about Randy," I said. "What about you?"

"I'm happier than I've ever been," she said. "Randy is a real calming influence."

I glanced over at Monk, snoozing away. It

was a shame he hadn't heard Sharona's remark.

"It's called being in love," I said.

"Which used to feel like the flu until Randy came along. He's the first man in my life who didn't give me headaches and cramps from the stress and a sore throat from the yelling."

"Are you working?"

"Yeah, as a private nurse for some people in town, dropping in on them each day, administering their meds and checking their vitals, that kind of thing. And I get to come home each night to a good man who treats me like a queen."

"You can't beat that," I said.

"No, I can't. I don't want to lose this life, Natalie, not after it took me so long to get it. That's why it's so important to me that Randy emerges from this scandal on top. It's why we need Adrian."

"Don't worry," I said. "Randy doesn't need to be concerned about neglecting the police department while he's running the local government. No crime will go unsolved while Mr. Monk is in town. He'll keep Summit clean."

"Thank you," she said.

"By the time we leave, Mr. Monk will have the birds cleaning up their own droppings."

"Oh God," she said in mock horror, "what have I done?"

CHAPTER SIX:
MR. MONK
ARRIVES IN NEW JERSEY

We touched down hard in Newark at two a.m. and the jolt awakened Monk, who sat up straight in his seat and gripped his armrests for dear life.

"Taking off is the part I hate most," Monk said.

"Then you can relax," I said, "because we've just landed."

Monk looked out the window and saw for himself that we were heading toward the terminal, not away from it. When he turned back to us, he saw Sharona smiling at him.

"Welcome to New Jersey," she said. "You slept the whole way."

"You slipped me a mickey," he said.

"I did," she said. "Do you feel an overpowering desire to score some crack?"

"I used to trust you," Monk said, then shifted his gaze to me. "Were you aware of what she was doing?"

"No," I said. "But I think you're treating

Sharona unfairly."

"She drugged me," Monk said. "That's an unforgivable betrayal."

"You didn't feel that way when you drugged your brother with sleeping pills, kidnapped him, and dragged him across state lines in a motor home," I said.

"Adrian did that?" Sharona said.

"He did," I said. "It was a birthday present for Ambrose."

"Some present," Sharona said.

"That was an entirely different situation," Monk said.

"No, it wasn't. You did it to get Ambrose from one place to another with as little drama and discomfort as possible," I said. "In fact, what you did was worse. You took him away against his will."

Monk squirmed a little in his seat. "I did it for his own good, to get him out of the house so he could experience new places he'd never been to before."

"Have you ever been to New Jersey?" I asked.

"Hell no," Monk said.

"I rest my case," I said.

"For the remainder of this trip, you're tasting all of my food and water before I do," Monk said.

"I'd be glad to, but we both know that

you're not going to eat or drink anything that I've tasted first. So you'll just have to take your chances. Or starve."

The stewardess announced that we'd arrived, told everybody they could make calls on their cell phones while we taxied for a few minutes, and relayed some information about connecting flights.

"Look at the bright side, Adrian," Sharona said. "We didn't crash. You're alive."

"In New Jersey," Monk said. "I might have been better off dead."

"How can you say that?" she said. "You don't know anything about New Jersey."

"I know it's so poisonous that there are over one hundred and twelve New Jersey locations on the EPA's priority cleanup list of the most toxic sites in the nation," Monk said. "With another twenty-nine under consideration to be added."

"How many does California have?"

"Ninety-six," Monk said. "But the only one near San Francisco is the Treasure Island Naval Shipyard, and it's out in the middle of the bay, far from me. Beyond that, the closest highly toxic site is across the bay in Alameda. The odds of me ever being in either place are infinitesimal. But in New Jersey, you can barely step outside your door without your foot landing in a steaming pile

71

of toxic waste."

"Is Summit on that list?" Sharona asked.

"No," Monk said.

"So what are you whining about?"

"The town isn't hermetically sealed. People in Summit are coming and going from elsewhere in New Jersey, bringing their toxic waste with them."

"And people come to San Francisco from all over the world," she said. "You're in no more danger here than you are there."

"At least in San Francisco, the odds of someone walking across a toxic waste site are substantially less," Monk said. "And nobody puts drugs in my drinks."

"As far as you know," I said and grinned mischievously.

"You're joking, right?" Monk asked.

I shrugged. Before he could pursue the matter any further, the plane came to a halt at the terminal and everyone got to their feet.

Summit Police Chief Randy Disher was waiting for us in the baggage claim area. He wore a crisply pressed, dark blue police uniform and a trooper's flat-brimmed hat, his silver badge sparkling in the fluorescent light of the drab terminal. Instead of evoking authority, the uniform only underscored

72

his natural boyishness. He looked like an excited kid on his way to a costume party.

Sharona picked up speed, ready to run into his arms, but he held up his palm in a halting motion.

"I'm on duty," he said.

"Your duty is to kiss me," she said and embraced him, planting a big kiss on his face. Disher immediately blushed with embarrassment.

"She has no respect for authority," Monk whispered to me and looked away. He hated displays of affection.

As soon as Sharona let go of Disher, I gave him a hug, too, only deepening his blush and Monk's discomfort.

"It's so good to see you," I said. "How does it feel to be back in uniform?"

"It's not the same thing at all," he said. "This is a chief's uniform. It feels very different from a patrolman's uniform."

"It looks the same to me," I said.

"It's not," he said. "I wear it to show solidarity with the men."

"And because it's a small department, so the chief has to roll on calls, too," Sharona said.

"In a strictly supervisory, chiefly capacity," Disher said, correcting her, then turned to us. "Thank you both so much for coming. I really, really appreciate this. It's almost like having family coming to visit."

"It is," I said.

Monk rolled his shoulders. "I'm not comfortable here."

"You're not comfortable anywhere, Adrian," Sharona said, "so that's like saying that you already feel right at home."

"I've got you set up at the best hotel in town," Disher said, "and it will be just the way you like it."

"Is it in San Francisco?" Monk said.

"No," Disher said.

"Then I won't like it," he said.

"I know this was hard for you, Monk, but I want you to know that it means a lot to me that you came here anyway. It speaks to the bond we forged in battle, fighting crime on the mean streets of Frisco."

"I was drugged," Monk said.

Sharona spotted our luggage on the baggage carousel, so we quickly gathered it up and lugged it to the Summit Police patrol car that was parked right outside the door. There were definitely some perks to being a cop.

Monk hesitated on the curb.

"Don't worry, Monk, I had it cleaned by a crime scene cleaning crew and completely detailed before coming here," Disher said, tossing our bags in the trunk. "It's the cleanest car you could possibly sit in."

That seemed to brighten Monk's mood considerably. He motioned to me for a wipe. I gave him one, which he used to open the door to the backseat. He sniffed the air inside and smiled.

"It's redolent of disinfectant," he said.

"Is that a good thing?"

"If only the whole world could smell like this," he said and slid inside. Disher nodded, pleased with himself. I winked at him and got in, too.

Within a minute of leaving the airport, the motion of the car and the stress of the long journey caught up with me and I fell asleep. Either that, or I blacked out from inhaling all the Lysol.

I awoke when the car stopped. I was briefly disoriented, but then remembered our flight and realized we were outside a hotel. I got out of the car and stretched my legs while Disher unloaded our bags.

I didn't know anything about the Claremont Hotel at that moment, and yet its entire past was evident in its architecture, each of its wings representing a distinct period in America's history.

The main structure, facing the street, was the original rustic hunting lodge built in the early 1900s. There was the stately and Romanesque 1930s wing, the space-age lines, cinder-block walls, and lava-rock accents of the 1960s expansion, and the cold, tinted glass and marble cladding of the 1980s section.

Monk and I followed Disher and Sharona inside. The lobby was dominated by a massive stone fireplace and had a high ceiling with lots of exposed, hand-hewed beams.

As we admired our surroundings, Disher got our keys from the waiflike woman at the front desk and came up to us.

"I've taken the liberty of checking you both into even-numbered rooms on the second floor of the newest wing, constructed in 1982," he said.

Carrying our bags, he led the way down a long, narrow hallway in the old wing and into a wider, more spacious one in the new extension. "I have to warn you, they say the place is haunted."

"There are no such things as ghosts," Monk said. "Only delusional people."

I agreed with Monk on that point, but I also liked a good ghost story.

"Is there a legend to go along with it?" I asked.

"Of course there is. They say a woman was robbed and murdered on this spot on a

76

foggy night in the 1800s. Now her ghost roams the halls in a swirl of fog, searching for her killer," Disher said. "Supposedly, if you look into her eyes and don't turn away, you're doomed to die the next day. So if you see her, be sure not to look at her face."

"Do you believe that story?" Monk asked.

"No, but we've had a few tourists call us about it over the years," Disher said. "Not since I've been here, though."

Monk rolled his shoulders. "What are the facts surrounding the murder?"

"Oh God," Sharona said. "It was two hundred years ago, Adrian. Do you really think you can solve it?"

"Someone should," he said. "It's long overdue."

"If it even happened," Sharona said. "It could just be a scary story people tell to add some character to this place."

"That's why I'm telling it," Disher said. "Forget about it, Monk. I've got more pressing cases for you to solve."

He led us up a set of stairs to the second floor, stopped in front of room 204, and handed Monk two key cards.

"I got you two adjoining rooms," Disher said.

"I don't need two rooms," Monk said.

"Yes, you do. Because if you open the door

between them, you will have two of everything and will be occupying a symmetrical space."

It was brilliant.

"Rooms should be symmetrical," Monk agreed.

"The two rooms are identical, one the mirror image of the other. I've had the rooms thoroughly cleaned by a team of crime scene cleaners and inspected by the health department," Disher said. "You'll find the signed certificate from the inspector on the desk inside."

Monk opened the door to his room. It smelled like an over-chlorinated pool and looked like any other basic hotel room, but he gazed upon it with wide-eyed appreciation, as if it were a penthouse suite. He picked up the certificate and admired it.

"May I keep this as a souvenir?" Monk asked.

"It's all yours," Disher said.

"And suitable for framing," Monk said.

"The refrigerator is full of Fiji water and there are four cases of it in the closet."

"Thank you, Randy."

"My pleasure, Monk. By the way, it's okay to call me Randy here, between us, but I'd appreciate it if you'd call me Chief in public."

"Of course, Chief," Monk said. "Where is Natalie going to be?"

"I've got her down the hall in room 208," Disher said.

Monk nodded, impressed. "Another fine room."

"You haven't seen it yet," I said.

"The number is good, and if it's anything like this one, it's top drawer."

"Get some rest, Monk. I'll be seeing you at ten a.m.," Disher said. "The police station is one block away. Just take a right out the lobby door."

Disher closed Monk's door and Sharona gave him a kiss on the cheek.

"That was amazing," Sharona said.

"What was?"

"How you handled Adrian," Sharona said.

"I've known him for years. It wasn't so hard," Disher said, then looked at me. "Now it's your turn."

"What do you mean? I don't require any special treatment," I said. "My needs are very simple."

"I know." He led me down to room 208 and handed me the key. "In addition to the usual treats and assortment of spirits in the minibar, I've also stocked the room with Pop-Tarts, Oreo cookies, Nacho Cheese Doritos, and cashew nuts. You'll find DVDs of every movie Hugh Jackman and Daniel Craig have ever made, the latest issues of *Esquire, Vanity Fair, Cosmo,* and *People,* and lots of bubble bath soap."

I was wowed. If he'd been this attentive to me a few years earlier, I might have snagged him for myself before Sharona ever got the chance.

"Hold on to him, Sharona," I said. "Hold on tight."

She took his arm. "I will."

I dragged my suitcase into my room, regarded the stack of DVDs, the magazines, and all the junk food, and flopped down on the comfy bed.

We'd only just arrived, and despite the very late hour, it was already beginning to feel like a vacation.

But that feeling wouldn't last long. About two hours, to be exact.

CHAPTER SEVEN:
MR. MONK IS HAUNTED

I was so tired when I went to bed that I didn't think a hand grenade going off outside the window could have awakened me. But it was something much quieter and more insidious that pulled me out of my deep sleep. . . .

It was a feeling, nagging and persistent at the edges of my consciousness, and a chill that made my skin tingle. Both sensations sent a message that was unmistakable.

There's someone else in the room.

I opened my eyes and saw a swirling, ethereal mist beside my bed. At first I thought I was still dreaming. I blinked hard and not only did the mist remain, but I could see something moving inside it.

No, not something.

Someone.

A woman.

And that's when her pale face burst through the haze, her yellow eyes blazing with fury, her sharp fangs bared and moist.

I shrieked, pulled the sheets up over my head, and buried my face in my pillow. I heard her heavy footsteps move away from the bed and I thanked God for sparing me.

And then I thought . . .

Footsteps? From a ghost?

It was possible. Some ghosts even drag chains behind them or ride headless on horseback.

But then I thought . . .

What the hell am I doing?

I was a grown woman, one who had stared down vicious killers, genuine flesh-and-blood, homicidal monsters, and yet there I was, cowering from something that didn't exist.

Except that I'd seen it. I'd stared into her yellow eyes, seen her pointy fangs.

Yellow eyes? Fangs?

What kind of ghost was that?

Disgusted with myself, I whipped back my sheets and got up, but my heart continued to pound with fear.

The room was still dark and heavy with mist. I staggered into the entryway just as the ghost burst out of my closet, went straight to the door, and began struggling with my dead bolt.

I grabbed for her. Instead of my hand

passing through her noncorporeal presence, I caught part of her arm.

She elbowed me hard in the chest, opened the door, and dashed out.

The blow knocked the wind out of me for a moment, and as I gasped for breath I heard a voice behind me.

"Don't worry, Natalie, she won't get far."

I turned around and saw something even more extraordinary than a yellow-eyed, fanged ghost standing in a cloud of cemetery fog beside my bed.

Adrian Monk was peering down at me from an opening in the ceiling of my closet.

"Mr. Monk? What are you doing up there?"

"I couldn't sleep," Monk said.

"So you decided to crawl around in the rafters?"

I peeked out the doorway into the hall. The ghost was running in her gossamer gown right toward two uniformed police officers who were emerging from the stairwell.

She spun around and came my way again. I ducked back into my room, waited until she was passing my open door, and then tackled her, straddling her back and pinning her facedown on the floor until the cops came running up.

"Having fun, ladies?" one of the officers asked. He was so muscular that I wasn't sure whether it was a Kevlar vest under his starched uniform or his beefy body. Even his cheeks looked ripped.

Only then, when I saw his leering, frat-boy grin, did I realize I was wearing only a T-shirt and panties. It wasn't my nakedness that bothered me as much as how flabby I was.

I really had to start going to the gym if I was going to run around hotels half-naked, tackling ghosts in front of muscle-bound cops.

"You're welcome to wrestle all you want," the other cop said. His neck was so thick that it appeared to have absorbed his chin. But it wasn't muscle in his case. He looked like a cop balloon that had been overinflated. "But could you please keep it quiet and behind closed doors?"

That's when Monk, lightly covered in dust and bits of insulation, staggered out of a closet down the hall.

"Someone call a paramedic," Monk said. "We have a deadly emergency."

"Who's hurt?" the chinless cop asked.

"I am," Monk said. "I'm caked in hantavirus."

An hour later, as morning was dawning, a sleepy-eyed Chief Disher, wearing an untucked, wrinkled shirt and jeans, his hair askew, sat across from us on a couch in the lobby.

Standing behind Disher were the two officers, who'd since been introduced to us as Raymond Lindero, the muscular one, and Walter Woodlake, the chubby one.

I'd put on a bathrobe and a pair of sweats and sat yawning next to Monk. He'd been given a clean bill of health by the two irritated paramedics, who assured him that despite his desperate protests to the contrary, no treatment was needed for hantavirus, which is carried by rat droppings, simply because he'd encountered a lot of dust in a crawl space.

"What do you think crawls in crawl spaces?" Monk said. "Rats."

"So see your doctor if you begin to show symptoms," said one of the paramedics as he packed up his stuff.

"You're suggesting that I wait to seek medical attention until I am already in my death throes? What kind of lazy, incompetent paramedics are you?"

"The kind who are leaving," the paramedic said and walked away with his partner.

Now, as eager as Monk was to go back to his room and shower the plague off his clothes, his desire to regale Disher and his police force with his brilliance was even stronger than his phobia.

That's because when Monk solves a mystery, it's one of the rare times when he feels utterly in control of the world around him, when everything seems to fit and balance is restored.

It's also the only time when he seems totally confident in himself, able to assert authority over his own phobias and insecurities.

So he indulges himself and we allow him to do so, no matter how long and frustrating the experience might be.

He started his story at the moment a few hours earlier when we'd left him in his hotel room.

Monk told us that the first thing he did was inspect his surroundings. He opened the drawers, looked under the furniture, and examined the closet.

He spotted an access door in the ceiling of the closet that he presumed led to some sort of crawl space. But it wasn't secured in any way, which he thought was odd. So he pulled over a desk chair, stood on it, and pushed against the door. It was locked from the other side.

"What's so strange about that?" Disher asked. "They obviously don't want guests crawling around in the ceiling."

"Then why have the access panels at all?" Monk asked.

"So they can get up into the crawl space for maintenance purposes," said Lindero, his impatience underscoring every word. I was mesmerized by the muscles coursing under his cheeks and decided that he could probably chew walnuts without shelling them first.

"Then it would be locked from the outside, not the inside," Monk said. "Therefore, I surmised that the panels aren't intended to allow access to the crawl space from the room, but rather the other way around."

At the time, it was an oddity that Monk filed away for later consideration. He had more pressing tasks to perform, things he believed everyone should do the moment they arrive at a hotel, like locate the emergency exits and the nearest cache of cleaning supplies.

"Why would you want to know where the cleaning supplies are?" Woodlake asked.

"In case you run out of the cleansers that you brought with you and a mess occurs."

"You leave it for the maid," Woodlake said.

"What if the maids are off duty?"

"You wait," Woodlake said.

"And I suppose if the building was burning, you'd wait for the firemen before fleeing from the nearest exit."

Woodlake started to reply, but was cut off by Disher. "Forget it, Woodlake. Let Monk continue."

Monk explained that he went down the hall, found a utility closet, opened it, and discovered two things that puzzled him — a padlocked access panel on the ceiling and, amid the cleaning supplies, a large, unmarked bottle of blue liquid that he determined from the smell and viscosity was a mixture of water and glycol.

"Then it all made sense to me," Monk said.

"What did?" Disher asked.

"The legend about the ghost, of course," Monk said. "So I went to see the woman at the front desk. Her name is Rhonda Dumetz and she's the daughter of the couple who own the hotel and who built the 1983 addition to the building that we are staying in."

"Yes, we know that," Lindero said. "We

live here."

"I informed her that Natalie always takes a sleeping pill after a late-night plane flight," Monk said, "and that she would likely need multiple wake-up calls in the morning in order to awaken from her deep, almost comatose slumber."

"I don't take sleeping pills," I said.

"I also asked if they had a safe," Monk said, ignoring my objection. "I told her that I was worried about Natalie's diamond ring, an old family heirloom that she keeps on her nightstand. I thought it might not be wise for her to wear it around town and draw the attention of local ruffians."

"I don't have a ring like that," I said.

"We don't have ruffians," Disher said.

Monk ignored us both. He explained that he went back to his room, but kept watch. An hour later, Rhonda Dumetz passed by in the hall. He opened his door a crack and saw her go into the utility closet.

"I immediately called the police, reported a violent altercation at the hotel, and went to the closet to investigate."

"There wasn't a violent altercation," Lindero said.

"But I knew one would occur because, as I expected, the access panel to the crawl space was unlocked, a ladder was deployed underneath it, and the bottle of glycol was missing."

Monk stopped, pleased with himself, a smile on his face. Disher and the cops stared at him.

"That's it?" Disher said.

"The rest is obvious," Monk said. "I'd solved the mystery."

"What mystery?" Woodlake asked.

"The ghost mystery," Monk said.

Disher rubbed his forehead, and for a moment it was as if I were looking at a younger version of Stottlemeyer. "I'd forgotten what this felt like."

"Solving a crime?" Monk asked.

"Following your reasoning," Disher said.

"The bottle of glycol mixture was the dead giveaway," Monk said. We all stared at him blankly. "None of you know what it's used for?"

The cops shrugged. I was too tired to shrug.

Monk shook his head in disappointment, disapproval, and intellectual superiority. It pissed me off, not that I needed much of an excuse to be irritable. I'd had only a couple of hours' sleep.

"You can't tell the difference between a Nacho Cheese Dorito and a Funyun," I said, "but you can identify glycol from smell and texture and you know what it is used for?"

"Of course," Monk said.

"Why would you possibly know that?" I asked.

"It's the formula used in haze machines to create the smoky atmosphere in buildings to safely train firemen and police officers on fire rescues," Monk said. "It's perfect for that purpose because it's water based, nonhazardous, dissipates quickly, and doesn't trip hydrocarbon sensors in fire detectors."

Now Disher nodded. "They use it at concerts and discos, too. You can get one for thirty dollars and creep out your house at Halloween."

"Or a hotel room to create the impression that a woman in white is a ghost," Monk said. "I followed Rhonda up into the crawl space. I discovered that there's a remote-controlled haze machine up there that she positioned next to the air vent in Natalie's room."

Now it all made sense to me, too, as did the colorful detail of the legend, the part about how looking at the ghost's face would lead to your own demise. That was meant to scare people away from taking too close a look at the ghost. There would be less of a chance, even with the mist and darkness, that anybody would recognize the ghost's face. It also explained the yellow eyes and fangs, two terrifying distractions to help you forget her actual facial features.

Monk continued his story. "Ordinarily, if Rhonda accidentally awakened a guest, she would escape through the closet, creating the illusion that she'd just disappeared. But I held the access door closed, so this time she had to flee out the door."

"Wait a minute," Woodlake said. "How did you know the ghost was Rhonda and that she'd make a play for the ring tonight?"

"Because she works nights and is thin enough to move easily through the crawl space and be convincing as a ghost," Monk said. "I knew she'd strike now because it was the only time that she could be certain that Natalie would take a sleeping pill and be deep enough asleep not to realize someone else was in the room."

Disher broke into a broad smile and turned to his officers. "See? Isn't Monk just like I said he'd be?"

The cops nodded in agreement.

"Mentally unstable," Woodlake said.

"Frustrating as hell," Lindero said.

"A damn good detective," Disher said, "who honed his skills working closely with me for years in Frisco."

"So how come you didn't solve the ghost mystery yourself?" Lindero asked.

"Because I was too busy rooting out corruption in city government to focus my attention on it. I'm only one man." Disher pinned his gaze on Lindero. "And until now there was nobody else in this department who even approached my level of expertise. But with Monk here, that's changed. Nothing is going to get past the eyes of justice."

"You can count on me," Monk said.

"Thank you, Monk," Disher said.

"If I don't die a miserable, drooling death from the hantavirus first." Monk stood up and gestured to the couch, where he'd left some dust and insulation behind. "That piece of furniture will need to be incinerated, of course."

"Of course," Disher said.

"If this is the best hotel in town, I wouldn't want to see the worst," Monk said and headed off to his room.

Disher looked at me and smiled. "It feels like old times."

CHAPTER EIGHT:
MR. MONK GOES TO WORK

The downside of drugging Monk for the flight to Newark was that he was almost fully rested but I was walloped with fatigue. I'd foolishly stayed up on the flight chatting with Sharona. And thanks to Monk sending a ghost to my room, the only sleep I'd had in twenty-four hours was a short nap.

While Monk showered, changed, and served himself a breakfast of Wheat Chex (which he'd packed for the trip, along with the spoon and bowl to eat them with), I waited for Lindero to remove the haze machine from the crawl space, and once I was sure nobody would be peeking at me through my air vents, I showered and went down to the lobby for some breakfast in the hotel's restaurant.

But the restaurant was closed and Officer Woodlake was busy trying to explain to a dozen outraged guests why cops were in the crawl space and why the owners of the hotel were too busy at the police station to run the kitchen.

So I had no one to blame but myself for having to scrounge up breakfast somewhere else.

I went outside and looked around. Down the street to my right, past some apartment buildings, was the police station, housed in a redbrick colonial building with imposing white columns supporting a portico.

To my left, at the corner of the next block, was a gas station mini-mart.

I headed over to the mini-mart, which had a fine selection of microwavable goodies in its freezer section. I zapped myself a sausage and cheese Hot Pocket, grabbed a shrink-wrapped cinnamon bun with an expiration date well into the next decade, and poured myself a large cup of highly caffeinated coffee.

I managed to eat most of my breakfast on the walk back to the hotel, and I did it without spilling anything on myself. It was a feat of physical prowess that ought to be an Olympic event and for which I certainly deserved a gold medal.

The cinnamon bun was so tasty that I was tempted to go back for another one. But then I thought about how strong and un-natural the chemicals must be that could keep it fresh for years and all the irreparable harm they might be doing to my own DNA.

On the plus side, I figured that maybe they'd keep me fresh into the next decade, too, but I was willing to settle for keeping me awake for the day.

When I got to the lobby, Monk was waiting for me. He looked upbeat and energized. Solving a crime and eating a bowlful of perfect squares of wheat often had that effect on him.

"I think I might live," he said.

"That's a relief," I said. "Ready to fight some crime and balance the scales of justice?"

Monk cocked his head. "Are you mocking me?"

"Ever so slightly."

"You do realize I am your employer."

"Right now, you're the guy who hid in my closet in the middle of the night and sent a woman to rob me while I slept."

"Because I wanted to protect the guests in the hotel from further harm."

"Because you were wide-awake with nothing to do and you wanted to get back at me for taking Sharona's side in the argument about drugging you."

"That would be petty," Monk said.

"Yes, it would," I said, and left it at that.

He was my boss, after all.

We walked the rest of the way in silence, mostly because the sidewalk was cut into squares and Monk was intent on stepping precisely in the center of each one. And counting them as he went along.

He kept walking after we reached the police station, two steps forward and one step back to be exact, so he would end his trek on an even number.

We approached the counter, where a pucker-faced old woman in a police uniform sat in front of the city seal on the wall. She looked like she'd been sucking on a particularly sour lemon for eighty years.

"May I help you?" she asked.

"I am Natalie Teeger, and this is Adrian Monk. We are here to see Chief Disher."

"Oh yes, we heard about you," she said, pinning her gaze on Monk. "You're afraid of germs."

"Isn't everyone?" he said.

"The only thing I'm afraid of is liberals," she said.

"What for?" I asked.

"They want to take away our guns. Without our weapons, we'd all be chum for the communists." She pushed her seat back from the counter so I could see she was wearing a holster holding a gun that was

97

only slightly smaller than an antiaircraft cannon.

"I thought the commies were all gone," I said. "What with the fall of the Soviet Union and everything that's happened in the last sixty years."

"Oh, they're here," she said. "There's evidence of their dangerous, insidious activities everywhere."

"Like what?"

"Buffet restaurants," she said.

"I agree," Monk said.

I looked at him in disbelief. "You *do?*"

"Buffets are very dangerous. Everyone eating out of the same dishes, handling the same serving utensils, mixing their entrées together on their plates. It's unsanitary."

"And un-American," she said. "It's dining socialism."

I didn't see how an all-you-can-eat buffet could be an example of socialism, but before I could pursue the matter further, Disher emerged in full uniform from the door that led into the back.

"I see you've met Evie," he said. "The longest-serving employee in the department. She was the dispatcher back in the day. Now she's our front-desk officer."

"The first line of defense against the public," she said.

"I thought that's who you are supposed to serve," I said.

"Only after Evie screens out the wackos," Disher said.

"And liberals," I said.

She narrowed her eyes at me. "They are easy to spot."

I wondered what gave me away. I wasn't wearing my VOTE OBAMA pin, or holding my NPR mug, or throwing myself in front of a tree to protect it from a bulldozer, so I decided it was because I wasn't wearing makeup. She'd pegged me as a hippie instead of just lazy.

"Evie, I want you to treat Natalie and Monk as two full-fledged members of our police force," he said. "They get total and complete access."

"Yes sir," she said, but it was clear she didn't agree. I could tell because her face puckered up again, as if she'd just started sucking on a fresh lemon.

"Lovely woman," I said as we walked through the door into a short hallway that led to the squad room.

"She's crusty but she doesn't miss much," Disher said. "More than I can say for most of my cops."

"She's also crazy," I said.

"People have said the same thing about

some other detectives I know," Disher said, casting a glance over his shoulder at Monk, who responded with a quizzical expression.

"I like her," he said. "She's vigilant."

"You've got to be with all those commies lurking around," I said.

The squad room consisted of several filing cabinets and four unoccupied metal desks with computer terminals, which were situated in front of Disher's glass-walled office. It was like the SFPD homicide division in miniature.

"Where is everybody?" I asked.

"Not counting me, Evie, and the dispatcher, we're only a six-man force," he said. "Two cops working three eight-hour shifts. Let me show you around."

He led us down a short hallway that branched off from the main squad room. We stopped in front of an observation window, which looked in on the one interrogation room. A middle-aged couple sat at a table in the room, looking miserable.

"Those two are Harold and Brenda Dumetz, the owners of the hotel," Disher said. "They were implicated by their daughter, Rhonda, in the burglary."

"She ratted out her own parents?" I said.

Monk shivered. "Please don't mention rats. It makes me want to shower again."

"She did it because they were going to hang her out to dry," Disher said. "They claimed not to know anything about what she was doing. But she says the ghost thing was entirely their idea and so was the surveillance."

"Surveillance?" I said.

"She claims all the rooms are wired for sound and video," Disher said. "They were blackmailing guests. Apparently, people in Manhattan sneak out here to the burbs to have their affairs where they won't be recognized."

"It's going to create quite a scandal once the tapes come out," I said.

"Just what we need," Disher said. "But we don't have the tapes yet. The Dumetzes have lawyered up and are keeping quiet. My guess is that they're going to use them as bargaining chips to make a deal with the DA."

"Maybe the DA is on one of those tapes," I said.

"It wouldn't surprise me, the way things have been going in this town since I got here."

He showed us the locker room, the radio room, and the holding cells, where Rhonda Dumetz sat on a concrete bench and glowered at me from behind the bars. She looked

101

scarier now than she did with the yellow contacts and plastic fangs.

We worked our way back to the squad room and over to a large map of Summit. There were about a dozen colored pins stuck in the map.

"These pins represent the locations of residential burglaries over the last few months," Disher said. "As you can see, they're all over town. And they're happening day and night."

"It's anarchy," Monk said.

"It's not quite that bad," Disher said. "But it has to stop. They're taking cash and electronics, mass-produced stuff like Rolex watches, but no paintings, rare books, or custom jewelry that needs to be fenced, which leads me to believe we're dealing with amateurs."

"These homes don't have alarms?"

"They do," Disher said. "But if the alarms go off, the burglars are gone before our cops get there."

"How do you know there's more than one burglar?" Monk asked.

"It's a guess, based on how much they're taking and how quickly they seem to be doing it. And on a couple of occasions, they've taken a big-screen TV, which requires more than one man to carry."

"What about neighbors?" I asked. "Nobody saw anything or anyone unusual?"

"Nope," Disher said. "And the burglars always seem to know when the house they're hitting is going to be unoccupied, even if it's only for an hour or two."

"So they have these places under surveillance," I said. "But nobody has spotted them watching."

Disher nodded. "We've even stepped up our neighborhood patrols during each shift, but if anything, the burglaries have only increased. It's as if the bad guys are mocking us."

"It's intolerable," Monk said.

"I'm glad you feel that way," Disher said. "Your dedication to your work is one of the big reasons I brought you out here."

"Oh, for God's sake, man up," Monk said, and began removing pins from the map and setting them on the desk in color-coordinated piles. "You're the chief of police."

"What are you doing?" Disher said.

"What you should have had the guts to do weeks ago as the leader of this force. You've got reds and blues and whites all mixed together. Pick a color and have the fortitude to stick with it, no matter what."

"I was talking about the robberies, not the

pins," Disher said.

"What kind of example are you setting for your men?" Monk said. "You need to demonstrate clarity of thought, steadfast resolve, and total command of the situation. You can't do that with multicolored pins unless each color represents a different kind of crime."

Disher picked up a stack of folders from the desk and handed them to me. "Here are the case files on each of the break-ins. You can take the map on the wall with you."

"Where are we going?" I asked.

"To buy new pins," Monk said.

"I'll buy new pins. You're going to the scenes of those burglaries. Maybe you'll spot something we missed." Disher reached into his pocket and put a set of keys in my hands. "These keys go to the car I picked you up in last night. It's parked out front. You're One-Adam-Four on the radio if you need to call in."

"You're putting us in a squad car?" I said. "But we're not cops."

"It's all I've got," Disher said. "And this way you can monitor the radio calls and go to any crime scene where your detecting might be needed, though things are pretty slow around here compared to Frisco."

"But what if someone on the street flags

us down and expects us to help them?" I asked.

"We do it," Monk said.

"No, you don't," Disher said. "You call in to the dispatcher and she'll send somebody out. You're not cops, even though I've given you free rein in the station and a police car."

"And you expect us to investigate and solve crimes," I said.

"Exactly. I'm glad that's clear," Disher said, then checked his watch. "I've got a meeting with the city accountant. Good luck."

He hurried off. I looked at Monk over my pile of folders. "Where to first?"

"The most recent crime scene," Monk said.

CHAPTER NINE:
MR. MONK AND THE POOP

This is going to sound silly, but even though I'd hung around cops for years as Monk's assistant, I was really excited about driving a police car. The moment I got behind the wheel, I felt a childlike sense of glee. I wanted to turn on the siren, drive fast, and arrest someone.

It was too cool.

I'd driven an unmarked police car before, when Monk was a scab during the SFPD police strike a few years back, but never a squad car. It was like trading up from a speedboat to a destroyer.

There were no gun turrets or rocket launchers on our vehicle, but it felt big and powerful anyway, like a car on steroids.

The rifle was missing from the gun rack, but otherwise the car was fully equipped, though I had no clue how to use the laptop built into the center console. That didn't matter to me as long as the lights and siren worked.

I knew I'd find an excuse to use them before our trip was over.

I put on my seat belt and glanced over at Monk in the passenger seat. He sighed contentedly, which for him meant he was as excited as I was.

"Let's roll," he said.

I started the car and the engine roared with more horsepower than anything I'd ever driven before. I held on tight to the steering wheel as if that would somehow rein in the car if it got out of control. I shifted the car into drive and tapped the gas pedal.

It was like lifting off in the space shuttle. I almost rear-ended the car in front of us on the road.

I eased up on the gas and took a deep breath. This was a car that wanted to go fast, smash through walls, and fly over the tops of hills with lots of loud action music blaring in the background.

Of course, it wasn't the car that wanted to do that, but the driver. I managed to hold my reckless desires in check and steered us slowly down Springfield Avenue, Summit's main drag, on our way to the scene of the last home burglary.

The street was lined with buildings made

of stone, brick, and concrete — buildings crafted in the Edwardian Classical style that was popularized in the 1920s and that personifies small-town America so much that Disneyland used it for its Main Street.

The newer buildings in Summit paid homage to the style without turning it into caricature, so they fit right in with the authentic stuff. The abundance of mature trees and old-style parking meters only added to the charm.

But, as Sharona had told me on the plane, the decidedly upscale nature of the restaurants, shops, and galleries, not to mention the preponderance of Range Rovers, BMWs, Lexuses, and Mercedes on the road, belied the small-town vibe.

As we cruised along, I could feel every person on the street looking at us but, in reality, nobody was.

I was simply self-conscious about being a stranger driving a cop car down the main drag of a town I'd never been in before. It was almost as if I was afraid someone would accuse me of pretending to be a cop.

Which, to be honest, was exactly what I was doing at that moment. I was pretending I was Angie Dickinson in *Police Woman* and that Monk was my crusty boss, which he was, so that part felt very authentic.

It was childish, I know, but I was having fun. I was deep into my imaginary episode, pretending to be scanning the streets for perps, pimps, and pushers, when Monk slammed his hand on the dashboard, startling me.

"Stop!" he yelled.

I stomped on the brakes, bringing the car to a sudden, jarring halt, which dug the seat-belt strap into my chest and sent a jolt of adrenaline into my bloodstream.

I was wide-awake, more so than I'd been in hours. For one terrifying moment, I was certain that I'd fallen asleep at the wheel and that Monk had saved me from running over a dog, or an old lady, or some kid on a bike.

But there was no one in front of us. In fact, there was nothing amiss at all that I could see.

"What's wrong? You scared the hell out of me, Mr. Monk."

"Pull over," Monk said. "Hurry."

I parked in a red zone, one of the perks of being in a cop car, and turned to face him, my heart pounding so hard in my chest that it felt like it was trying to escape. "What's the big emergency?"

"You might want to call for backup," Monk said.

"Is there a robbery in progress?"

"No," he said.

"An assault taking place?"

"No," he said.

"Then what do we need backup for?"

"An unspeakable crime," he said.

I looked around and identified only one thing that could provoke such an exaggerated response. "Are you talking about that dog peeing against the tree?"

"Worse," Monk said and pointed out the window.

A few doors down was a gallery with some sculptures in the window. The place was called Poop and was tucked between a café and a clothing store.

"It's just a name," I said.

"It's a profanity," he said.

"Poop?"

"Sssh," Monk said. "You're in a police car."

"What does that have to do with anything?"

"We should be setting an example by being law-abiding citizens."

"No one can hear us," I said. "And even if they could, there's no law against saying 'poop.' "

"Sssh," Monk said. "Pop the trunk."

"Why?"

"Would you please just do it?"

I did. He got out of the car and so did I. He went to the trunk. He took out two gas masks and a bullhorn.

"Prepare yourself," Monk said, handing me a gas mask. "This could get ugly."

I tossed the mask back in the trunk and slammed it shut. "Don't you think you're overreacting? It's just a cheeky name for a gallery."

"It's much, much worse than that," Monk said. "This could quite possibly be Summit's Chernobyl."

"What are you talking about?"

Monk began creeping up cautiously on the Poop storefront.

"Have you seen what they sell?"

"Art," I said.

"Look closer," he said.

I walked ahead of him and up to the galley's front window. There were four items on display.

There was something that looked like an ossified pile of soft-serve ice cream, about one cone's worth, on a piece of polished marble. A little placard in front of it read:

AUTHENTIC COPROLITE (DINOSAUR POOP). 65 MILLION YEARS OLD. CUT AND POLISHED. $1,275.

The next item was a bronze watch laid

atop a piece of jagged stone like a lizard sunning itself. It was a very masculine, pre-distressed watch with styling that made me think of mud-caked Jeeps, guys in khaki, and the grassy plains of Africa. The watch face had an organic texture and was the color of a dried leaf. The placard beside it read:

FINE SWISS TIMEPIECE WITH JURASSIC COPROLITE (DINOSAUR POOP) FACE AND AMERICAN CANE TOAD STRAP. $12,000.

Beside it was a crude, two-foot-tall version of Michelangelo's *David,* sculpted out of what looked like straw and clay and protected in a glass box. Its placard read:

PANDA POO DAVID BY STANLEY HUNG, IMPORTED FROM CHENGDU, CHINA. $25,000.

And finally, fanned out like peacock feathers, was an array of multicolored, very pulpy paper. The tiny placard beside the paper read:

WIDE SELECTION OF ELEPHANT, RHINO, AND BISON DUNG STATIONERY NOW AVAILABLE!

It was disgusting and yet strangely fascinating.

I took the excrement art as intentionally outrageous, a heavy-handed attempt to be shocking, but I had no idea what to make

112

of the fossilized dino droppings, or the dung watch, or the crappy paper.

It made me very curious about the store, which I suppose was the whole intention of the window display. I wanted to see what other poopy products they were selling, but first I had to deal with Monk, who I feared was probably on the verge of a complete nervous breakdown.

I took a deep breath and turned to face his bullhorn as he made an announcement, nearly scaring the poop out of me.

"Attention poo-poo felons, this is the police. You are completely surrounded. Come out with your hands up and thoroughly washed."

His words were heard up and down the street. People began pouring out of the buildings all around us. Monk turned to address them with his bullhorn.

"Go back inside. You must remain indoors for your own safety. You don't want to be on the street when the Poop door opens."

Nobody was listening. In fact, even more people came out.

"Mr. Monk —," I began, but then he yelled into his bullhorn again.

"What's wrong with you people? Take cover. This is a toxic emergency."

I yanked the bullhorn out of his hand.

"That's enough, Mr. Monk."

That was when a woman emerged from Poop. Monk let out a cry of alarm and slipped his gas mask over his face.

She appeared to be about my age but carried herself with an elegance and grace that I could never pull off. She had long blond hair, piercing blue eyes, and perfect skin. She was immaculately dressed in a silk blouse and slacks and approached us with a genuinely warm smile, as if she hadn't been summoned by a bullhorn, and seemingly oblivious to the crowd coming out of the café, the clothing store, and buildings all around.

"Is there a problem?" She asked the question without a trace of anger or embarrassment and because of that, I liked her immediately.

If anything, she was amused.

"You're under arrest," Monk said.

"We aren't cops, Mr. Monk," I said, then turned to the woman. "I am so sorry about this."

Monk looked at me in shock. "You're apologizing to her? This woman is the most heinous, despicable, and deadly criminal I have ever encountered."

"Oh my," she said. "This may be the worst first impression I've ever made."

She didn't seem upset but I spoke up quickly, eager to reassure her that she wasn't in any trouble.

"My name is Natalie Teeger and this is Adrian Monk. We've just arrived from San Francisco. We're consultants with the Summit Police Department and the sentiments that Mr. Monk has been expressing are his own. He is repulsed by even the idea of excrement."

"Of course he is," she said. "Most people are. That's why I opened Poop here two years ago, to enlighten, amuse, and educate people about the natural, and enduring, value of excrement in our lives."

"You've been here for *two years?*" Monk said. "And nobody has stopped you?"

"Quite the contrary," she said. "I was just elected president of the Summit Chamber of Commerce."

"I knew this city was corrupt," he said. "But this is beyond comprehension. It ends now. You're going down, Poo Lady."

"My name is Ellen Morse," she said. "Won't you please come in and let me show you around?"

"No. Way. In. Hell," Monk said. "In fact, I'm almost certain that *is* hell."

"I'd be glad to," I said to Morse and took a step toward her.

Monk grabbed my arm. "It's suicide."

"You're overreacting," I said, and yanked my arm free.

"Am I?" Monk was trembling with anger. "You're about to enter a building full of poop. Wall-to-wall dung. It's like walking into a nuclear reactor, only not as clean. I won't let you do it."

"How do you intend to stop me?"

He balled his hands into fists. "Brute force."

"I can take you, Mr. Monk."

"You wouldn't dare."

"I wouldn't even have to throw a punch. I'd just have to sneeze. Or spit."

"I wish I had a Taser," he said.

"You'd Tase me?"

"You'd thank me later," he said. "Now you won't live to."

"I'll be out in a few minutes," I said. "Maybe I'll buy you something."

Morse held the door open for me and I walked inside.

CHAPTER TEN:
MR. MONK GOES TO HELL

Poop had the ambience of an art gallery coupled with the hippie vibe of a Marin County health food store. It was an open space, with exposed beams and pipes, artwork on display here and there, hardwood floors, and several rows of shelves composed of boards propped on the feet of many old folding ladders. Speakers piped in the white noise of nature — burbling springs, birdcalls, and wind rustling the leaves of tall trees. The air was heavy with floral incense.

"Everything sold here is derived from solid animal waste," Morse said. "We have the items divided into four sections — art and jewelry, food and nutrition, health care products, and stationery."

I gave her a look. "Did you say *food?*"

"I did," she replied with a sly smile.

"People eat poop?"

"They do," she said.

117

"Sane people?" As soon as I said it, I realized I must have sounded like Monk.

She laughed and led me to a shelf lined with bottles containing a golden red liquid. "Are you familiar with argan oil?"

"Sure," I said. "I had it once on a salad at Le Guerre, a fancy French-Moroccan restaurant in San Francisco."

"It's crap," she said.

"I thought it was very tasty," I said. "It's strong, but it really brings out the flavor of meat and cheese."

"What I mean is, the oil is poop."

"You're kidding me," I said.

"It comes from goats in southern Morocco, who climb into the argan trees, eat the fruit, and excrete the nuts, which are collected, roasted, and pressed to make the oil."

She handed me a bottle. It was priced at almost forty dollars. I examined the label.

"They don't say anything about it being goat crap on the bottle," I said.

"You wouldn't eat it if they did," she said. "Or put it on your hair or use it to moisturize your skin."

I cringed at the thought that I'd been putting poop in my hair or down my throat. She smiled at my discomfort.

"I can see what you're thinking. You're

118

picturing yourself sticking a spoon in a pile of steaming dung or slathering it in your hair with your bare hands," she said. "It's revolting and it makes you sick."

"I'm surprised to hear you say that," I said, "considering that you sell the stuff."

"The excrement used in argan oil, or any of the food or health care products that I sell here, has been so refined that there are no toxic elements remaining. But the facts don't matter. We are conditioned from a very early age to revile excrement, despite its many practical and even vital uses. It's a totally Western bias," she said. "In India, for instance, cow dung is revered. A new home is considered blessed, and the occupants destined to be prosperous, only after a cow has defecated in the living room. And once they move in, they smear dung on their front porches to welcome and honor their guests."

"As enlightened as you are about poop, you must still be at least a little revolted by it, too, or you wouldn't burn incense to hide the smell."

"Do you like the incense?"

"It's better than sniffing L'Air du Crap," I said.

"It is crap," she said. "The incense is

imported from India. It's floral-scented cow dung."

I began to regret leaving my gas mask behind. "Is that healthy?"

"Indians think so," she said. "They believe dung is antiseptic and pure because it comes from the sacred beast."

"But is it?"

"They have practiced their beliefs for centuries without harm," she said. "They wash their bodies with dung soap, brush their teeth with dung toothpaste, and they aren't sick and dying, so you tell me."

India was definitely a country Monk should never visit under any circumstances. And even though I'm a lot more liberal minded than Monk, I decided that if I ever visited India, I'd take plenty of soap and toothpaste with me and a pair of old, comfortable shoes I wouldn't mind parting with when I left the country.

And if Indians were really immersing themselves in so much dung, it certainly explained why most of the customer support operators I talked to in Mumbai were always so surly. I would be surly, too, if I had to deal with that much crap, literally and figuratively, every day.

I was still thinking about all the implications of such a poop-centric life when the front door of the store flew open and Monk burst in, wearing his gas mask and holding the other one in his hand.

I guess he'd gathered up his courage and given himself a running start to ensure that he would actually make it through the door, even if he had second thoughts on the way. But his momentum carried him right up to a display of portraits painted on dried cow patties, where he came to a dead stop.

He shrieked, staggered back, and bumped into a pedestal holding an enormous pile of fossilized dino dung.

He yelped, spun around, and came face-to-face with a shelf of Panchagayva Herbal Soap, which the packaging stated in bold letters was MADE FROM PURE COW DUNG, URINE, GHEE, CURD, AND MILK.

His eyes went wide with horror. I hurried over and put my arm around his shoulder, hugging him to my side and pulling him slowly back, away from the display.

"I'm right here, Mr. Monk," I said reassuringly in his ear.

"I came to rescue you," he said feebly, handing me the gas mask, his hand shaking. He sounded like Darth Vader having an anxiety attack.

"It's all right," I said, taking the mask from him. "I'm okay."

121

"Good," he said. "Now you can rescue me."

I was genuinely touched by his bravery. It was like Superman diving into a pool of kryptonite to save Lois Lane.

"You're safe," I said.

"She's right," Morse said. "You have nothing to fear from poop."

Monk turned to her, pinning her with a look of absolute hatred. "Excrement is among the most dangerous substances known to man, deadlier than radiation, and responsible for more deaths than guns, AIDS, cancer, car accidents, malaria, and smoking combined."

"*Human* waste, Mr. Monk," she said. "But even that has positive uses. In London, they burn it to create electricity. In Calcutta, they use it for fish farms and fertilizing crops."

"Poo-poo causes millions of deaths every year," Monk said, his face bright red with anger. "It's a highly toxic breeding ground for cholera, typhoid, salmonella, E. coli, influenza, dysentery, candida, cryptosporidium —"

"Again, you're talking largely about human waste," she said, interrupting him. "Cattle dung and bird guano are extraordinarily versatile and can be used for such things as fuel, fertilizer, batteries, insulation, moisturizer, paper, soap, roofing, food, gunpowder, and explosives. What other resource on earth is so useful, cheap, plentiful, safe, and renewable?"

"Take a good look at her, Natalie," he said. "She's the devil."

I was about to speak when I was interrupted by another woman's voice.

"Put a cork in it, Adrian."

We turned to see Sharona coming into the store, her face tight with irritation.

"What are you doing here?" Monk asked.

"Randy called me," she said. "He said it was an emergency."

"It certainly is," Monk said. "But where's the backup?"

"I think I can handle you on my own," Sharona said.

"Forget about me," Monk said. "What about the hazmat team, Homeland Security, the Environmental Protection Agency, and the strike force from the Centers for Disease Control?"

Sharona ignored Monk and approached Morse. "I am so sorry about this, Ellen."

"You know this she-devil?" Monk said to Sharona.

"It's our fault," she continued. "We invited Adrian here but we were so caught up in everything else that we totally forgot about your store. We should have told him to stay away. At the very least, we should have given you some warning."

"So that's how she's gotten away with her crimes," Monk said. "You've been tipping her off before the authorities showed up. Does Randy know that he's sleeping with the enemy?"

"It's quite all right, Sharona," Morse said. "No harm done."

"No harm?" Monk said, his voice cracking. "You're selling people poo and telling them it's soap!"

The instant the words were out of his mouth, he seemed to remember where he was. He grabbed my arm and dragged me to the door. This time I let him.

Once we got outside, he yanked off his gas mask and took in deep breaths of air, as if he'd just escaped from a burning building. I looked around. The crowd had dispersed and life seemed to be back to normal on the street.

"I can't believe what I've seen and heard," Monk said. "It's like I stepped into a parallel world. The poo-niverse."

"I know you don't agree with Ellen Morse's philosophy, but she seems like a good person."

Monk looked at me with concern. "The

fumes and sleep deprivation have obviously gotten to you. Take deep breaths and let them out slowly."

Sharona emerged from Poop and marched over to Monk. "What were you thinking, standing on the street, screaming at people with a bullhorn? This could have turned into a major embarrassment for Randy."

"It already is," Monk said. "That store is an outrage, an affront to human decency and public health. How could Randy have let that place stand?"

"You may not like it, Adrian, but there is nothing illegal about what Ellen is selling."

"It's toxic waste," Monk said. "There *are* laws about that. But you're protecting her. First, you drug me. Now you're standing up for Satan. I don't know you anymore."

"Oh, spare me the drama," Sharona said. "You're supposed to be solving crimes, not harassing shopkeepers."

"What she's doing *is* a crime," he said. "Against humanity."

I sighed. I really didn't want to get in the middle of this but I had no choice.

"I know you find Ellen Morse's business highly objectionable, Mr. Monk, and that it goes against everything you believe in. But she has the same right to express her beliefs, in her case through art and commerce, as

125

you have to express yours, which you do in the way you lead your life," I said. "We are a country built on those fundamental freedoms and if you are truly dedicated to enforcing the law and protecting people, then you'll defend her right to offend you."

Both Monk and Sharona stared at me.

"Is this where we're supposed to pledge allegiance to the flag?" Sharona asked. "Or start singing 'The Star-Spangled Banner'?"

"I thought you'd appreciate my help," I said. "Frankly, I thought my defense of Ellen Morse wasn't only persuasive but deeply moving."

"That speech was way, way over the top," Monk said. "Even for you."

"For *me*?"

"It's important to stay calm in a crisis and not become overwrought," Monk said. "You have to maintain your perspective or you won't be able to think clearly."

"And you are?" I asked.

"I'm obviously the only one around here who is. You've been behaving irrationally since I had you pull over. But at least you have an excuse. You're suffering from sleep deprivation and the shock of confronting unspeakable horrors." Monk looked at Sharona. "But you don't have an excuse.

You're a nurse. You took a Hippocratic Oath."

"I don't recall poop being part of it," Sharona said.

" 'I will prevent disease whenever I can, for prevention is preferable to cure,' " Monk said. "That's just one key poop part."

"You've memorized the Hippocratic Oath?" I said.

"I swore to it," he said.

"But you aren't a doctor," I said.

"I kill germs," Monk said. "The oath is my license to kill."

"The name is Monk," I said. "Adrian Monk."

"Yes, that's who I am. Are you delirious?"

"No," I said. "I was joking."

"My name is a joke?"

"You disappoint me, Mr. Monk," Sharona said, following my lead into the world of Bond. "You're nothing but a stupid policeman."

"I won't stand here and be insulted," Monk said to Sharona and then turned back to me. "Do you think you're clearheaded enough to drive?"

"Yes," I said. "But Sharona wasn't insulting you. She was quoting *Dr. No.*"

"If he's the doctor who told her that poop is good for you, he should have his medical license revoked. Let's go," Monk said, turning his back on Sharona and heading for the car. "The sooner we solve the crimes around here, the sooner we can go home. We're one big step closer already."

I gave her a wave good-bye and hurried after him.

"How is that possible?" I said. "You haven't opened any of the files or visited a single crime scene yet."

"Yes, but now I know who is responsible."

"You're going to say Ellen Morse, aren't you?"

"That's right — the dark sorceress of the poo-niverse," Monk said. "And I am going to take her down."

Chapter Eleven:
Mr. Monk
and the Burglary

The house that was most recently hit by the wave of residential burglaries was probably a hundred years old, two stories tall, and had a broad front porch adorned with a pair of very inviting, comfy wicker rocking chairs that faced the front lawn and the tree-lined street. I wanted to curl up in one of those chairs and take a nap while Monk did his investigating.

My lack of sleep was eroding my energy and I could feel myself slowing down, like a windup doll that needed a few twists of its key.

The houses were all big, homey in an old-fashioned, Norman Rockwell kind of way that made me feel safe and secure. It was almost like the neighborhood was cuddling me.

Of course, it was an illusion. The burglary of this home, which had occurred only a few days ago, proved the street wasn't as safe as it seemed.

I had the case file open in front of me and I summarized the facts from the police report in a running commentary as I lagged lazily behind Monk, who walked around the perimeter of the house, framing what he saw with his hands, cocking his head from side to side.

The burglary had happened at noon on Tuesday. The Roslands, a couple with two kids, lived in the house, but they weren't home at the time of the burglary. The husband was working in Manhattan, the kids were at school, and the wife was having lunch in Summit with friends.

The burglars got into the house by prying open a first-floor window, which was equipped with a broken alarm sensor. They stole two iPads, several watches, a laptop computer, and five thousand dollars in cash.

"Randy should be fired for letting that woman stay in business," Monk said.

"Forget about her," I said, fighting back a yawn. "Concentrate on solving these burglaries."

"This whole town could end up being evacuated and quarantined as unsafe for human life," Monk said. "And Randy is worried about a few burglaries? Where's his sense of priorities?"

"Your priority, Mr. Monk, is helping Randy solve these crimes, which you are not going to be able to do if you can't get your mind off of Ellen Morse."

"She did this," Monk said, stopping in front of the window that had been pried open. The window frame had since been replaced and, I assumed, a new sensor had been installed. Of course, it was a little late now.

"How can you say that?"

"Where did Mrs. Rosland have lunch?"

I checked the file. "The Buttercup Pantry."

"Which is right next door to Poop. That's how Morse knew that Mrs. Rosland was out of the house and roughly when she'd return."

"How did Morse know the sensor in the window frame was broken?"

"Maybe she didn't and just chose the window because it was easier to open than one of the doors."

"Then she was taking a big risk. She was assuming that if a siren went off, the police wouldn't get here in time and that it wouldn't draw the attention of the neighbors."

Monk looked over his shoulder at one of the neighboring houses. An old man was watching us from a second-floor window.

He was wearing a bathrobe over a cardigan sweater and had a face like a raisin.

"How come he didn't see anything?" Monk asked. "Is he blind?"

That was a good question. I scanned the police report for details from their canvass of the neighborhood.

"It says here that Mr. Baker was in the hospital that day. He'd been taken away by an ambulance the previous evening with chest pains. Turned out it was indigestion but they kept him overnight for observation anyway." I closed the file. "So if Ellen Morse is the burglar, how did she know that he'd be gone, too?"

"Maybe she gave him a bottle of that Moroccan poo-oil that night," Monk said, cringing just from the thought of it.

"Let's ask him," I said, eager to rule Morse out as a suspect so Monk could focus and solve the crime so I could finally get some sleep.

But as I turned to go next door, I heard an alarm go off in the distance, perhaps a block or two away, judging by how loud it was.

I looked at Monk, who cocked his head like a dog. His ears even seemed to perk up.

"It's a home alarm," he said. "Another burglary."

"Or it's someone setting off their own alarm by accident, or it's the wind shaking a window, or it's someone who forgot their code," I said. "Those alarms go off in my neighborhood all the time. It's like car alarms. Who pays attention to them anymore?"

"Let's call the dispatcher and see," he said.

We hurried to our patrol car. I got inside, picked up the radio handset, and checked in.

I won't lie to you, I got a real thrill out of identifying myself as "One-Adam-Four" and asking if there was a 211 in progress in the vicinity of our 10-20.

"Ten-four, One-Adam-Four," the dispatcher said. "We have an alarm call indicating a possible two-one-one in progress at 218 Primrose Lane."

I typed the address into our GPS. The house was only a few blocks away. Monk snatched the mike from me and called in.

"Ten-four, Dispatch. Unit One-Adam-Four responding, Code Two."

He replaced the handset and looked at me. "What are you waiting for? Hit it."

"But we aren't cops. We don't have badges and we don't have weapons."

"But we're nearby, we have moral authority, and we have the police car."

And the siren. Logic be damned, it was too good an opportunity to pass up.

I switched on the lights, turned on the siren, and floored the gas pedal, burning rubber as I peeled out, pinning Monk to the back of his seat.

He didn't complain. He was getting as big a thrill out of the action as I was, if not bigger.

I was wide-awake now, the siren amping up my pulse and giving my bloodstream a shot of adrenaline. With the GPS as my guide, I sped to the scene, taking the turns fast and hard, reveling in the screech of the tires sliding on the asphalt and the fishtailing of the car.

It was fantastic.

As I rounded the final corner, I saw a cop car that had come from the opposite direction and was already parked in front of the house. Two officers were getting out of the car as I skidded to a stop, our front bumpers nearly touching.

The cops were Raymond Lindero and Walter Woodlake, the guys we'd met at the hotel earlier that morning. They didn't look too happy to see us. To be fair to them, having two civilians ride up in a black-and-white for a possible burglary-in-progress call wasn't something they were used to.

But I didn't want to give them too much time to think about it or they might send us back to our car. I approached them, trying to exude all the confidence and authority that I didn't feel.

"What've we got, guys?" I had to raise my voice to be heard over the shrill alarm. I noticed that nobody was coming out onto the street or peering at us through their windows.

"We just arrived ourselves," Lindero said. I was once again distracted by his muscles. A great white shark would probably spit him out because he was too tough to chew. "You know what we know."

"You got here fast," Monk said.

"It's a small town," Woodlake said, his cheeks red. He was already catching his breath and he was just getting out of his car. "It ain't San Francisco."

"Our shift is just about over," Lindero said. "We were on our way to the station to clock out."

"Have you seen any cars speeding away?" Monk asked. "Anyone running off on foot?"

"Nope," Woodlake said. "Have you?"

"Maybe this is a false alarm," I said. "A bird flying into a window or something."

"Or the bad guys are jumping the back fence while we're standing here chatting."

Lindero drew his gun and headed for the backyard.

Woodlake drew his weapon and went to the front door, probably because that required the least amount of exertion. Monk followed Lindero and I followed Monk.

Lindero opened the gate and crept along the side of the house, which was lined with rosebushes, to the backyard, where there were more rosebushes, a freshly watered lawn, and a broad patio with a dining set, chaise lounges, a barbecue, and an outdoor pizza oven. That backyard was better furnished than my entire house.

There was a sliding glass door leading to the kitchen. The glass pane beside the latch was broken.

Lindero grabbed the latch with his free hand, gently lifting the door as he slid it open so it wouldn't catch, either because the door was warped or the track was. I had the same problem with my sliding door at home and it drove me crazy.

He stepped cautiously into the kitchen, careful to avoid the broken glass, and we followed him.

The kitchen was recently remodeled and had stainless-steel appliances, an industrial-style stove, marble countertops, and dark-stained wood cabinets with fancy moldings.

"Hello? Anyone home?" Lindero called out. "This is the police."

It was a futile gesture. If anyone was in the house, it would have been hard for them to hear his voice over the alarm.

Monk paused to look at the sliding door, then bent down, took a pair of tweezers from his jacket pocket, and picked up a little round washer from amid the broken glass.

Out of habit, I grabbed a baggie from my purse and held it open for him. Meanwhile, Lindero went to the front door and let in his partner, who typed the security code given to law enforcement agencies into the panel, shutting off the alarm.

The silence was a welcome relief.

Monk dropped the washer into the baggie and went into the entry hall to join the two officers. I followed close behind. From the hall, there was the living room to our left, a study to our right, and a grand staircase curving up to the second floor.

Lindero went up the stairs while Woodlake took the less strenuous path and peeked into the living room.

Monk glanced into the study, which had been ransacked. The desk drawers were open and the floor was covered with books, which had been swept off the shelves that lined the room.

137

Lindero came back down the stairs, holstering his weapon. "All clear."

Woodlake came out of the living room and holstered his weapon, too. "Ditto."

He reached for the mike on his shoulder, which was connected to the walkie-talkie on his belt, and called the dispatcher to report that the house was clear and to request a forensics unit to process the scene.

"Do you know the people who live here?" Monk asked.

Lindero picked up an *Architectural Digest* from a side table and looked at the subscription label. "David and Heather McAfee? Nope. Why would I?"

"You said it's a small town."

"It isn't that small," Lindero said, tossing the magazine back on the table.

"So you can't tell us what's missing," Monk said.

"It'd be hard to, since we've never been in this house before," Lindero said in a slow, patronizing tone, as if talking to a complete moron. "Why? Have you already deduced what's been taken?"

"No, but if it follows the pattern of the other crimes, what's going to be missing will be electronics, jewelry, and loose cash." Monk squatted down in the doorway to the study, took out his tweezers again, and picked up a strand of yellow lint flecked with blue from the carpet.

I handed the baggie with the washer in it to Lindero to hold on to while I reached into my purse for another baggie, which I held open for Monk.

"What's this?" Lindero asked, holding the baggie up to his face.

"A washer," Monk said as he plucked up several more strands of lint and dropped them into my baggie.

"I can see that," Lindero said. "Why are we bagging it?"

"Because it's how the burglars temporarily foiled the alarm system, which is an old Amtek 670," Monk said. "The sensor is a metal rod embedded in the top of the sliding door that makes contact with a magnet in the frame. If that magnetic field is broken, the alarm goes off. The burglar slipped that washer in between the door and the sensor."

It was so ridiculously simple and low-tech.

"The washer stuck to the magnet and maintained the connection when he opened the door," I said. "So why did the alarm go off anyway?"

"In the burglar's hurry to get out, he forgot that the track was warped," Monk said. "He dislodged the washer when the sliding door got stuck as he jerked it open."

"How come neither the alarm nor our siren attracted any attention?" I asked the two cops. "It's like this street is deserted."

"Have you taken a good look at these homes?" Woodlake said. "They cost a fortune to own and maintain. Most of the people who live on this block are married professionals who both work in the city."

"If they've got kids, they're in private school or in day care or with their nannies," Lindero said. "And nothing is going to tear those nannies away from their telenovelas."

Woodlake glanced at his watch. "This would happen right as our shift was ending. Just our damn luck, Ray. And we aren't even going to get overtime for it."

"Why not?" I asked.

"The mayor and chief, who now happen to be the same guy, suspended overtime payments for all city workers because of the scandal," Woodlake said. "There's no money."

"It's okay, you can go," Monk said. "We'll secure the scene until the forensics team gets here."

"You will?" Lindero asked.

"I know you've had a long shift," Monk said. "I was there at the start, remember?"

"How can I forget?" Lindero said, handing the baggie back to me and giving me a grin. "The image is seared into my memory. I don't often get to see a catfight between two women, at least not without a cover charge and a two-drink minimum."

"You're a classy guy," I said.

The cops walked out the front door and Monk headed to the backyard. I trailed after him. Those chaise lounges suddenly looked very, very inviting.

Monk crouched beside the grass and seemed to be studying the blades.

"What are you thinking?"

"The grass is wet," Monk said. "But there are no wet footsteps or mud in the house. There don't appear to be any footprints in the grass or in the dirt along the fence."

"So the burglars came from the street, just like we did."

Monk stood up and rolled his shoulders. "But how did they get away?"

The forensics team arrived ten minutes later, just as I was dozing off in one of the chaise lounges.

Monk asked me to drive him back to the police station because he wanted to go through the case files and examine the map. We stopped at Office Depot and picked up some pins on the way.

By the time we got to the station, my adrenaline high had worn off completely, my energy was sapped, and I could barely keep my eyes open.

I went to Disher's empty office and collapsed on his couch, which was upholstered with the same vinyl as the backseat of a 1975 Ford Country Squire station wagon and no, I'm not going to tell you how I know that. But I wouldn't have cared if it was upholstered with sandpaper. I was so tired that the floor would have seemed inviting to me.

I curled up and instantly fell asleep.

It felt like five seconds later when Monk shook me awake. But it was getting dark outside, so at least four or five hours had passed. I was hungry, groggy, and not entirely sure where I was.

"You need to get up now," he said.

"Why?" I said, turning my back to him, drawing my knees up against my chest, and pressing my face into the warm vinyl where it had been before.

He rolled me back over. "There's been another burglary."

"Have someone else take you," I said. "I'm sleeping."

"This time someone was home," Monk said. "And she was killed."

CHAPTER TWELVE:
MR. MONK AND THE PAIN

The crime scene on Hobart Avenue was only a couple of blocks away, but I used the siren to get us there anyway. I'm sure it didn't shave more than a minute or two off our journey, but that's not why I did it. I needed the adrenaline kick that driving fast would give me to cut through my grogginess. What I really needed was a couple of Red Bulls or about thirty cups of coffee, but Monk was in too big of a hurry to let me stop by 7-Eleven or Starbucks on the way.

The neighborhood where the homicide had occurred was a lot like the one we'd been to earlier that day. This time, though, there were a couple of dozen people on the sidewalks, watching the police activity. House alarms might not draw attention, but portable lights, a morgue wagon, cop cars, and a forensics unit always do.

Disher met us as we got out of the car.

He had a grim expression on his face, yet I also detected a glimmer of excitement in his eyes.

"This is the first murder in Summit since I got this job," he said. "The whole city is going to be watching how this goes down."

And I knew that for a former big-city homicide detective like Randy Disher investigating this murder was going to be a lot more exciting than writing speeding tickets, chasing shoplifters, solving break-ins, or being interim mayor.

It was tragic, of course, that someone had died, but perhaps for the first time since Disher had arrived in Summit, he was on familiar ground.

"Don't worry, Chief. Mr. Monk has solved every murder he's ever investigated," I said.

"I'm not exactly a newbie at this, Natalie. There are a lot of guys sitting on death row in San Quentin ruing the day that they ran up against this badass hombre." He poked himself in the chest with his thumb just in case we weren't sure which badass hombre he was talking about. "It's that reputation as a relentless lawman that got me this job."

"Of course. I didn't mean to imply otherwise," I said.

"But I am spread a little thin now," he said. "So I'm grateful to have a couple of

144

seasoned pros at my side on this one. We need to catch this perp fast."

I was ridiculously flattered that he included me in that statement.

"Then you need to talk to Ellen Morse," Monk said.

"How did you know about her?" Disher asked.

I felt my heart skip a beat. "She's dead?"

"No, she's the Goldmans' next-door neighbor," Disher said. "She's the one who called it in."

"A coincidence?" Monk said. "I don't think so."

"So who is the victim?" I asked.

"Pamela Goldman," Disher said. "Her husband, Joel, is some kind of famous financial guru. Writes books and does motivational seminars on how to get rich quick or increase the riches that you already have."

Disher led us to the house, which was in the center of a corner lot. It was classic Georgian style with some Cape Cod flourishes. The two-story, pitched-roof home was white and symmetrical, with wood siding and decorative shutters and — with the exception of the chimneys — not a touch of stone. The two flat-top, one-story additions on either end were lined with low, ornamental balustrades, giving the home an almost nautical look, a place to stand and look out at the sea.

But there was no sea. Instead, the balconies overlooked an expanse of perfectly manicured grass and a curving driveway that led back to a detached garage, which appeared to be in the process of being remodeled into a guesthouse. The area around the garage was covered with construction materials — sacks of cement mix, rolls of fiberglass insulation, stacks of wood, and pallets of drywall, among other things. An enormous trash bin was nearly overflowing with garbage.

"Joel Goldman came home early tonight on the 5:17 train out of Penn Station, ran into Ellen on the street on his walk home, so they headed back together," Disher said. "He invited her in and they found his wife's body in the kitchen. Ellen called 911."

"Morse did it," Monk said.

"She couldn't have," Disher said. "The ME puts the time of death at around lunchtime. She was at her store all day. We have witnesses."

"So she's in on it with the husband," Monk said. "They were having an extramarital sex affair."

"Joel Goldman was in his office, doing a

146

live Skype webinar, interacting directly with people from all over the world, at the time his wife was killed," Disher said. "There's no way he could have done it."

"Maybe Morse has an identical twin sister," Monk said. "Or he has an identical twin brother."

Disher nodded, mulling the idea, because it was just the kind of theory he would have come up with himself. "That's a possibility. I'll look into that. Good thinking, Monk."

"No, it's not," I said. "It's absolutely ridiculous."

"Oh really?" Monk said. "And how many impossible murders have you solved?"

"I've seen you solve enough of them to know that identical twins is not the answer to this one," I said. "You aren't thinking clearly, Mr. Monk. You're biased against Morse because she sells crap."

"Who wouldn't be?"

I gestured to Disher. "He's not."

Monk narrowed his eyes at Disher. "That's right. Why haven't you done your duty and arrested her?"

"For murder?"

"For selling people poop," Monk said.

"Because there's no law against it," Disher said. "Besides, Dino Dung is cool."

"There's nothing stylish, trendy, artistic,

culturally significant, or personally enhancing about a toxic pile of extremely old, extremely disgusting fossilized excrement."

"Unless it's from a *dinosaur*," Disher said. "Imagine owning something that actually came from a T. rex's ass."

"It would be like owning a chunk of radioactive waste," Monk said.

"It's not the same thing at all," Disher said. "The closest comparison would be owning a piece of a meteor. Now imagine if that piece of space rock was eaten by a Brontosaurus and he crapped it out."

"I can't," Monk said, cringing.

"Prehistoric meteor dino dung," Disher said. "That'd be priceless."

I smiled to myself. It was nice to know that power and authority hadn't changed Disher at all.

We walked along the driveway to the backyard. Monk glowered at the mess around the garage as if it were a tethered wild animal straining against its chain.

A man in a business suit sat crying on the edge of a chaise lounge, face in his hands, a uniformed cop standing beside him, looking very uncomfortable, unsure what to do around so much grief. It didn't take a detective to figure out that it had to be Joel Goldman on the chaise.

I spoke up. "Were there any signs of a break-in?"

Disher gestured to the house. "The glass is broken on the French doors."

"It fits the MO of the other burglaries," I said. "Was Mrs. Goldman supposed to be somewhere today?"

"As a matter of fact, yes," Disher said. "She had a hair appointment that got canceled, so she came back home."

"And walked in on the burglars," I said. "How come the alarm didn't go off when they broke in?"

"Because it wasn't on. She set it when she left the house at eleven a.m., but then she must have come back in for her car keys or something, because she deactivated it thirty seconds later and forgot to set it again when she went back out."

It was a fatal mistake.

We stepped through the French doors into the kitchen, where Pamela Goldman's body was covered with a sheet. Monk squatted down and lifted the sheet so we could get a look at her.

She was maybe in her forties, casually dressed in jeans and a loose-fitting blouse, with long brown hair that was now thickly matted with dried blood. She'd been killed by a blow to the back of the head with the ever-popular blunt object.

"Have you found the murder weapon?" Monk asked.

"It was a rolling pin," Disher said. "The intruder probably just grabbed the nearest object and clobbered her with it."

I glanced over at Joel Goldman, who seemed to have collected himself a bit. He dabbed his face with a handkerchief. His Brioni suit was perfectly tailored to his lean body and his hair was as neatly trimmed as his clothes. Everything about him was clean, crisp, and refined, except for his bloodshot eyes and wet cheeks. Grief was messy, disorganized, and rough.

Disher followed my gaze and took a deep breath. "I hate this part of the job. It never gets any easier."

He headed over to Goldman and we tagged along.

"Mr. Goldman, I'm Chief Disher. I'm terribly sorry for your loss. I want to assure you that finding whoever is responsible for this is my top priority."

"I still can't believe this is happening," Goldman said. "This is a nice town, a safe neighborhood."

"Do you feel up to answering a few questions?" Disher asked.

"What can I possibly tell you that could help?"

"You'd be surprised." Disher gestured to us. "This is Adrian Monk, a homicide consultant to the San Francisco Police Department, and his assistant, Natalie Teeger. They're working with me on this."

Monk tipped his head toward the garage. "Where are the construction workers?"

"There was no one today," Goldman said. "I've been doing it myself and hiring day laborers."

"On your own?" Disher asked.

"I built a cabin at Spirit Lake from scratch, so I figured it wouldn't be any harder converting the garage into a home office. Once it's done, I won't have to make the commute into the city anymore, and Pamela and I can spend more time together. . . ."

His voice drifted off as he realized he was describing a dream that was never going to come true.

Disher took out his notebook. "These day laborers, were they always the same people or new ones each time?"

"A mix," Goldman said. "They huddle on the corner outside of the Home Depot. I honk, they climb into the car, and I pay them cash at the end of the day. A couple of

151

the guys have been back here a few times. You don't think one of them is responsible for this . . . ?"

"It's one possibility," Disher said.

"That would make it my fault that she's dead," Goldman said, lowering his head.

"You can't think that way," I said.

"Was anything taken?" Monk asked.

Goldman's head shot up, his eyes flashing with anger.

"How the hell should I know? The most important thing in my life was just taken from me. Do you think I stopped to check if my stereo was still there? Do you think I even give a damn? How can you ask me something like that?"

"Mr. Monk meant no offense," Disher began, but Goldman interrupted him.

"Do you have any idea what this feels like?" Goldman snapped at Monk. "Do you?"

"Yes," Monk said, then glanced at me. "We both do."

It was a commonality that we rarely acknowledged, much less discussed. There was too much pain there. But it was one of the many things that created a bond between us that was much more complex than just employer and employee.

"Mr. Monk's wife was murdered," I said.

152

"My husband was killed in Kosovo."

Goldman looked at us as if seeing us for the first time. Even Disher was looking at us differently. I'm sure he rarely, if ever, thought about that aspect of our lives. But it was never far from my mind or, I'm sure, from Monk's.

"Oh my God, I'm so sorry." Goldman swallowed hard.

"It's all right," Monk said.

Goldman regarded him with a plaintive, almost pleading look. "Tell me, please, how will I ever get past the pain?"

Monk rolled his shoulders. "You won't."

CHAPTER THIRTEEN: MR. MONK AND THE SECOND ROOM

I leaned against the police car while Pamela Goldman's corpse was wheeled out to the morgue van in a body bag. Disher and two of his officers canvassed the neighborhood looking for possible witnesses, and Monk roamed around inside the Goldman house, trying to deduce what might have been taken. I couldn't see the backyard, but I assumed Joel Goldman was still there, sitting on the chaise lounge, in a state of shock.

I was too tired to do much of anything, and was seriously considering sneaking away for a Big Mac and fries, when Ellen Morse walked over from her house with two mugs of hot coffee, one of which she handed to me.

"You look like you could use this," she said.

"You mean I look like a zombie," I said, taking the mug.

"I know you've had a long day."

I took a sip of the coffee. It had the rich, silky taste of fine cocoa crossed with a dark, bitter roast and had enough caffeine that I felt my heart race, my eyes dilate, and my energy level jack up before the fluid had even reached my throat.

"This coffee is incredible," I said.

"It ought to be. It's Kopi Luwak, the rarest, most expensive coffee in the Western world. Only five hundred pounds of it are made annually."

"What did I do to deserve this?"

"It's what you're *going* to do," she said. "You and Mr. Monk are going to catch whoever killed Pamela Goldman."

"Do you have any idea who that might be?"

She shook her head and took a sip of her coffee. "Pamela was an angel. She spent all of her time raising money for local schools, museums, the arts. She was a giver, not a taker. I'm not a detective, but I'm sure that she wasn't killed because of who she was, but what she walked into."

"Have you seen anyone suspicious hanging around the house lately?"

"Joel has brought in a lot of day workers to help him out with his garage project. I don't want to sound racist or superficial, but some of them were people I'd never

155

invite into my car, much less lead to my home, where they could see all the material things I have that they don't."

Which, apparently, included a supply of the priciest coffee in the United States. I was savoring it. The flavor was amazing, incredibly full-bodied, by far the best coffee I'd ever had. I was so alert now, thanks to the caffeine, that I could probably have heard the flutter of a butterfly's wings from a hundred yards away.

I wondered if it would be rude to ask for a refill.

"I've never had anything like this coffee before," I said. "Where did you find it?"

"In my store," she said.

My stomach cramped. "Your store?"

"I import the Kopi Luwak from Indonesia, where ironically it's known as 'the poor man's coffee' because it's gathered from the ground by people without any land of their own on which to grow coffee bushes."

I relaxed a bit. "So it's made from fallen coffee beans."

"Yes and no. There's an animal called a civet that forages on the big coffee plantations, eating the fruit of the coffee bush, then later poops out the undigested beans, which are gathered up, roasted, and ground into coffee."

So I'd just guzzled a mug of civet poop. I handed her back the empty cup and fought back the urge to vomit. "Do not tell Mr. Monk about this. *Ever.*"

"Why not?"

"Because he'll have you arrested for poisoning me and then take me to the ER to have my stomach pumped."

She smiled. "Do you think that I've poisoned you?"

"I certainly wouldn't have sipped from that mug if you'd told me it was hot liquid crap."

"But you thought it was delicious before you knew that the coffee beans had passed through an animal before being processed and reaching your cup," she said. "So why does it make any difference now? Why is it any more disgusting than drinking cow's milk?"

"Mr. Monk thinks that's poison, too."

"Yes, but do you?"

"No, I'm fine with milk. Sausages, too. But from now on, I'm not eating or drinking anything you give me until you've disclosed whether or not it came out of some animal's butt. You picked a very odd and inappropriate time to play a trick on me."

"That wasn't what I intended," she said.

"I thought I was doing you a favor. Kopi Luwak is a rare and expensive delicacy, sought after and savored by the finest gourmands in the world."

"Well, I'm not one of them. I wouldn't know the difference between a fine bottle of wine and a Two-Buck Chuck from Trader Joe's, but as open-minded as I am, I draw the line at drinking actual crap."

"I apologize," she said.

"No harm done," I said, my stomach churning. "I hope."

"Don't worry, Natalie. The coffee is safe and perfectly healthy, full of antioxidants. The washing, roasting, and brewing process leaves it as clean as bottled spring water."

Monk emerged from the house, froze for a moment when he saw who I was talking to, then marched over.

"Bottled water happens to be Mr. Monk's favorite drink," I said.

"You're joking," she said, following my gaze.

"Nope," I said. "In fact, he's a bottled water connoisseur. He can sip a glass and tell you how old the water is, where it came from, and the minerals that it contains."

"Incredible," she said.

Monk stopped in front of us and glowered at Morse. "Do you have a twin sister?"

"I'm an only child," Morse said.

"Are you having an extramarital sex affair with Joel Goldman?"

"Of course not," she said. "How can you even ask me a question as rude as that?"

"Because anyone who washes herself with poop is clinically insane, has no moral or ethical scruples, and wouldn't think twice about committing adultery or killing another human being."

"You may be impolite but at least you're honest," she said. "I'm going to change your mind about me yet, Adrian."

"Not as long as you keep selling excrement."

"I'd like to invite both of you to my house for dinner tomorrow night," she said.

"I don't think that's such a good idea," I said.

"I promise that nothing on the menu will be predigested," she said.

"Gee, that sounds enticing," Monk said. "But I'd rather have dinner with Charles Manson than break bread with you, and by 'break,' of course, I mean cut into even halves."

"You are adorable," she said.

"You are reprehensible," he said.

I spoke up. "All this talk of food reminds me that I haven't eaten since breakfast and

I don't think Mr. Monk has, either. So if you'll excuse us, Ellen, I think we'll head for the nearest set of Golden Arches that we can find."

I opened the car door for Monk and practically shoved him inside, then got in myself and drove us away. My stomach growled so loudly it sounded like a small animal was in the car with us. Apparently, drinking a cup of hot civet poop hadn't diminished my appetite. If anything, it had stimulated it.

"Was anything missing in the house?" I asked.

"It appears some jewelry and cash were taken," Monk said. "It's consistent with the previous burglaries."

"But something isn't sitting right with you."

"It's her," Monk said.

"I don't think that she's been burglarizing houses and that Pamela Goldman caught her in the act and was killed for it."

"Why not?"

"Ellen Morse would have to be awfully stupid to burglarize her next-door neighbor's house."

"Maybe she did it because she's fiendishly clever. She anticipated that someone like you would think that she'd be too smart to burglarize her own neighbor and would rule her out as a suspect. It's a shrewd ploy and you're falling for it."

"You're forgetting that she has an alibi. She was seen in her store at the time of the murder."

Monk waved it off. "I've heard better."

I sighed because I knew what was coming and was already tired of it. Actually, I was just plain exhausted all the way around.

"You're going to mention the guy in outer space again, aren't you?"

"And the one in the coma. Those were top-notch, ironclad alibis, a lot more clever and challenging to crack than 'I was in my store all day selling excrement.' "

"Okay, let's say she was able to be in two places at once."

"That's the first sensible thing you've said all day."

"When did she burglarize the other house today?"

"Which other house?"

"David and Heather McAfee's. The one where you found the washer and the lint. Are you suggesting that after we left her store, Morse went out and immediately burglarized the McAfee house and then hit the Goldman place a couple of hours later?"

"Why not?"

"She'd have to be crazy," I said.

Monk gave me a look. "I think we've clearly established that fact beyond any reasonable doubt."

I found a McDonald's and parked out front. I knew Monk would like the restaurant because it served the same items, in the same way, with exactly the same flavor, no matter which location you visited. He liked consistency.

The only thing that was different was the layout of each individual restaurant, but as disconcerting as that was, he could always depend on them being impeccably clean inside. The place reeked of cleaning supplies and, unfortunately, most of the food tasted like it as well.

I ordered two Big Macs, french fries, and a Coke for myself and got Monk a Big Mac minus the bun (he hated the "chaos of sesame seeds") and not assembled. He preferred all the ingredients boxed separately. I also got him an order of french fries, which I knew he would trim with his knife and fork so all the pieces were the same size.

For a beverage, he had one of the bottles of Fiji water I kept in my ridiculously large purse, the kind mothers with newborns carry around to lug all of their baby stuff.

The fact was, I had a lot of the same

things in my purse that those mothers have in theirs. Disinfectant wipes, baggies, and even some snacks — little packets of Wheat Thins that I'd forgotten all about until that moment. I could have helped myself to Monk's snacks instead of starving all day.

We took our food to a booth and ate in silence, mostly because I was too intent on devouring my meal. I ate it so fast that I didn't even taste it, which was probably a good thing, considering where we were dining.

Monk ate carefully and methodically with his knife and fork, as if performing surgery on the food rather than eating it. I could see that the lack of sleep, lack of food, and the stress of his long day were beginning to take their toll on him. He looked pale, there were dark circles under his eyes, and he was moving more slowly than usual.

"What did you do while I took my nap?" I asked.

"I read through all the files on the burglaries and looked for patterns and inconsistencies."

"What did you find?"

"That I couldn't stop thinking about Ellen Morse," Monk said. "It just shows how corrupt this city really was that she was allowed to open that business on their main street. What I can't understand is why Randy has gone along with it."

"See, this is exactly what I warned you about. You're letting your revulsion of Ellen Morse's business cloud your judgment. You aren't going to be able to think clearly, or solve crimes, as long as she's on your mind."

"Unless she's guilty."

"But what if she's not? Then your inability to stop thinking about her might give a killer the opportunity to get away with murder and cause Randy to lose his job."

"You're right," Monk said.

"I know I am."

"She has to go."

"That's not what I was getting at."

"We have to run her out of town for the good of the community," Monk said. "Unless I can arrest her for burglary and murder first."

"I don't think you're getting my point."

Monk yawned. "But all of that will have to wait until tomorrow. I'm too tired to restore the balance of the universe tonight. Do you mind if we go back to the hotel?"

"Not at all," I said.

We dropped the police car at the station. It was a nice night and we walked to the Claremont Hotel in comfortable silence.

We said our good nights and went up to our rooms.

The effects of the flight, the spotty bits of sleep since then, the periodic jolts of caffeine and adrenaline in between, and the junk food binge all worked together to completely screw up my internal clock and my metabolism.

I was dead tired yet wide-awake.

I know that sounds like a contradiction, but it wasn't.

My eyes burned and my body was exhausted but my mind was too jacked up to sleep. I could almost hear the neurons firing in my skull.

I tossed and turned in bed in my tank top and panties for what felt like an eternity before I finally gave up and turned on the TV, flipping the channels through endless reruns of various versions of *CSI* and *Law & Order,* feeling nostalgic for the time when there used to be other shows on the air besides those two and their procedural, character-free progeny.

But somehow the kaleidoscope of *CSI* and *Law & Order* had a hypnotic effect on me and after a time — it could have been minutes or hours — I found myself locked in a strange trance, floating somewhere between consciousness and sleep, caught in a seemingly endless loop of heavy-headed David Caruso whipping off his sunglasses and Sam Waterston shaking his shar-pei face in dour disapproval.

And I might have stayed that way forever, my eyes wide, my jaw hanging open, drool running down my chin, if not for the rainstorm.

In my room.

I didn't even hear the explosion, or feel the fire, that made the sprinklers in the ceiling go off.

I just felt the cold water, which snapped me out of my stupor and into another one: several long seconds of extreme disorientation as I tried to figure out who I was, where I was, why it was raining indoors, and what that shrill alarm was that was making my ears hurt.

And then it all clicked.

Fire.

And then something else clicked.

Monk.

I threw off the sheets, ran to my door, and opened it. The hallway was thick with smoke and as I turned toward Monk's room, I saw fire licking out of what remained of his door.

Oh my God, no!

I ran in terror to his room. I was almost

166

there when the door to the hotel room between his and mine flew open, releasing a blast of hot air, and Monk tumbled out fully dressed and wide-eyed, soaking wet and shaken, flames nipping after him like angry dogs.

That's when I remembered. . . .

He had two rooms.

Without saying a word, I grabbed his hand and ran with him to the stairwell.

We rushed down the two flights as fast as we could and out the emergency exit to the parking lot, where a dozen other soaked hotel guests had already gathered and stood staring at the flames coming out of the windows of what had been Monk's rooms.

He looked at me. "I definitely would not recommend this hotel to other travelers."

CHAPTER FOURTEEN:
MR. MONK IN THE ATTIC

The first police officers to arrive, our friends Walter Woodlake and Raymond Lindero, were on the scene moments later, followed in short order by the fire trucks, an ambulance, and Randy Disher.

Monk covered me with his jacket, heavy and soaked with water, less out of courtesy than his own extreme discomfort at my near-nakedness.

Officer Lindero didn't have a problem with it, though. He couldn't resist leering at me and making a comment before running into the hotel with Officer Woodlake to help evacuate the guests.

"Last night you were wrestling women, tonight it's the wet T-shirt follies. What's it going be tomorrow? You're like a one-woman Pussycat Lounge."

My response was a profanity that amused the officers and shocked Monk, who asked, "Are you suffering from post-traumatic stress disorder?"

I turned to him.

"I was awakened last night by an intruder and tonight by a fire and both times I had to endure obnoxious remarks from those two police officers while I was half-naked. How do you think I should have responded?"

"Those remarks could have been avoided if you hadn't gone to bed in an indecent state."

"This is how I sleep," I said.

"What you do in the privacy of your home is one thing, and still something you should reconsider, but when you're traveling, you need to change your behavior."

"I am not going to go to bed fully dressed," I said.

"Then you have no reason to complain," he said. "If you dress like a stripper, you will be treated like one."

"Thanks for the understanding," I said.

The paramedics began handing out blankets to all of the drenched and shivering hotel guests in the parking lot. I gladly took one and gave Monk his jacket back.

Because the fire department got there so quickly, they were able to quash the flames within minutes and limit the actual fire damage to the rooms that Monk had occupied. But the water and smoke damage was extensive. Nobody would be sleeping in that wing of the hotel for a while.

Monk and I leaned on the hood of a police car for the next hour or so and watched the firemen mop up as the officers took statements from the hotel guests.

Disher huddled with the fire chief, presumably getting briefed on the details of the fire. There was no question that the blaze was intentional or who was supposed to get incinerated.

We'd had a very hectic twenty hours, causing far more trouble for Randy than we'd resolved. I'm sure Randy was thinking the same thing and asking himself whether it had been such a great idea to invite us to Summit after all.

Sharona drove up and rushed over to us carrying a laundry bag over her shoulder.

"Are you both okay?" she asked.

"We're wet, but we're fine," I said.

"I brought you some clothes," she said, handing me the bag. "They might not fit just right, but they're better than nothing."

"Thank you," I said.

"I am not wearing someone else's clothes," Monk said.

Sharona glared at him. "They're clean, Adrian."

"Not if someone else has been wearing them."

"Randy has been wearing them," she said.

"Randy is someone else."

"Randy isn't some hobo, and I washed the clothes myself."

"I don't wear used clothing," Monk said. "Nobody should. It's unsanitary and disgusting."

"So you'd rather stay in those soaking-wet clothes and catch your death from cold."

"Without question," Monk said and turned to me. "You should follow my lead on this."

Sharona spoke up. "Those are my clothes that I'm lending her."

Monk looked at me sternly. "Need I say more?"

"I am not some kind of skank," Sharona said.

"I will be glad to wear your clothes," I said. "And I appreciate your bringing them down here in the middle of the night for us."

"It was the least I could do," Sharona said. "You both could have been killed and it would have been my fault."

"You're right," Monk said.

"That's cruel, Mr. Monk, and unfair."

"It's accurate," he said.

171

"You owe her an apology," I said.

"She's the one who dragged me across the country to this toxic, excrement-strewn hellhole of corruption," he said. "We wouldn't be here to be killed if it wasn't for her. That's a fact."

"Oh, come on, Mr. Monk. This is not the first time someone has tried to kill us. I don't like it, but if you're going after murderers, you've got to expect that occasionally they're going to come after you, too."

Monk turned to Sharona. "She has PTSD."

"She's telling you to stop whining and I agree with her," Sharona said to him and then looked at me. "I had no idea you were so tough."

"A burglar attacked me in my home and I killed him in self-defense. That's how I met Mr. Monk and ended up working for him. In the years since then, I've seen a lot of death and looked into the eyes of more than a few killers. If that didn't make me tougher, I would have quit this job a long time ago."

Sharona shook her head. "You didn't stay because you got tougher. You stayed because you enjoy it."

"I don't like being scared, and I certainly don't like violence and death," I said, "but

172

yes, I suppose it's true that I've grown to like the work."

"Of course you do," Monk said. "You work for me and I'm a very easygoing, likable person."

"And she likes the rush," Sharona said.

I shrugged. "It beats staying home and folding laundry."

Monk gave me a look. "When have you *ever* folded laundry?"

Disher finished his talk with the fire chief and came over to us.

"The chief says the incendiary device was a Molotov cocktail that was thrown through the window. It ignited the curtains and the bedsheets and spread rapidly from there," Disher said. "You're lucky you were in the other room, Monk, or you'd be toast."

"Luck had nothing to do with it," Monk said. "I slept in room 204 last night, so I had to sleep in room 206 tonight."

"Why?" Disher said.

"Balance," Sharona said. "Adrian had two rooms, therefore he had to alternate which room he slept in."

I could see that Disher still didn't get it.

"It's not enough that both rooms are even-numbered, adjacent, and symmetrical," I said, "but the time he spends in them has to be as well."

"I wasn't raised by apes," Monk said.

"Fine. Whatever," Disher said. "I don't get how you managed to drive someone into a murderous rage in just one day."

"I've seen it happen in five minutes," Sharona said.

"I've seen it happen in two," I said.

"Ask Ellen Morse," Monk said. "She has plenty of motive to want me dead. I told her I was going to take her down and she knew that I meant it."

"Don't be ridiculous, Adrian. Ellen didn't throw a Molotov cocktail through your window," Sharona said. "And besides, how would she have known which room you were staying in?"

"Sharona is right," Disher said. "Only the police and the hotel staff knew that."

"Then it's got to be the hotel owners," I said. "It's Monk's fault that their ghost scam was exposed and they were arrested. Thanks to him, they can kiss their hotel business good-bye, as well as their freedom. Speaking of which, are they still in jail?"

Disher shook his head. "They were released on bail this afternoon." He motioned over Officers Woodlake and Lindero, who were chatting with a couple of firemen.

Woodlake gestured to us as he approached. "I thought these two were supposed to lower the crime rate around here, Chief, not jack it up."

"Did I ask for your opinion, Woodlake?" Disher said. "I want you two to go find Harold, Brenda, and Rhonda Dumetz and bring them in for questioning. Find out where they've been the last few hours and secure their home and cars for the forensics unit."

"Yes sir," Lindero said. He gave a little salute and got into the driver's seat of the police car we were leaning against. Woodlake got in on the passenger side. We stepped away and they drove off.

Monk glanced up at his hotel room, then over at a line of pine trees that was midway between the building and the street. He rolled his shoulders and tipped his head from side to side.

It was his tell.

Disher studied him. "What are you thinking, Monk?"

He was thinking that he'd solved a mystery. What I didn't know was which one it was or how the hell he'd done it.

"I'm thinking I need to go to 218 Primrose Lane right now," he said.

"What's there?" Sharona asked.

"The home of David and Heather McAfee," Monk said. "They were burglarized

175

yesterday morning."

"It's three a.m., Monk," Disher said. "Can't this wait until morning?"

"Not if you want to end the spree of burglaries, catch a killer, and capture an arsonist."

Monk had solved all three mysteries, but there must have been one last piece of evidence that he needed to prove it, and it was at the McAfees' house.

I knew he wouldn't tell me what it was, so I didn't bother asking.

I ducked into the ambulance and changed out of my wet and smoky clothes into a pair of Sharona's tight jeans and a scoop-necked shirt. It was more scooped than I was either comfortable with or had the bosom for, so I put a sweater over it, too.

I emerged from the ambulance and rejoined Sharona and Monk, who regarded me with a bewildered expression on his face. I guess it was odd for him to see me dressed like his former assistant. But Sharona nodded with approval.

"You know something? This fire may have been a blessing in disguise," Sharona said. "That's a terrific look for you. You ought to burn the rest of your clothes when you get home."

"I've been telling her that for years," Monk said.

"You don't have to burn clothes that get stained," I said.

"No, you don't," Monk said. "You can bury them, shred them, or send them into outer space."

"If we did that, our first extraterrestrial encounter might be with some bug-eyed alien race wearing our secondhand clothes," I said. "Imagine E.T. in stained Ralph Lauren. Do we really want that?"

Sharona laughed. "Now you sound like Randy."

"His way of thinking is infectious," I said.

"So are a lot of other things about him," Monk said. "Which is another reason I don't want to wear his dirty clothes."

Sharona groaned and went back home to get some sleep while Disher wrapped things up at the hotel, then drove the two of us over to the McAfees' house.

Disher knocked on the front door, which was answered by a very groggy barefoot man in striped pajamas and a bathrobe.

"Sorry to wake you up, Mr. McAfee. I'm Police Chief Disher, and we're here about —" Disher turned to Monk. "What *are* we here about?"

"Your attic, Mr. McAfee," Monk said,

stepping up beside Disher. "I need to see it."

"Why?" McAfee yawned. "There's nothing up there except baby clothes, Christmas decorations, and old paperbacks. Can't this wait until morning?"

"It's a matter of life and death," Monk said. "Or we wouldn't be here."

The man sighed. "Come on in. I'll get the ladder."

McAfee put on a pair of slippers, went to the garage, and got the ladder, which he brought into the house and carried upstairs.

All of this ruckus naturally woke up his wife and two young kids, who stood in the hallway as McAfee climbed the ladder, opened the trapdoor into the attic, and disappeared inside.

Monk dropped his blanket and went up the ladder behind McAfee, just high enough to peek inside the attic.

"Why is that man all wet?" the little girl asked her mother.

"Maybe it's raining outside," Heather McAfee said.

"It's not, Mom," the little boy said.

"Maybe he ran through some sprinklers," the little girl said.

Monk came right back down again.

"That's it?" Disher said.

"I'm all done." Monk picked up the blanket and wrapped it around himself again. "We can go back to the station now."

"What did you see up there that was so important?"

"Insulation," he said.

"I could have told you they had insulation," Disher said. "All houses have it."

"But you couldn't have told me what kind. This house was recently remodeled and re-insulated with sprayed cellulose instead of blanketed with fiberglass."

"What difference does that make?" Disher asked.

"A big difference," Heather McAfee said. "It's the greenest insulation on the market, made almost entirely from recycled paper that's treated with fire retardant. If everyone went green, we could save the ozone layer and our children from skin cancer."

"I appreciate your desire to conserve resources, limit greenhouse gases, and recycle stuff," Disher said to her, then shifted his gaze back to Monk. "But I don't see what that has to do with the burglary in this house yesterday."

"It proves who did it," Monk said.

CHAPTER FIFTEEN: MR. MONK PROVES HIS CASE

The three of us went back to the police station. Disher and I remained in the dark about who the felon was because Monk refused to tell us. He was saving it for the right dramatic moment and, despite my weariness, irritability, and discomfort, I wasn't going to try to deprive him of that pleasure. He'd earned it. Disher seemed to have the same attitude — one born from long experience — because he didn't press Monk for answers, either.

Evie was waiting for us when we came in. I didn't expect to see her there so late at night. She held a dark blue police uniform that was wrapped in plastic.

"The chief asked me to get this for you," she said, presenting the uniform to Monk. "It's brand-new, never worn, and is about your size."

Monk accepted it with a smile and turned to Randy. "Thank you, Chief."

"No problem, Monk," Disher said.

"For the record, I don't approve of this one bit," Evie said. "He's impersonating a police officer."

"Monk won't be wearing the badge, or the hat, or carrying a weapon," Disher said.

"He'll just be wearing the uniform and driving one of our police cars," she said.

"Exactly," Disher said.

"If it makes you feel better," Monk said, "I am a former San Francisco police officer who rose up to the rank of homicide detective. I still meet all the legal, professional, and physical requirements to serve."

"What about the psychological ones?"

"Do you?" I asked her.

She reached behind the counter and I flinched, half expecting her to come out with her gun. But instead she pulled out my soggy purse.

"The firemen were able to recover this from your room," she said and tossed it to me. It was like catching a leather bucket full of water and I got nice and wet.

"Thanks," I said.

Disher pointed Monk to the side door.

"You can go change out of those wet clothes in the locker room down the hall. I'll see to it that nobody comes in." Monk headed off to change. Disher turned back to Evie. "Are Lindero and Woodlake back yet?"

She nodded. "They brought the Dumetz family clan in with them. The forensics unit is on the way out to the Dumetz place and we're having the Dumetzes' cars towed in."

"Good work," Disher said. "I really appreciate your coming in to help out."

"It's what I live for," she said.

She was so sour-faced I couldn't tell whether she meant it or if she was being sarcastic, not that it really mattered. I followed Disher down the hall into the squad room, which was occupied only by Lindero and Woodlake, who sat at their facing desks doing paperwork.

Lindero looked up as we came in. "We've got the Dumetz family in the interrogation room."

"Did they give you any trouble?" Disher asked.

"Docile as lambs," Lindero said. "They claim we woke 'em and that they've been home all night."

"But they can't corroborate that," Woodlake added.

"In the morning, once the stores open up, I want you to visit the businesses along Springfield Avenue and get their exterior security camera footage from tonight,"

Disher said. "Maybe one of the cameras got a shot of the Dumetzes' car passing by around the time of the firebombing or caught them on foot."

"Will do," Lindero said.

Monk came in wearing the uniform, which seemed to have imbued his stride with a heroic swagger. Either that, or he had a nasty case of hemorrhoids, which I considered highly doubtful.

"When you brought the Dumetz family in," Monk said to the officers, "did you tell them they have the right to remain silent, that anything they say can and will be used against them in a court of law, and that they had the right to have a lawyer present during questioning?"

"Of course," Woodlake said.

"Did you understand those rights?" Monk asked.

"You mean did *they* understand them," Lindero said.

"No," Monk said, "I meant you."

"Yes, we understood what we were saying," Woodlake said.

"Good. That will save us some time and trouble," Monk said. "You're both under arrest."

Lindero laughed. "What for?"

"Burglary and murder," Monk said.

Disher took a seat on the edge of a desk and rubbed his brow. For a moment, he could have been Captain Stottlemeyer. It was uncanny.

I felt his pain. I'm sure the last thing Disher needed in the wake of a city hall corruption scandal was another one in the police department. But that was what he had now, even if he hadn't quite accepted it yet.

"Please, Monk, tell me you're joking," Disher said.

"I don't joke about murder. In fact, I don't joke about anything, though I do know a few knee-slappers. Here's one: A drunken man is walking down the street, with one foot on the sidewalk and one in the gutter. A police officer stops him and says, 'You're under arrest for public drunkenness.' The drunk says, 'Are you sure I'm drunk?' The police officer says, 'Yes, I am.' The drunk sighs with relief. 'Thank God. I thought I was crippled.' "

Monk slapped his knee and waited for us to laugh. None of us did.

Lindero pointed at him. "That man is mentally ill."

Woodlake stood up and walked up to Monk, invading his personal space. "Where do you come off calling us burglars and killers? In case you haven't noticed, we're the good guys."

Monk took a big step back. "You're supposed to be, but you're not. The reason the burglars are always gone by the time you get there is because you're them."

Lindero swiveled his seat around so he could face us. "Let me get this straight, because it's fun for me to try to think like an insane person. You're saying that because the burglars were gone when the police showed up, that means the police must be the burglars."

When he put it like that, it did sound silly. But it didn't to me when I considered the theory in light of what I knew about the burglaries, and what I'd witnessed firsthand when we arrived at the McAfees' house.

Monk didn't let Lindero's objection slow him down. He plowed on with his summation.

"There's more. Being police officers on patrol is also how you're able to case the homes you're planning to break into without anyone noticing anything unusual and it's how you're able to track the movements of the various residents," Monk said. "For instance, thanks to your patrols, you knew that the Roslands' house would be unoccupied in the afternoon and you knew that their nosy elderly neighbor, Mr. Baker, was hospitalized, giving you a window of opportunity to burgle the home without being seen. It's why you didn't see anyone flee from the McAfees' house, and neither did we, and why there were no signs of the burglar's escape across the wet grass."

Woodlake shook his head and looked over at Disher. "Do we really have to stay here and listen to this craziness, Chief?"

Disher sighed and glanced at Monk. "I have to admit, Monk, you're not making a very convincing case. If you're going to accuse two cops of being dirty, you better have solid, irrefutable evidence to back it up."

"Officer Lindero told us that he'd never been to the McAfees' home before," Monk said, then turned to Lindero. "And yet you knew the rear door didn't slide properly on its track before you opened it."

That was true. He did.

Lindero shrugged. "I have a good eye for doors that aren't plumb. If being able to tell when something is crooked is a crime, then you're a master criminal."

"He's got a point, Monk," Disher said.

"I also found this at the house." Monk pulled a plastic evidence baggie from his pocket and handed it to Disher. "I just picked it up from the clerk in the evidence room. It's one of the many yellow fibers collected at the crime scene."

"What's a bunch of lint prove?" Woodlake asked.

"It's not lint," Monk said. "It's fiberglass strands from the insulation at the Claremont Hotel. It stuck to Officer Lindero's uniform when he was up in the crawl space and later he tracked it into the McAfees' house when he burgled it."

"That's your evidence? Bits of insulation?" Lindero said. "You'll find that same insulation in thousands of homes."

"But not the McAfees'," Monk said. "They have sprayed cellulose insulation."

That got Disher's attention. Now he, too, saw the pieces falling into place. He straightened and looked hard at his two officers. They noticed.

"This is hooey, Chief," Lindero said. "Monk can't prove those strands came from me or from the Claremont."

"Actually, I can." Monk took the baggie from Disher and held it up in front of Woodlake's face to demonstrate his point. "If you'll look closely, you'll notice the fiberglass strands are stained with blue. It's from the glycol in the fog machines they had up in the crawl space." Monk handed the baggie back to Disher, then tipped his head toward Lindero. "And speaking of stains, you've got some pine sap on your uniform from when you climbed the tree outside the hotel to throw the Molotov cocktail into my room."

"Well, hell's bells." Lindero drew his weapon and aimed it at Monk.

"That's not a very wise move, Ray," Disher said.

"It's the only one I've got left," Lindero said, rising from his seat. "Don't just stand there, Walt. Get the chief's gun and give it to me."

Woodlake did as he was told, but he didn't seem to have his heart in it. His shoulders were slumped and he looked like he might burst into tears at any moment.

"You could just give up," Disher said.

"I'm not a quitter. I always go down fighting. Cuff yourself to the radiator, Chief," Lindero said, then tossed his cuffs to Woodlake, who caught them. "Cuff Monk and his lady friend to the radiator, too, Walt."

"What's your plan?" Disher asked, as he went over to the radiator and looped his cuffs through it.

"I'm not sure yet," Lindero said, "but I know a big part of it involves not getting arrested and going to prison."

"I don't see a scenario where that's pos-

188

sible," Disher said, then looked over at Walt, who led Monk to the radiator. "Do you, Woodlake?"

"All we wanted to do was make a few extra bucks," Woodlake said as he cuffed Monk. "Everyone is getting rich in this town except us."

"I'm not," Disher said.

"Because you're a fool," Lindero said. "Why do you think the city hired you?"

"Yet I still managed to bring the corrupt politicians down," Disher said. "And now two thieving killer cops."

"You're handcuffed to a radiator," Lindero said.

"But it's still over for you both," Disher said.

"And it wasn't you who figured us out." Lindero gestured to Monk. "It was him."

"I brought him here to solve the burglaries and he did," Disher said. "And the murder, too."

"We never killed anyone," Woodlake said, taking out his cuffs and approaching me.

"So I suppose Pamela Goldman beat herself to death and that Molotov cocktail threw itself into Mr. Monk's hotel room," I said. "Wake up, Walt. You're out of luck. You're just making a bad, bad situation even worse for yourself."

"I don't see how it can get any worse than it already is." Woodlake took me by the arm and started to lead me over to the radiator.

"Hold up, Walt. Just cuff her hands behind her back," Lindero said.

"Why?"

"We're bringing her with us," Lindero said.

I certainly didn't like the sound of that, or the way Lindero leered at me when he said it. Or the thought of what might happen to me when they decided they didn't need a hostage anymore.

"Take me instead," Monk said.

Lindero laughed. "I'd rather go to prison."

"Okay," Monk said. "It's a deal. I'm sure glad that's over."

"You really are a strange guy," Lindero said. "So smart and yet so clueless. I knew you'd be trouble."

"But you thought you could scare him off with a Molotov cocktail," I said.

"The man is scared of dust," Lindero said. "So yeah, I figured a firebomb might send him running back to Frisco. Or, worst case, bagged and shipped to the morgue."

Woodlake cuffed my hands behind my back. "I don't think this is such a good idea, Ray."

"We need some insurance and I like the

way she looks in her underwear. You got a better suggestion?" Lindero asked. Woodlake didn't say anything. "That's what I thought. There's a roll of duct tape in the closet. Tape their mouths shut and let's go."

Woodlake went to the closet for the tape.

"Do you have any idea where that tape has been?" Monk asked.

"In the closet," Lindero said.

"Has it been disinfected lately?"

"Who disinfects duct tape?" Lindero said.

"Who doesn't?" Monk asked.

"We don't." Woodlake came out of the closet and tore a strip off the dusty roll as he approached Monk.

"Wait, wait. I think I speak for myself and for the chief when I say that there's no need to put that tape on our mouths," Monk said. "Our lips are sealed for at least an hour."

"Not good enough," Woodlake said.

"Two hours," Monk said.

"We can't trust you to keep quiet," Woodlake said.

"Okay, then shoot us," Monk said.

"What?" Disher said.

"It's better than suffering a slow, painful, drooling death," Monk said.

"It's duct tape," Disher said. "It's harmless."

Monk turned to Disher to argue the point

191

and Woodlake slapped the duct tape over his mouth.

"Thank you," Disher said.

Woodlake taped Disher's mouth shut, Lindero grabbed me by the arm, jabbed his gun into my side, and we backed up toward the door. I was scared but I felt worse for Monk than I did for myself. He looked terrified.

Lindero stopped. I felt his body tense up. Woodlake turned and stared at something in the hallway behind Lindero.

"That's a .357 Magnum in your back, Ray," I heard Evie say behind us. "You so much as twitch and I'll fire, snapping your spine. You'll spend the rest of your miserable life in a wheelchair, crapping into a colostomy bag."

"Maybe you didn't notice that I have a hostage," Lindero said. "I'll shoot her."

"Go ahead," Evie said. "I'll sleep better at night with one less commie to worry about."

He knew she meant it and so did I.

Lindero dropped his gun on the floor and kicked it aside. Woodlake took his gun slowly out of his holster and tossed it on a desk. It was over.

CHAPTER SIXTEEN:
MR. MONK TAKES A NAP

"You can't get hantavirus from duct tape," the irritated paramedic said, closing his medical bag. It was the same guy who'd come to our hotel the previous morning.

"You can't know that until you've had the duct tape tested," Monk said. Before the paramedics arrived, he'd washed his mouth out with Scope and brushed his teeth two dozen times (luckily I had Scope and a Gertler 4000, his favorite toothbrush, in a sealed package in my purse for emergencies). Now he sat on the edge of the couch. I sat beside him while the paramedic crouched in front of him.

"I'm a paramedic, not Dr. House," the paramedic said, rising to his feet in front of Monk.

"This is how the Black Death got started," Monk said, sitting up.

"They didn't have duct tape in the Middle Ages," the paramedic said.

"But they had rats, ignorance of proper hygiene, and careless physicians," Monk said.

"Next time you call, you'd better really be sick or injured." The paramedic headed for the door, his partner in tow. "Or we'll file charges against you for fraudulent calls."

"So I shouldn't call you until I'm in my death throes," Monk said, "the Grim Reaper standing over me with his scythe dripping with my fresh blood."

"Now you're getting the point," the paramedic said and walked out.

Monk shook his head. "They are as corrupt as Lindero and Woodlake."

"Not quite," I said. "They haven't killed anyone."

"They have by their inaction and laziness," Monk said. "When I drop dead in six months, foaming at the mouth with the plague, I want those two prosecuted as accessories to murder after the fact. Make a note of that."

"Will do," I said.

"You aren't making a note," he said.

"My notebook is sopping wet, so I've made a mental note instead."

"You'll forget," he said.

"I'll remember," I said.

"I'll haunt you if you don't."

194

"It's an empty threat," I said. "You're going to haunt me anyway."

Monk nodded. "True."

Disher was busy interrogating Lindero and Woodlake and preparing for the scandal that would erupt once the media learned about what had happened. So Sharona came to take us back to their house before the reporters showed up. With the hotel shut down, there was nowhere else for us to stay except with Randy and Sharona.

Their place was a very cozy two-story Craftsman with lots of stone and exposed wood beams. The interior décor was eclectic, but not by design. It was a mishmash of Disher's bachelor pad furnishings and Sharona's single-mom furniture and, as a result, was very much a picture of their pasts and their new beginning. For me, it made the house a home. I found it charming and welcoming.

Monk hated it because nothing matched. He liked symmetry, consistency, and uniformity, none of which was present in the intermingling of Sharona's and Disher's lives and possessions. Life wasn't neat.

That was a reality Monk could not, and would not, accept. But at least he was polite about it.

"You live like animals," he said.

195

"We love like animals, too," Sharona said with a mischievous grin, "so I hope you're a sound sleeper."

That completely grossed him out. He covered his ears and began singing "100 Bottles of Windex on the Wall" to clear his head.

He deserved it.

Sharona showed him to her son Benjy's room, where Monk would be staying. The room was decorated with comic book posters and filled with shelves of graphic novels, DVDs, and CDs. Benjy was about the same age as my daughter, Julie, and was traveling through Europe with some of his friends before figuring out what he wanted to do with his life.

I'd be bunking on the leather couch in the den, Disher's man cave, which was dominated by a huge flat-screen TV, a PlayStation, and a Wii. There was also a computer in the corner that Sharona told me I was welcome to use.

With the sleeping arrangements assigned, Sharona declared that the first order of business would be to go out and buy us some clothes and toiletries (on the city's dime, of course).

Monk disagreed with Sharona's priorities. He felt that the immediate crisis was

196

"detoxifying and disinfecting" their "domestic cesspool" of a home.

In other words, he wanted to clean the place.

Sharona didn't take offense. In fact, she thought it was a great idea and so did I. Nothing relaxed Monk more than cleaning, and it would keep him occupied and out of trouble for the rest of the day and perhaps well into the night, if he didn't collapse from exhaustion first.

Her only requirements were that Monk had to promise to stay out of their bedroom, not to incinerate anything, and not to throw out any dirty, flawed, or mismatched dishes or clothing.

Monk was fine with avoiding their bedroom but he chafed against the rest.

"Perhaps I should save all the filth, grime, and fungus for you, too," he said. "You can sell it at Ellen Morse's store."

But he ultimately agreed to her terms.

She made us waffles for breakfast, much to Monk's delight, and then she and I headed out to the Short Hills Mall, leaving him with the dishes, which he was happy to wash.

I have to admit that it was a pleasure to get away from Monk for a while. Being cooped up with him nonstop, and with virtually no sleep, for almost three straight days had been exhausting on physical, emotional, and psychological levels.

And Sharona understood, better than just about anyone else could, exactly what I was going through.

So she took charge at the mall. I didn't have to explain Monk's peculiar needs when it came to clothing and toiletries. They were as much second nature to her as they were to me. She even still remembered his measurements.

Shopping for him was easy. He wore the same thing every day. White shirts that were a hundred percent cotton with exactly eight buttons, a size sixteen neck and a thirty-two-inch sleeve. Pleated and cuffed pants with a thirty-four-inch waist and a thirty-four-inch inseam. Brown Hush Puppies loafers, size ten.

We purchased four identical sets of clothes for him because three sets was an uneven number and two sets was too few.

Then it was time to go clothes shopping for me.

I was too tired to fight Sharona when she picked out stuff that was brighter, tighter, and more revealing than I would ordinarily purchase for myself. I figured it was her money, or at least the city's, and if it made her happy to dress me like her twin sister, so be it. I'd give the stuff to Goodwill when I got home. Besides, I didn't get much, since I figured now that Monk had brought the crime wave in Summit to an end, we'd be heading back home in a day or two.

With the clothes shopping out of the way, we got all of our toiletries and bought Monk his essentials — a thousand packets of Wet Ones disinfectant wipes, a couple of hundred Ziploc baggies, a box of latex gloves, a pocket-size can of Lysol Disinfectant Spray, a small tape measure, and a key chain–size level.

We lugged everything to the car, then treated ourselves to an early lunch at the California Pizza Kitchen in the mall.

But as soon as I sat down in the booth, I found myself struggling to stay awake.

Sharona told me how worried she was that Disher could lose his job now that the police department had been tarnished not just with scandal but with murder.

I'm sure I would have offered sympathy and good advice if I hadn't been fighting just to stay awake. As it was, I barely heard a word that she said. I was so tired I couldn't even eat. Chewing would have taken too much energy.

Sharona saw that I was fading fast, so she

had our food wrapped up to go and hustled me to the car.

I fell asleep on the drive back to the house, and Sharona told me later she'd been tempted to leave me in the driveway in her car with the windows rolled down. But she shook me half-awake, something I don't remember at all, and led me sleepwalking inside, where I collapsed on the couch in the den.

What I didn't know was that Monk had fallen asleep, too, sitting in a recliner, wearing an apron over his police uniform and clutching a feather duster in his rubber-gloved hands as if it were a teddy bear.

It turned out to be a good thing that both Monk and I slept through most of the day, tucked away in seclusion at Sharona and Disher's house. It kept us both out of the public eye and away from the news media, which had been provoked into a frenzy by the arrest of two police officers for murder, arson, burglary, and a bunch of other charges in a town that had already made headlines for rampant corruption in its city hall.

While I was dreaming of sleeping in a huge canopy bed with big fluffy pillows and thick white comforters in a room with wide-open windows, the thin drapes fluttering in the breeze off the impossibly blue waters of the Mediterranean — yes, I dreamed of sleeping, that's how exciting my fantasy life was — poor Chief Randy Disher was being grilled by reporters and the irate New Jersey state attorney general. Disher was doing his best to save his reputation and persuade the outraged and anxious authorities in Trenton not to swoop in and take over Summit.

But as we were soon to find out, by the time he came home for dinner, he'd managed to accomplish both, not because he was media savvy or politically adept, but through honesty and some quick improvisation born out of sheer desperation.

I was awakened by the smell of food. I sat up on the couch feeling stiff and heavy-headed, like one of the *Peanuts* characters, only I wasn't nearly as animated. My stomach growled, angrily demanding attention. So I got up and staggered in my stocking feet into the kitchen, where Sharona, Disher, and Monk were gathered, preparing spaghetti and meatballs. I knew without even looking that each noodle would be the same length and that each meatball would be perfectly round.

Sharona unwrapped our uneaten salads from lunch and put them into bowls so they

201

could be shared while Disher set the table.

Monk wore a KISS THE COOK apron over his uniform and was carefully laying out noodles on the plates when he saw me come in.

"No shirt, no shoes, no service," he said.

"This isn't a restaurant, Adrian," Sharona said.

"The germs and bacteria on her fungal feet don't know the difference," Monk said.

I didn't have the energy or the will to argue, so I went back to the den, put on my shoes, and when I returned, the food was already on the table.

I sat down and looked at my plate. The twenty noodles, two meatballs, and dollop of sauce were all served separately. I mixed them together, eliciting a gasp and a look of disapproval from Monk.

"You're a guest in someone's home, not a hobo in a railroad car," Monk said, then turned to Sharona and Disher. "I apologize for her lack of manners."

"No apology necessary," Sharona said as she combined her spaghetti with the meatballs and sauce. "We're all animals here."

Monk turned away, only to be assaulted by the sight of Disher doing the same thing. "Is this Summit? Or Sodom and Gomorrah?"

"You sound like the people who were on my back today," Disher said.

"Seems to me they have good reason," Monk said.

"Mr. Monk, you're talking to a close friend who has welcomed you as a guest in his home. How can you be so insensitive and rude?" I turned to Sharona and Disher. "I apologize for his lack of manners."

"No apology necessary," Disher said. "Because Monk is right."

"Of course I am," Monk said.

"The corruption in this town is so widespread," Disher continued, "I was certain that after people heard about Lindero and Woodlake, they'd march on police headquarters with torches and the authorities in Trenton would invade."

"So why haven't they?" Sharona asked.

"Because I told everybody that I have things under control and that the arrest of Lindero and Woodlake proves it. I rooted out the corruption in city hall first and then I brought in two experienced law enforcement professionals from outside New Jersey to do the same thing in my own department."

"That's a brilliant spin on events," I said. "I had no idea you were such an adept politician."

"I never had a chance to prove it before," Disher said. "My leadership qualities were squelched in Frisco. Here I have a chance to shine."

"Or become the object of national ridicule," Monk said.

"Thanks for the support," Disher said.

"How can you say you're rooting out corruption when you have a store on your main street that's selling excrement?" Monk asked.

"Ellen's store is the least of my problems," Disher said.

"It should be your top priority," Monk said. "It's emblematic of the rot that permeates this city and is a beacon for criminals, perverts, and lunatics."

"I'm proud of you, Randy," Sharona said, reaching across the table and giving his hand a squeeze. "When this is all over, the public may elect you mayor."

"I don't want the job," Disher said. "I'm a cop."

"Speaking of cops," I said, "how did it go with Lindero and Woodlake?"

"Lindero lawyered up fast, but Woodlake cracked the second he was alone in the interrogation room. He wants to cut a deal and get a lesser sentence in return for testifying against Lindero."

"There is no honor among thieves," Sharona said.

"And you can find them all shopping at Poop," Monk said.

"Woodlake says the reason they only stole cash, assembly-line jewelry, and electronics was so they wouldn't have to work with any fences to move their merchandise," Disher said. "They didn't want crooks to know that they were, well, crooks themselves. So they simply sold the stuff on craigslist, eBay, and other places like that under fake names."

"Which one of them killed Pamela Goldman?" Sharona asked.

"Apparently neither one of them," Disher said. "Woodlake admits they're burglars but says they aren't killers."

"So they lobbed that Molotov cocktail into Mr. Monk's room because they thought he was chilly," I said.

"It was meant to scare him off," Disher said, "not kill him."

"So I suppose Woodlake says Pamela's death was an accident," Sharona said. "Or that it was her fault for walking in on them unannounced."

"Nope," Disher said. "He says they didn't kill her."

"Of course he does," Monk said. "But the evidence says otherwise."

"He says they didn't burglarize that house, either," Disher said, "and that they have an alibi for the time of the killing."

"Is it convincing?" Sharona asked.

"No, but it's a new one on me," Disher said. "Woodlake says they were busy burglarizing another house at the time she was killed."

"Have you tried to confirm it?" I asked.

"Not yet," Disher said. "That'll be your job when your shift starts tomorrow."

"Shift?" I said.

Disher reached into his pocket and tossed something shiny across the table to me. I caught it out of reflex. It was a badge.

"Welcome to the Summit Police Department," Disher said.

CHAPTER SEVENTEEN:
MR. MONK AND THE BADGE

Disher tossed a badge to Monk, too.

Monk caught it, immediately pinned it on his uniform, and then smiled with pride.

"Wait a minute," I said. "You're telling me we're actually detectives of the Summit Police Department now?"

"No," Disher said. "Of course not."

I sighed with relief. "That's good to hear. For a minute there, you had me worried."

"We can't afford detectives," he said. "You're uniformed police officers."

"Cool," Monk said.

"No, it's not, it's insane. We can't be police officers," I said.

"With Lindero and Woodlake in jail, I've lost a third of my force," Disher said. "I need two officers I can depend on and I need them now. I have nowhere else to turn."

"You're not thinking this through," I said. "We haven't been trained."

207

"I have," Monk said.

"I haven't," I said.

"You've been working as a de facto San Francisco homicide detective for years now," Disher said to me. "I know you can do the job."

I turned to Sharona. "Talk to him."

"I already did, while you were napping," she said. "I told him what you said to Adrian outside the hotel this morning."

"I told him to stop whining."

"You told him that he should be used to the risks that come with the job because you certainly were. You told me that you've adjusted to the horrible violence that you see and that it doesn't unnerve you to look a killer in the eye. And you conceded to us both that you actually like detective work. That, and everything Stottlemeyer told Randy before about your skills, convinced him that he was doing the right thing."

I stared at her. "I can't believe you're in on this with him."

"It makes more sense than two civilians driving around in a squad car," she said. "And you can't do any worse than Lindero and Woodlake."

"That's not the point," I said. "You can't just put civilians in a uniform, hand them badges, give them guns, and call them cops."

"Sure I can," Disher said. "I'm the mayor and the chief of police. I can make my cat a cop if I want to."

Monk stood up abruptly. "You have a cat?"

"It was a figure of speech," Sharona said. "We don't have a pet."

"You shouldn't mention a cat if you don't own a cat," Monk said. "Someone could get hurt."

"How could that possibly get anybody hurt?" Sharona said.

"It's like yelling 'Fire' in a crowded theater. It could spark a panic."

"Forget about the nonexistent cat, Mr. Monk," I said. "Focus on what really matters. Randy wants us to be cops."

"That's Chief Disher to you, Officer Teeger," Disher said.

"He's right," Monk said. "Disrespecting the chief is not the best way to start your career as a police officer."

"I don't want to be a police officer," I said. "I already have a job. I'm Mr. Monk's assistant."

"And he's going to work temporarily for me as a cop, with full pay and benefits," Disher said, turning to him. "Aren't you?"

"I'd be glad to, Chief," Monk said. "I think I can do a lot of good in this town."

"Oh God," Sharona said. "Maybe this

isn't such a good idea."

"It's the smartest thing Chief Disher has done since he took on this job," Monk said.

Disher turned back to me. "So if you're going to assist him, and drive him around, you're going to have to be a cop, too."

I shook my head. I felt like the only sane person in a lunatic asylum. Of course, doesn't every crazy person think she is the one person who isn't?

"It's more than wearing a badge and driving a car," I said as adamantly as I could. "You're giving me a loaded gun."

"You have the right to own a gun," Disher said. "It's in the Constitution."

"But what if I have to use it?" I said. "You have no idea if I can shoot."

"You're forgetting who you're talking to," Disher said. "I know that you are capable of using deadly force and that your husband, a professional soldier, trained you to shoot. And I've seen you handle a gun."

All of that was true, but it didn't make his idea of hiring me as a cop any less insane.

Since common sense, logic, and rational argument weren't convincing him, I decided to take an entirely different approach.

"Okay, what do you think is going to happen when the media hear about you handing out badges and guns to two civilians from out of town?"

"I already told them," Disher said.

"You did?" I said.

"And it received a very enthusiastic response."

"It did?" I was astonished.

"Frankly, I think telling everybody that I was bringing in two experienced pros from San Francisco as interim police officers is what saved me from being tarred and feathered. Although your positions are only temporary, you'll be getting full pay and benefits for as long as you're on the job."

"How long are we talking about?" I asked.

"A week or two," Disher said. "Maybe three. Four, tops."

"Did it occur to you that I have a life back in San Francisco that I might not be able to put on hold for a month?"

Disher, Sharona, and Monk all looked at me now as if I'd just made the stupidest comment in the history of stupid comments.

"Who are you kidding?" Sharona said. "You're single and unattached, your daughter is away at college, and your full-time job is the guy sitting next to you."

"Okay," I said. "Did it occur to you to do me the courtesy of asking me first if I was willing to be an interim cop before you announced it to the press?"

"No, it didn't," Disher said. "And do you know why?"

"Because you were improvising and didn't think things through?" I said.

"Because I know you're going to love it," Disher said.

After dinner, Disher gave Monk and me each two big binders that contained all of the local laws and ordinances, as well as the police procedures unique to the Summit force.

Monk and I remained at the kitchen table long into the night, going over our binders together. I was surprised by how much of the material I already knew from my years working with, and closely observing, the San Francisco police. The stuff that deviated from what I knew was minor and not that hard to memorize.

Monk was still in his uniform and wearing his badge like an excited child trying out his superhero costume before Halloween. But he also looked very comfortable in it, as if it were his usual attire. I wondered how I'd look in my uniform, which was wrapped in plastic and draped over a chair in the den. Would I look gawky and uncomfortable or would I look confident and relaxed?

While I read the material in the binders, I kept stealing glances at the badge on the table.

My badge.

And resisting the urge to hold it, or, an even geekier move, pin it on my shirt.

Even though my appointment to the Summit police force was temporary, it was a tangible affirmation of my skills and it seemed like a natural next step in a personal evolution that had begun two years back, when I realized that not only did I enjoy detective work, but I might actually be good at it.

Despite all of my protestations to the contrary, I was thrilled at the chance to experience being a uniformed cop. I couldn't remember the last time I had felt such giddy anxiety about something. I couldn't wait until morning and yet, at the same time, I was terrified.

But it was a healthy, invigorating terror. It was the fear of facing a challenge and not knowing how or if I would overcome it, but that if I did, I would become a new person.

I wasn't kidding myself, though. There were real risks involved in this — for me and, to be honest, for the people of Summit as well.

They give cops guns because the job

requires them to put themselves in mortal danger to enforce the law, protect the public, and prevent crime.

So if I messed up, I could get myself or some innocent bystander killed.

And even if I did everything right, I could find myself in a situation where I might be required to kill someone in self-defense or to save the lives of others.

Disher had to know all of that when he gave me the badge. That meant he had more confidence in me than I had ever realized, perhaps even more than I had in myself.

I was thinking about all these things when I became aware that Monk was looking at me. I met his gaze. He smiled.

"Don't worry, Natalie. You're going to be an excellent police officer."

"How do you know?"

"Because you had the best training officer imaginable," he said.

"Captain Stottlemeyer?"

"No."

"Randy?"

"No."

"Lieutenant Devlin?"

"No."

"Steve McGarrett?"

"No," he said, glowering now. "I was referring to me."

I knew who he was referring to all along, of course. But I couldn't resist teasing him for being so smug.

"I'm sorry, Mr. Monk. That never occurred to me. I don't think of you as a cop."

"I may have given up my badge, but I've never stopped behaving like a police officer. You probably aren't even aware how much you've absorbed simply from observing me and being in my presence for so long, not to mention all the time you've spent with the other people you referred to, though I can't vouch for that Steve guy, whoever he is."

"You're not worried about me watching your back out there on the street?"

"Of course not," Monk said. "You've already been doing it for years."

"But this is different," I said. "I'm going to be armed."

"So am I," Monk said.

That hadn't occurred to me. I'd been so caught up thinking about how all this affected me that I'd forgotten that Monk had been given a badge and a gun, too.

At first the thought of an armed Adrian Monk was pretty scary. But then I remembered that he was a trained police officer after all and that I'd seen him use a gun before. And he'd never hesitated to use

215

deadly force when the situation demanded it. In fact, only a few months earlier, he'd saved his brother, Ambrose, from certain death by shooting a killer.

I knew Monk wouldn't think twice about using a gun to protect me or someone else. The question was, would I be able to?

I stood in front of the bathroom mirror, looking at myself in my police uniform. I wasn't wearing the holster yet, but just the badge and the blues were impressive. I practiced my look of casual confidence.

"Good morning, sir. Let me see your license and registration."

I took a step back and tried my hardest, coldest cop stare.

"Assume the position, scumbag," I said. "Make a move and I'll blow your tiny little goldfish brain into the next zip code."

I didn't sound half as tough or confident as Evie did when she pressed her gun into Lindero's back. I'd have to work on being more menacing, though it helps if you are actually holding a loaded gun. I knew that from experience.

There was a knock on the door. I opened it to see Sharona standing there, a smile on her face.

"You need the bathroom?" I asked.

"Nope," she said. "Adrian is anxious to get to work. He says we're running ten seconds behind schedule already."

"Yikes," I said.

"May I give you a little advice?"

"Sure," I said.

"I'd skip the goldfish bit," she said. "Too wordy. Just tell him you'll blow his brains out."

I felt myself blushing. "You must think I'm ridiculous."

"If I did, I wouldn't have let Randy give you the badge," she said. "You're going to do just fine."

"I hope you're right," I said.

"It's Adrian I'm worried about," she said.

"I've got his back," I said.

"I know," she said. "That's the other reason you had to take this job. I'm afraid that having a badge might go to Adrian's head."

"Gee, you think?" I said. "I'll make sure he enforces Summit's laws and not his own."

"Good luck with that," she said.

I took a deep breath and let it out slowly.

"This is not what I expected when I got on that plane three days ago."

"But you expected murder and arson?"

I nodded. "Not specifically, but yeah, I

figured I'd run into some violence and a few corpses. You can't go anywhere with Mr. Monk without people getting killed all around you. I've accepted it as a fact of life."

"More like a fact of death," she said.

"Point taken," I said.

"This is ordinarily a very peaceful town," Sharona said. "You two shouldn't have too much excitement. My guess is that Adrian has already solved the biggest crimes we're likely to see around here for a long time to come."

"I hope you're right," I said. I took another deep breath and stepped out of the bathroom.

Monk was waiting at the front door in his uniform, shifting his weight impatiently. "We're almost two minutes behind schedule."

"I'll get you there on time," Sharona said, grabbing her car keys so she could drive us to work. "Though I might have to break the speed limit to do it."

"Not with two police officers in the car, you won't," Monk said.

"You'd ticket me?" Sharona said.

"With pleasure," Monk said.

And I knew he meant it.

CHAPTER EIGHTEEN:
MR. MONK IN BLUE

My leather duty belt was loaded with stuff
— handcuffs, pepper spray, a portable radio,
latex gloves, a flashlight, a Taser, an expand-
able baton, a leather notebook, spare ammo
magazines, a side-handle baton, and a .40-
caliber Glock. It seemed like the only things
I didn't have on my belt that I might need
were a whip, a flamethrower, a harpoon
gun, a crowbar, and maybe a few power
tools.

Stottlemeyer once told me that more cops
ended up on disability because of the strain
put on their backs by their belts than from
all other injuries sustained in the line of
duty combined.

I thought he was joking but now I knew
that he was serious. I'd had the belt on for
only thirty seconds and already my back
ached.

But as I stood in front of the mirror in the
locker room, my hands above my hips, I had

to suppress a grin.

I looked formidable.

Then again, anybody wearing that uniform, badge, and duty belt would look tough.

Even Adrian Monk.

I found him on the other side of the locker room, standing in front of another mirror, striking the same pose that I had. Only the tough-guy effect was undercut by the pocket-size can of Lysol that he'd wedged into his belt in place of the flashlight and the disinfectant-wipe packets bulging out of his breast pocket.

"Ready to roll?" I asked him.

"Yes, but just so there's no confusion out there on the mean streets, let me remind you that I'm the senior officer here."

"Gotcha. But just so we're clear, let me remind you that you aren't my boss now. Randy Disher is. So until this job is over, we're partners, not employer and employee."

Monk cocked his head. "So that means I don't have to pay you while you're on the Summit Police Department payroll."

"I suppose it does," I said.

That made him smile. "Then I'm absolutely fine with it."

We'd see if he still felt that way once we

were out on the street and I wasn't assisting him anymore.

We strode from the locker room into the hallway, where Evie was waiting for us, shaking her head with disapproval.

"Here's the address of the home that Lindero and Woodlake say they were burglarizing at the time Pamela Goldman was killed." She handed me a slip of paper.

"Thanks, we'll check it out," I said. "You don't approve of our being cops, do you?"

"No, I don't," she said. "But it's better than having two civilians driving around in a police car. At least now you will be doing something useful, assuming you don't shoot someone by accident."

"We'll try to keep the shooting to a minimum," I said and we walked out.

It was a completely different feeling driving out of the station parking lot in the patrol car that morning, now that I was in uniform and carrying all that stuff.

This time it was infinitely cooler and the *Police Woman* theme was blaring so loud in my head that it was as if the orchestra were in the backseat. It felt like I was in the opening credits of my own series.

As we cruised down Springfield Avenue, I kept my eyes peeled for criminals, people in distress, crimes in progress, and suspicious activity of any kind.

"Pull over," Monk said.

He was staring at the Poop storefront.

"What for?"

"To enforce the law," he said.

"Do you see a crime being committed or someone in trouble?"

"I see an affront to human decency."

I nodded and kept driving.

He turned to me. "I told you to stop."

"And I ignored you," I said.

"You haven't been on the job for five minutes and already you're committing insubordination."

"I don't work for you," I said. "Remember?"

"I am your senior officer."

"But not my boss. Chief Disher specifically ordered me to keep you from harassing Ellen Morse," I said. "And that's what I'm doing. So unless you see someone robbing her store or vandalizing it, we're moving on."

Monk looked away from me, folded his arms across his chest, and sulked until we got to 4374 Brewster Street, the home of one Blake Prosser, according to the note Evie gave us.

Prosser's place was a low-slung and

sprawling house that had been restored to all of its original 1960s space-age glory. The sharp corners and aerodynamic roofline reminded me of *The Jetsons,* a cartoon I watched when I was a kid. But instead of a personal flying saucer in the driveway, Prosser had a new Jaguar that was every bit as sleek as his house.

I parked beside the Jag and we got out, which isn't so easy when you're carrying a sporting goods store and an armory around your waist.

I knocked on the front door. After a moment, Prosser opened it. He was in his thirties, his black hair wet and slicked back, and from the way he was dressed, it looked like he'd made a wrong turn on his way to Miami. He wore an off-white silk shirt with a light floral pattern, opened wide to show off his undershirt and a gold chain around his neck, as well as white slacks and white loafers without socks.

"How can I help you, Officers?" he asked, flashing a set of teeth the same shade of white as his pants.

"You could put on socks," Monk said.

"Has there been a complaint about my feet?"

"There is now," Monk said.

"We're investigating a burglary, Mr.

Prosser," I said.

"Where?" he asked.

"Here," I said. "May we come in?"

"Of course," he said and stepped aside, looking confused. We walked past him into the wide, marbled-floored entry hall. I couldn't help noticing that by the door he had a Louis Vuitton briefcase that was probably worth more than my car.

His home had a very open floor plan. The entry hall led into a vast family room dominated by a massive flat-screen TV beside a high-end stereo system, gaming consoles, and an impressive computer setup. The adjacent kitchen was filled with countertop appliances, from an espresso machine to a smoothie maker.

"I love gadgets," he said, following my gaze. "Fortunately, I'm in the electronics business, so I can get my hands on just about any gizmo that comes along."

"Are you missing anything?" I asked.

"No, I'm not," he said.

"You're missing a pair of socks," Monk said.

"I can assure you that they weren't stolen," Prosser said, adjusting the Rolex on his wrist so I'd notice it. The man was flirting with me with his accessories. "It was a choice."

"A bad one," Monk said. "Unless you're a fan of foot fungus."

"So you're certain that your home wasn't broken into," I said.

"Absolutely certain," he said. "Everything is accounted for. Why do you ask?"

"You have a broken window," Monk said, pointing to the dining room, where a side window had a pane covered with cardboard and duct tape.

"Oh, that. A bird flew into it," Prosser said. "It happens all the time in this neighborhood, as you probably know. They get drunk on the berries from the trees on the street. Maybe you should cite them for flying drunk."

Prosser was joking but Monk had no sense of humor. And I could see from the way Monk's hand was suspended over his ticket book, he was actually tempted by Prosser's suggestion.

"Is that why you're here?" Prosser asked. "Because you saw a broken window?"

"Actually," I said, "we got a report that this house was burglarized yesterday."

"You did? From whom?"

"Two burglars," Monk said.

"That doesn't make a lot of sense. Why would they confess to a crime that they didn't commit?"

"To avoid going to prison for a crime that they did," Monk said.

"I've got a lot of high-end electronics in here," Prosser said, gesturing to the TV. "Like that sixty-five-inch, 3-D Triax flatscreen." The way he said it, and the way he looked at me while he said it, he might as well have been describing a particular part of his body. But I didn't measure a man's virility by the size of his screen. "Don't you think I would have called the police myself if someone had broken in and stolen anything?"

"Yes, of course," I said. "We're just being diligent."

"Which is why we urge you, in the strongest possible terms, and in the name of God, to wear socks," Monk said.

"I'll take that under advisement." Prosser smiled and opened the front door for us. "Now if you don't mind, I've got a lot of work to do. But if you're looking for a deal on an iPad or a PlayStation, stop on by. Consider me your friend in the electronics biz."

"Thank you for your time," I said.

We walked past him out to our patrol car just in time to see a bird fly into the windshield, stagger back in a daze, then lift off again in a zigzagging path down the street.

Monk shook his head in disgust. "Stores selling excrement. Cops breaking into homes. People wearing shoes without socks. Birds flying around drunk. The downfall of Western civilization is beginning right here in Summit. I hope we're not too late to stop it."

"You and I are going to save Western civilization from ruination," I said. "Do you really think that's possible?"

"I'm confident that we can do it," Monk said.

"Don't you think that's a little ambitious?"

"We'll do it one sock at a time, if necessary."

"You may want to call for backup," Monk said as we drove up to a house not far from Prosser's place. We were responding to a domestic disturbance call. The front lawn and shrubs were covered with men's shirts, slacks, underwear, ties, and socks.

A disheveled guy in a wrinkled business suit stood on the front walk, holding his briefcase and looking up in exasperation at the second-floor windows of the house.

Several of his neighbors were out on their front lawns, watching the drama unfold, coffee cups in their hands. I guess it beat watching *Good Morning America.*

"What do we need backup for?" I said to Monk. "This doesn't strike me as a dangerous situation."

"Look at the size of that mess. Everything has to be gathered up, cleaned, and folded. That's more than a two-man job."

"It's not our problem," I said.

"It's disorderly conduct," he said.

"It's disorder," I said. "Not conduct."

"Throwing it out the window was the conduct."

"Throwing clothes out the window isn't a criminal offense," I said.

"It has to be," he said.

"It isn't," I said.

"My God, is there no law at all in this town?"

"There's a law against disturbing the peace," I said. "That's why we're here."

"The peace of not having clothes strewn over shrubbery," he said.

"I don't think so," I said.

"Well, that's the way I'm going to interpret it."

I parked in the driveway and we got out. The man turned and groaned when he saw us.

"You really don't need to be here," he said. "I've got it all under control."

"It doesn't look like it to me," Monk said. "Your yard is a mess."

"She's a drama queen, that's all," the man said. "You can go. It's all over."

"You're done fighting?" I said.

"Probably. There are no more clothes left for her to toss out. She's out of ammo."

That was when a computer monitor sailed out of an upstairs window. I shoved the man aside and the monitor smashed on the ground where we'd been standing.

"Now you've gone too far," he yelled, pointing at the broken glass and plastic. "That was a seven-hundred-dollar monitor, you crazy bitch!"

"You'd better open your umbrella, Dave!" A woman in a pink bathrobe leaned out of an upstairs window. "Because I'm just getting started."

She pulled a ring off her finger and threw it out. Dave chased after it into the shrubs.

"That's a five-thousand-dollar diamond," he said. "Are you insane?"

"You throw one more thing out the window and I'll place you under arrest," Monk said.

"Me?" she yelled. "I'm not the adulterer. I'm not the one who spent the night banging his secretary."

Dave emerged from the bushes, holding

the ring. "I told you, Martha — I pulled an all-nighter working late on the big presentation. Nothing happened. It's all in your imagination."

Monk rolled his shoulders and looked up at Martha. "Come down here right now and bring the shampoo and soap from your shower with you."

"What for?" she said.

"Because I'm the law," Monk said, then turned to Dave. "How long have you been up?"

"Twenty-four hours straight, sweating at my desk, slaving over a massive presentation I have to deliver in Pittsburgh next Tuesday. And you know why I do it? To provide for my family. And this is the thanks I get."

Martha came out, her feet in big furry slippers. She was holding a shampoo bottle in one hand and an eroded bar of soap in the other.

"He's a lying pig," she said.

Monk sniffed the shampoo and then sniffed the bar of soap. "Yes, he is."

"How can you say that?" Dave said. "You don't have any of the facts."

"I know that you had an extramarital sex affair with your secretary and that you showered afterward so your wife wouldn't

230

smell her on you," Monk said. "You thought you were being smart using the same brands of shampoo and soap as you have at home, but that was also your mistake. If you'd really spent all night sweating over your work, you wouldn't still have those distinctive fragrances on you."

"It's strong soap," he said. "That's why I use it. Read the box. It says it offers twenty-four-hour protection."

"Perhaps," Monk said. "But you also took your clothes off to have your extramarital sex affair and washed them to be absolutely certain you wouldn't bring home a stray hair of hers or, perhaps, of one of her pets. The wrinkles on your shirt aren't from working but from not ironing your clothes after they came out of the spin dry."

Dave laughed, a little too heartily. "My God, you're as crazy as Martha. That's pure fantasy."

"Your secretary uses fabric softener when she washes clothes." Monk picked up a shirt from a juniper bush. "Your wife doesn't."

"You can't tell that from just looking at a shirt," Dave said.

"You can if you aren't blind," Monk said.

That would make 99.9 percent of us blind compared to Monk, but regardless, it was obvious from the look on Dave's face that he was guilty as charged.

Monk pointed at Dave. "You're leaving. But first you're going to neatly fold all of these clothes and take them with you. Be sure to wash them before you wear them."

"Why should I bother to fold them if they're just going into the wash?"

Monk got up in his face. "Because you don't want me to shoot you."

"You're crazy," Dave muttered.

"Then you'd better hope I don't stop you on your way out of here and find a single item of clothing unfolded." Monk looked over at Martha. "And I expect you to clean up after that computer monitor."

"Yes sir," she said.

Monk nodded and marched to the car. I tried to suppress a smile as I got into the driver's seat.

"Aren't you the tough guy," I said, starting the car.

"I hate cheaters," he said.

"I don't like adulterers much myself," I said.

"I can't stand people who try to shirk their obligation to fold their clothes," Monk said. "There are some lines you simply can't cross."

CHAPTER NINETEEN:
MR. MONK
PROTECTS AND SERVES

I called Disher and let him know that the alibi that Woodlake gave him for Pamela Goldman's murder didn't hold up — not that he was expecting that it would.

Now that the Goldman murder and the string of home burglaries were solved, Disher was hopeful that law enforcement in Summit would go back to the usual mundane dribble of petty crimes and misdemeanors.

Since Prosser's house was only a few blocks from the Goldman residence, I decided to cruise by and see how Joel Goldman was doing. Goldman was a stranger to me, but the grief and anger he was feeling were not.

I remembered all too clearly how I'd felt when I learned that my husband's plane had been shot down over Kosovo. At least I didn't have to see him being carried out of our own home in a body bag. I couldn't imagine what that must have felt like.

When we pulled into Goldman's driveway, I could see him carrying drywall into the garage that he was converting into a home office.

I took the radio and called the dispatcher to let her know we were Code 6 at the Goldman residence, which basically meant we'd left our car to investigate something.

"What are we doing here?" Monk asked.

"Showing a victim that we care," I said and got out of the car.

We walked down the driveway to the garage, where I could hear Goldman working inside with his nail gun, most likely securing the drywall.

"Mr. Goldman?" I called out between nail firings.

Goldman emerged wearing leather work gloves, his sweatshirt and jeans covered with dust. He seemed bewildered to see us.

"When did you become police officers?" he said.

"This morning," I said. "It's only temporary. There's a manpower shortage on the force."

"That's because two police officers were arrested yesterday for burglarizing your home and murdering your wife," Monk said.

"I know all about that," Goldman said. "I

had a dozen reporters outside of my house last night, jockeying for the best position for their live shots on the eleven o'clock news."

"I'm sorry," I said.

"Don't be." Goldman turned to Monk. "I understand from Chief Disher that I have you to thank for solving the case."

"It wasn't very hard," Monk said. "I once solved a case where the murderer's alibi was that he was in a coma at the time of the killing."

"Really?" Goldman said.

"This was a no-brainer," Monk said.

I spoke up quickly. "Not that he's diminishing, in any way, your horrible loss."

"I know he's not. I want to apologize for the way I treated you yesterday." Goldman took off one of his work gloves and held his sweaty hand out to Monk. "I am forever in your debt."

Monk hesitated, staring at Goldman's moist hand as if it were covered with maggots.

I took Monk's arm by the elbow and forced him to extend his hand toward Goldman, who shook it.

"Mr. Monk appreciates it," I said.

"If there is ever anything I can do for you," Goldman said, "don't hesitate to ask."

"You could wash your hands." Monk took

a disinfectant-wipe packet from his pocket and tore it open.

"Okay, I will," Goldman said and nodded toward the house. "I'm going to do it right now."

Monk vigorously wiped his hands with the moist towelette. "You'll thank me later."

"I believe I just did," Goldman said.

"You'll thank me again," Monk said.

Goldman went inside. I'm sure he was grateful for the polite excuse to get as far away from us as he could. The last thing Goldman needed to deal with today, less than twenty-four hours after his wife's murder, was Monk's eccentricities.

Monk held the wipe out to me but I ignored him and started walking down the driveway to the car.

"You're supposed to take this," he said, hurrying after me with the wipe, and the packet it came in, held at arm's length.

"That's your problem, not mine," I said. "You've got a pocket full of baggies. Use one of them."

He stopped and took a baggie out of his pocket. He dropped his used towelette into the baggie, sealed it tight, then tossed it into the Dumpster beside Goldman's garage.

I got in the car, called the dispatcher, and reported that we were back on patrol.

Monk got in and we drove off.

"Did it seem odd to you that he was working on his home office the morning after his wife was killed?" he asked.

"Not at all. What did you do after you got the news that Trudy had been killed?"

"Sobbed uncontrollably," he said.

"And after that?"

"Kept sobbing," he said.

"After that?"

"Sobbed some more."

"What did you do after the sobbing?"

"I cleaned the house," he said.

"Because you were trying to restore order in your life."

"Because the house was a mess," he said.

"I heard that you cleaned nonstop for three weeks until you finally collapsed from exhaustion, dehydration, and sleep deprivation and had to be hospitalized."

"It was a very big mess," he said. "It was work that needed to be done."

"So is the renovation of Joel Goldman's garage into a home office."

"What does he need his home office for now?"

"It's got nothing to do with whether or not he needs a home office, Mr. Monk. He's desperate to occupy himself, to go through the motions, *any* motions, to distract himself

237

from the overwhelming grief and pain that he's feeling. Maybe this is his way of restoring order to his life."

Monk looked at me. "What did you do after the sobbing?"

"I focused all of my attention on Julie," I said. "I absorbed myself completely in mothering her. Actually, smothering her is more like it, but she survived. And thanks to her, so did I."

"I had Sharona," Monk said.

"And Joel Goldman has his home office," I said.

"What's he going to do when he finishes it?"

I shrugged. "Maybe he won't."

"That's ridiculous," he said.

"Have you ever heard of the Winchester Mystery House in San Jose?"

"Nope," Monk said.

"It was owned by the guy who made the Winchester rifle. After he died, his widow, Sarah, kept remodeling and adding on to her Victorian mansion. The work continued every day until her own death thirty-eight years later. The house has two ballrooms, forty bedrooms, ten thousand windowpanes, forty-seven fireplaces, three elevators, six kitchens — more than a hundred and sixty rooms in all. She thought the never-ending construction would appease and confound the spirits of all the people killed by her husband's weapons."

"She was a fruitcake," Monk said.

"She was carrying a lot of grief," I said. "Who knows, today we might have witnessed the beginning of the Goldman Mystery House."

The next few hours lived up to Disher's hopes. Monk wrote a few parking tickets, cited some people for spitting, and chastised others for letting their dogs urinate on the street.

One elderly woman who was walking her poodle took genuine offense at being admonished by Monk.

"My dog has been doing his business on this street for ten years," she said.

"You should be ashamed of yourself and your dog," Monk said. "There are laws against public urination."

"For people," she said.

"Urine is urine," he said. "Do you think your dog's is any less disgusting and unpleasant? Do you think people appreciate having their streets soaked in dog pee? It's barbaric."

"Where would you have my dog relieve himself?"

"In a bathroom," Monk said. "Like any

other civilized creature."

"A dog isn't a civilized creature," she said.

"Yours certainly isn't," Monk said. "You shouldn't own a dog if you aren't going to properly train it."

"I've never seen a dog use a toilet in my life," she said.

"Of course not," Monk said. "That's why we have bathroom doors."

"That's outrageous," she said.

"Don't press your luck, lady," Monk said. "You're lucky I'm letting you walk away without a ticket."

"For what?"

"Public urination, of course," he said. "You ought to crank up the volume on your hearing aid before you go out."

"I don't have a hearing aid," she said.

"Then maybe you should get one," Monk said.

The woman stormed off in a huff rather than continue engaging Monk in debate. So he turned his attention to using his tape measure to determine whether parked cars were equally spaced between one another. If they weren't, he left a warning citation under the windshield. But drivers with the misfortune of parking while we were there had to endure Monk's directing them into place. He wouldn't let them leave until their cars were perfectly centered between the other vehicles.

While he did that, I stood around and tried to look confident and coplike as his backup.

It was an important job. There was always the chance that one of the drivers might become frustrated enough to shoot him. I wasn't parking my car but I was tempted to shoot him myself just listening to him give drivers directions.

I suppose I could have stopped him, but I knew it was making him happy. So I let him indulge himself. He deserved it for all the good he'd done in Summit over the last couple of days.

And for me.

Thanks to him, I was a cop, and I didn't even have to spend a single day at the police academy.

CHAPTER TWENTY:
MR. MONK
ACCEPTS AN INVITATION

Monk was on the sidewalk on Springfield Avenue, directing foot traffic, making sure people stayed in their invisible lanes, when I spotted Ellen Morse coming our way, a friendly smile on her face.

"Here comes Ellen Morse," I said.

Monk looked up with a scowl on his face. "The she-devil."

"This would be a good time to apologize to her."

"For what?"

"For accusing her of having an affair with Joel Goldman and implying that she was involved in his wife's murder."

"She could have been," he said.

"But she wasn't," I said. "You like to say that you're always right when it comes to homicide, but this time you were wrong."

"I never *officially* declared that she was the one."

"You were wrong."

"It doesn't count because she sells poop soap," he said.

"You were wrong."

"She sells poop paper," he said.

"You were wrong."

"For God's sake, Natalie, she's pure evil."

That was when Morse reached us. "Congratulations on joining the Summit police force. You're the talk of the town."

"That will settle down soon," I said.

"I doubt it," she said. "The cars on the street have never been parked by make, model, and color before. People will be talking about this for a long time."

"I apologize," Monk said through gritted teeth.

"I kind of like it," Morse said. "I'm a very orderly person myself."

"It's not about the cars," I said and gently nudged him. "Tell her what you're sorry for."

"For suggesting you had an extramarital sex affair with your neighbor," Monk said. "But I'm categorically, absolutely, and definitively not apologizing for condemning you for being a poop purveyor."

"That's very nice of you," she said. "However, I won't accept your apology unless you come to my house for dinner tonight."

"Will you be serving hot buttered poop,

poop salad, and cow patty cookies?" Monk asked.

"Not tonight," she said with a smile. "See you at seven."

"What can we bring?" I asked.

"Gas masks, gloves, our own eating utensils, and penicillin," Monk said.

She laughed, though she probably didn't realize that he was being serious. But nothing Monk said seemed to offend her. If anything, it only seemed to make him more endearing in her eyes.

"Just bring your charm and good humor," she said and ambled on toward her store.

"I hope you're happy," Monk said to me.

I was.

We got back in the car and went on patrol. Over the next couple of hours, we gave out a few tickets for traffic violations and Monk laid down the law to some jaywalkers.

After that, we were dispatched to the home of Yasmine Dugoni, a three-hundred-pound woman with varicose veins who was wearing a loud, floral housedress and who had reported an act of terrorism. It turned out to be the toilet-papering of a tree in her front yard while she was at work.

Monk was outraged by the crime.

"This is what happens when you have a

store in town that sells poop," he opined to me.

I didn't see the correlation.

I thought it had more to do with the fact, which I learned from the dispatcher, that Mrs. Dugoni had called the police 153 times in the last year to report the neighborhood kids for loud music, reckless driving, indecent exposure, curfew violations, and scores of other charges.

Considering how much she'd harassed those kids, I thought she was getting off lightly.

And I told her so.

"They're criminals," she said.

"They're kids," I said. "Being kids. If they were truly criminals, they would have done something worse and more permanent. This was harmless. My advice, Mrs. Dugoni, is to buy some drapes and some earplugs. That way you won't see the kids or hear them and you won't have anything to yell at them about anymore. If you stop yelling at them, you won't have to worry about them toilet-papering your tree again."

"They're terrorists," she said.

"And you're just like the woman who took Toto away from Dorothy," I said. "Only a lot heavier."

I marched back to the car. Monk came up

beside me.

"You weren't very sensitive to her concerns," Monk said.

"Like you were with the old lady and her dog?"

"That was different," Monk said. "The old lady was perpetrating a crime but this woman was a victim."

"Her tree was toilet-papered," I said. "Big deal."

"It's harrowing. I know the terror from firsthand experience." He stopped and looked me in the eye. "My trees have been toilet-papered. Not once, but many times. It's like having a cross burned on your lawn."

"It's not the same thing at all," I said.

"This is worse."

"How is this worse?"

"It's toilet paper," Monk said. "Think about what it's used for."

He cringed. I got in the car. I realized that Monk was right about one thing. I was unusually short-tempered with Mrs. Dugoni. I realized it was because we'd completely skipped lunch in our zeal to enforce the law.

The gas station mini-mart where I'd bought myself breakfast the other day was only a block away, so I drove us over there.

Just thinking about a Hot Pocket made my stomach growl loud enough for Monk to hear it.

He cringed again. He hates anything that reminds him that I have a body or that he does.

I pulled into the parking lot of the Low-P Gas Station & Food Mart.

"What are we stopping here for?" Monk asked.

"I'm getting a snack," I said. "You want anything?"

"Perhaps a package of Wheat Thins," he said. "Or Ritz Crackers and a bottle of Fiji water, please."

He liked Wheat Thins because they were perfectly square and Ritz Crackers because they were perfectly round.

I got out and went into the mini-mart.

There was a different guy behind the counter this time. This guy was in his thirties, lanky, unshaven, and when I came in, his eyes widened to E.T. proportions. Cops have that effect on people. Even if you've never committed a crime in your life, you are bound to feel guilty of something when you're facing a cop.

I smiled to put him at ease. "Got any Wheat Thins or Ritz Crackers?"

"Over there." He gestured in the general

direction of the rear of the store. Since there were only three aisles, that didn't narrow things down much.

"Thanks," I said. But as I turned to go down the aisle, I saw packets of Ritz Crackers right below the counter, along with several kinds of chips and candy.

I almost said something to the clerk about the crackers being right under his nose, but a twinge between my shoulder blades stopped me and kept me moving down the aisle and pretending I hadn't seen them at all.

I went to the freezer, slid open the glass door, and surveyed the selection of Hot Pockets, but it was only a show. I didn't care about the Hot Pockets anymore. My heart pounded hard in my chest and I began to sweat.

I stole a glance at a mirror up near the ceiling to my right. It was angled in such a way that the clerk could see what was going on in the back of the store. It also allowed me to see him watching me intently, occasionally shifting his gaze to the storeroom door that was to my left. The door was ajar, and I could see someone's foot, clad in a tennis shoe, tapping the floor nervously.

My throat went dry. It was as if the air had been sucked out of the place, the rest of the world had vanished, and all that still existed was that mini-mart, the guy at the counter, and whoever was in the storeroom.

I slammed the refrigerator door shut, hoping the action had drawn so much attention that nobody would notice that I'd unsnapped the clasp over my gun with my other hand at the same time.

I walked down the middle aisle where the cleaning supplies happened to be, grabbed a can of Lysol on impulse, and strode up to the front counter, my heart beating so rapidly that I thought it might burst out of my chest like that creature in *Alien* and run squealing out the door.

Relax, Natalie.

I set the can of Lysol on the counter between me and the cashier and smiled at him like the friendly officer that I was. It was in that instant that I knew what I was going to do, though maybe on some subconscious level I'd known it before.

"Guess what — the Ritz Crackers are right here," I said and pointed below the counter to a rack in front of me.

"Really?" the cashier said.

"Yeah, take a look."

As he leaned forward, I picked up the can of Lysol with my left hand and sprayed him in the eyes. He shrieked and staggered back.

With my right hand, I drew my gun and aimed it at the storeroom door.

"Drop your weapon and come out with your hands up," I said to whoever was back there. In my peripheral vision I could see the cashier rubbing his eyes, tears streaming down his face. So I sprayed him again to keep him occupied, eliciting another shriek and filling the room with a linen-fresh odor. But no one emerged from the storeroom. The only movement was that tapping foot.

"I am going to start shooting in three seconds. These are armor-piercing bullets," I said. "What do you think they'll do to that thin wooden door and your skull?"

They weren't armor-piercing bullets, but I didn't think whoever was behind the door knew that.

At least I hoped he didn't.

And I hoped I'd sounded tough instead of silly. It's not easy to deliver lines like that without sounding ridiculous. Clint Eastwood is probably the only guy who can get away with it. Even at eightysomething years old, he's one scary guy.

Me at fortysomething, far less so.

The door opened slowly and a man came out, thin and jittery and sweating from every pore, his hands on his head.

As he stepped out, I saw that the man

who'd waited on me the other day was on the floor behind him, wide-eyed and terrified, duct tape over his mouth and around his wrists and ankles.

Monk ran in then, his gun drawn, and saw me holding two robbers at bay with a Lysol can in one hand and a Glock in the other.

He smiled and nodded with approval.

"That's what I call law enforcement," he said.

We booked the two robbers at the station and we were on our way back to the squad room to write up our reports when Evie stopped me in the hallway.

"I was wrong about you," she said. "You've got stones."

"Thanks," I said.

Evie looked at Monk. "You, I'm not so sure about."

She continued on to wherever she was going and we continued on to the squad room, where we found Disher waiting for us.

"I just heard what happened at the gas station," Disher said. "Fantastic job, Natalie. How did you know a break-in was going down and that the proprietor was tied up in the back room?"

"The cashier didn't know where the crackers were," I said.

"That was it?"

"And I had a twinge between my shoulder blades," I said.

He pointed at me. "That's what I was looking for. I told you that you had a cop's instincts."

"Did you hear about the Lysol?" Monk asked Disher.

"I did," Disher said.

"That was her Monk instincts kicking in," he said.

Disher nodded. "I have no doubt."

"I do," I said.

Monk looked at me. "Of all the items in the store that you could have grabbed, you picked the Lysol disinfectant cleanser. That's significant."

"I picked it because I knew it would sting his eyes but not cause permanent damage."

"You picked it because it was the cleanest option," Monk said.

"I'm proud of you, too, Monk," Disher said. "Downtown Summit has never looked so organized. I've had dozens of calls."

"People are grateful," Monk said.

"Mostly they're irate. But what matters is that you've shifted everybody's attention away from Lindero and Woodlake. By the way, the two of them are sticking to their story. They insist that Prosser is lying."

"What possible reason would Prosser have to lie about being burglarized?" Monk asked.

"None," Disher said. "Lindero and Woodlake are idiots. I don't know why I didn't see it before."

"You inherited them from the previous chief," I said. "They weren't your hires. You were still getting settled in when the city hall corruption scandal broke. You never had a chance to really get to know your officers."

"The chief is responsible for the actions of the officers in his department. There are no excuses. But at least there won't be any doubt of their guilt. We served search warrants on their apartments and a storage unit that they'd rented outside of town. We recovered a truckload of electronics and jewelry. Our evidence room is stuffed with it."

"Case closed," Monk said. "You can put it all behind you now and look to the future."

"That's the good news," Disher said. "Tomorrow I'll put the word out on the cop grapevine that we're soliciting applications for two new officers, though it's going to be hard to top you two."

"Thank you, Chief," I said.

"Want a ride home for dinner?" Disher asked.

"We've still got some reports to fill out and then we have other plans," I said. "Ellen Morse invited us over for dinner."

"Cool," Disher said. "You can ask her my question."

"What question?"

"How much a meteor fragment pooped out by a dinosaur would be worth."

"Oh my God," Monk said. "How can you even imagine such a thing?"

"I bet it's the Holy Grail of Poop," Disher said.

"Do you know what the Holy Grail is?" Monk said.

"I know for poop it's got to be a chunk of meteor fragment gobbled by a mighty T. rex and blown out of his dino-butt."

"The Holy Grail is the chalice that Jesus drank from at the Last Supper," Monk said. "So a Holy Grail of Poop would be a chalice of excrement."

"Who says a Holy Grail has to be a chalice?"

"God says so," Monk said.

"When did he say that?"

"When he didn't say it was dinosaur poop."

I smiled to myself and went to a computer

to write up my report while they continued their ridiculous argument. It didn't irritate me. Quite the contrary. I found it comforting, like an old, familiar song.

CHAPTER TWENTY-ONE:
MR. MONK GOES TO DINNER

It wasn't until I started working on my report and had to recount every detail of what went down in the mini-mart that I realized how dangerous the situation had been and how reckless I'd been. And then I began to think about all the other deadly ways it could have played out.

I looked up and saw Monk studying me. He'd already finished his report because he didn't have as much to say. He'd been in the car and didn't realize anything was amiss until he saw me, through the mini-mart window, draw my gun.

"Having second thoughts?" he asked.

"Hell yes," I said. "What was I thinking in there?"

"You were thinking a robbery was in progress, lives might be in jeopardy, and you stopped it."

"No, I didn't think that. I didn't think at all. I just had a feeling and I went with it."

256

"There's nothing wrong with that."

"Of course there is. What if my feeling was just acid indigestion, dry skin, or fatigue? What if the cashier was new or stupid and didn't know where the crackers were? What if the guy in the storage room was a legitimate employee? I would have assaulted a guy for nothing and aimed a gun at an innocent person. And what if that innocent person had, in fear, made a sudden move that I misinterpreted as aggression? I could have killed someone."

"That's not what happened," he said.

"It could have," I said.

"But it didn't," he said. "Your instincts were right. The place was being robbed."

"Even so, what if the Lysol spray hadn't temporarily blinded the cashier? What if the guy in the storeroom had come out shooting?"

"You would have shot back," Monk said.

"Would I?" I asked. "And if I had, what if the proprietor had got caught in the cross fire? I didn't even know he was back there until it was over."

"But there was no shoot-out and no one was injured."

"There could have been," I said.

"You did the right thing, Natalie."

"I'm not so sure," I said. "Maybe instead

of acting like Dirty Harry, I should have pretended not to see a thing, then come back out to the car and called for backup."

"And it could have become a dangerous hostage situation instead," Monk said. "And when we all stormed in, everyone could have been killed in the melee."

"You don't know that," I said.

"You're right, I don't. But these dire hypotheticals are pointless. The fact is that you stopped a robbery in progress and subdued the assailants."

I shook my head. "It could just as easily have become a bloodbath. I don't know if I am ready for this."

"Clearly you are," Monk said.

"How can you say that?"

"Because you instinctively went for the Lysol."

"I went for my gun," I said.

"You went for the Lysol first," Monk said.

"I could have shot someone," I said.

"But first you disinfected the scene with Lysol, proving how levelheaded and conscientious you are. You have nothing to worry about."

"So why don't I feel better about this?"

"Because you're a good cop."

"You can't know that," I said. "I've only worn a uniform and a badge for one day."

"I know it because you're second-guessing your actions. A hard-charging wannabe cop who is just in it for the thrills wouldn't be. You understand the consequences of what you're doing out there."

"Someone could get killed," I said. "By me."

"That's true," Monk said. "But if it happens, I know it will be someone who would have killed you first if given the chance. Or me. Or somebody else."

"Thank you, Mr. Monk," I said.

"You're welcome," he said. "Partner."

We submitted our reports, changed back into the street clothes we'd brought with us that morning, and drove our squad car over to Ellen Morse's house. It was weird to be back in the squad car again without our uniforms on, but it was the only transportation we had.

We pulled up to the curb in front of her house.

"Pop the trunk," Monk said.

"What for?"

"So I can get my hazmat suit, of course."

"Ellen has invited us to her home for dinner. You are not walking into her house wearing a gas mask and gloves. It's beyond rude."

"You expect me to walk in there unprotected when there could be poop on the floors, poop on the walls, and poop in the air? The house itself could be made out of bricks of dung."

"It's a chance you're going to have to take."

"Why?"

"Because it's the polite thing to do."

"You're talking to me about polite?" Monk said. "It's considered polite to bathe regularly with soap, not wash yourself in excrement. She's the one who is impolite."

"Millions of people in India bathe with the soap that she sells in her store."

"Have you smelled the people who use that soap?"

"No, have you?"

"Perhaps there's a reason they are on the other side of the planet and we're here," Monk said.

"That's stupid and racist," I said.

"That's no way to talk to your boss," he said.

"You're not my boss, remember? You're my partner. Now get out or we're going to be late and I don't think you can live with that."

It was a low blow, but an effective one. He couldn't tolerate being late, even if it was to the home of the devil herself.

We went up the front walk to Ellen's door, Monk trailing behind me. My guess was that if she opened her door and a torrent of poop spilled out, he wanted to be sure I got hit with it first and he had time to run.

I rang the bell. She opened the door and made a show of checking her watch.

"Six fifty-eight," she said. "You're early. I thought I told you to be here at seven."

"We can wait," Monk said. "Or we can leave and not come back."

"I'm joking, Adrian. Where's your sense of humor?"

"I don't know," he said. "I'm still looking."

She laughed and beckoned us inside. "That's more like it."

What she didn't realize was that he was being serious.

I stepped inside. Monk hesitated, trying to get a good look at the interior from the safety of the porch first.

I'm sure that what Monk saw in the entry hall and adjoining living room surprised him as much as it did me.

The furniture was all matching sets, seemingly arranged with laser-guided precision according to exact mathematical calculations that guaranteed that each piece would not only be centered but set in perfectly equal and balanced relation to every other piece.

The works of art on the walls were in identical frames and arranged by size in symmetrical groupings. Even the images within those frames, whether they were painted, sketched, or photographed, were symmetrical.

It all felt manufactured and synthetic, as if I'd walked into a home designed, built, and occupied by androids.

It made that open house in San Francisco, the one dressed for showing, seem lived in and authentic by comparison (minus the dead Realtor, of course).

"You have a beautiful home," Monk said, stepping inside. "So warm and comfortable."

Only if you find the ambience of mausoleums, hospital operating rooms, and morgues relaxing, which Monk did, primarily because they were so stainless and sterile.

"Thank you, Adrian," she said.

I couldn't believe what I was seeing. It was as if she and Monk shared the same interior decorator, a supercomputer or perhaps some alien being that had never actually been in an earthling's home before but was nonetheless trying to create one.

I'm sure he didn't expect that. I certainly didn't.

"It's perhaps the nicest home I've ever seen," he said, looking awed. You would have thought we were touring the Palace of Versailles.

"I'm truly flattered," she said.

The décor had to be a show for Monk's benefit. But if it was, she'd pulled off a monumental undertaking that was accomplished with extraordinary speed and care.

"Is this really how you live?" I asked her.

"Oh, of course not," she said, closing the door behind her.

I sighed with relief. "I didn't think so."

"I stashed all of my coprolites and dung art away so I wouldn't offend Adrian."

"And the rest of this?" I said, sweeping my arm to indicate the entire house.

"I'm sorry I didn't have a chance to clean up," she said. "But I barely had time to hide the art and make dinner as it is. I hope you brought your appetites."

She led us into the living room, where there was a bottle of white wine for us and a bottle of Fiji water for Monk, and some hors d'oeuvres, a bowl full of roasted almonds and an assortment of canapés — toasted squares of bread topped with minced olives, mushrooms, shrimp, deviled eggs, and slices of cheese.

Monk and I sat down on the couch and I gobbled up a bunch of the canapés. Once they were in my mouth, I realized I was ravenous. I'd never gotten that Hot Pocket I went into the mini-mart to buy.

"Delicious," I said, and I am ashamed to admit that my mouth may have been full at the time.

It took all the self-control I had not to scarf down all the canapés then and there, so I reached for a handful of almonds to fill my hand and my mouth.

Monk eyed the food suspiciously, which Ellen noticed with obvious amusement.

"I assure you that nothing I will be serving you tonight was made with anything predigested, and that includes the dishware," Ellen said, opening the wine and filling our glasses before taking a seat across the coffee table from us.

"Was everything washed with real soap, including the plates and the linens?" Monk asked.

She nodded. "With common, brand-name dish soaps and laundry detergents found in any grocery store."

With that disclaimer, Monk bravely reached for an olive canapé and ate it. I took two more of the shrimp ones and another handful of almonds.

"Very tasty," he said and took another, popping it in his mouth.

"I grew the olives and mushrooms myself in my own garden," Ellen said.

Monk suddenly went pale. "Using fertilizer?"

She smiled. "They were grown in soil enriched by a compost heap made up of decomposed organic matter like banana peels, grass clippings, eggshells, leaves, potato skins, uneaten fruit that went bad in my refrigerator, coffee grounds, that sort of thing. No chemicals and no excrement were used."

Then again, her coffee grounds probably included beans that had once passed through the intestinal tract of a civet, but I didn't see any need to make that clarification. I took a sip of the wine and it was delicious, so I hoped it was covered in her disclaimer and wasn't derived from rare grapes crapped by some exotic animal I'd never heard of.

"You're obviously a woman who appreciates cleanliness, order, and balance," Monk said. "So how can you possibly peddle poop, much less surround yourself with it?"

"That's exactly why I can," she said.

"That makes no sense," Monk said.

"It does if you understand my approach to life. For one thing, I can't stand waste."

"Neither can I," he said.

"I prize efficiency and order."

"Me, too," Monk said, then turned to me. "Now we are getting somewhere."

"That's why I believe that anything and everything that *can* be recycled *should* be recycled, and that includes the excrement from all living things."

"Okay, now you're talking crazy," Monk said. "It's sad because you were doing so well before."

"I'm a big believer in the importance of symmetry and circles," she said.

"Now you're talking sense again. Hold on to those concepts and you'll finally begin to see reason."

"I try my best to lead a balanced life."

"Of course you do," Monk said. "It's only natural. Balance is something we should all strive to achieve."

"That's exactly what I'm getting at, Adrian. When we use something and recycle what's left of it, and then that product is itself recycled, and if that process is continually repeated, it creates a perfect circle and a natural balance. But when there is waste, when something is just thrown away, that circle is broken and an imbalance is created. And so it is with poop. If we can find ways to recycle it for energy, art, fertilizer, gunpowder, food, soap, paper, and other products, then that circle, and that balance, are maintained."

There was a long silence, broken only by the sound of me eating the remaining canapés and washing them down with wine. Finally, Monk rolled his shoulders and spoke.

"You're right."

I stared at him now, shocked. "She is?"

"Her argument makes a kind of sense," he said. "It would make perfect sense if it didn't include one thing."

"What's that?" Morse asked.

"Poop," Monk said.

"Don't think of poop as something repulsive and unhealthy that was extruded by a creature," Morse said.

"But that's exactly what it is," he said. "So if you want to keep clean, how can you have poop everywhere? It's an untenable contradiction."

"I've adjusted my thinking," she said.

"You mean you've lost your mind," he said.

I would have chided Monk for insulting our hostess in her own home, but my mouth was full, so speaking up at that precise moment wouldn't have been too polite, either.

Besides, she clearly wasn't offended by his remark. If anything, she found it compelling. She leaned forward, narrowing the distance between them, and looked him in the eye.

"Think of poop as a by-product in the process of manufacturing a product or creating energy, like sawdust or scrap metal or a banana peel," Morse said. "If you do, you'll see it as something left over, a part that no longer fits anywhere, that has to be organized and reintegrated in some way or the natural balance is thrown completely out of whack."

Monk cocked his head and looked at her for a long moment.

"I'll try," he said.

CHAPTER TWENTY-TWO:
MR. MONK
CHANGES HIS MIND

It would have been huge if all Monk had done was agree to consider someone else's point of view on a matter that he'd already had a strong opinion about.

That alone would have represented a major breakthrough for him.

But what he'd done actually went way, way beyond that, because the subject he'd agreed to reconsider was . . .

Poop.

Something that had to be at the top of his list of things that he reviled and feared the most.

The fact that he'd agreed to even consider adjusting his beliefs about something he found so repugnant was truly a miracle, one that probably never could have happened before Trudy's murder was solved.

It was such a big moment, such a Monk milestone, that I wouldn't have been surprised if Dr. Kroger, his late shrink, had risen from the grave and knocked on the door to congratulate him.

But if Monk recognized the profound significance of this moment, he didn't show it at all. He sat calmly through dinner, politely complimenting Ellen Morse on her homemade ravioli and fresh asparagus, all the spears the same size and set side by side on our plates.

It was the perfect meal for Monk, who'd hated her so vehemently just an hour ago, and yet there he was, being slowly charmed by her.

Maybe she really was the devil.

Monk was now at ease around Ellen Morse but I was becoming seriously creeped out, not by her take on poop but by the obsessive-compulsive way she lived in her home, especially since she didn't seem to express those tendencies in any other aspect of her life — at least not as far as I'd seen.

Who was this woman?

So I grilled her — politely, of course.

Under my relentless questioning, she told us that her parents were outspoken liberals with shared political views but sharply different personalities. Her father was a buttoned-down mathematician, very organized and rational, while her mother was a free-spirited dancer/performance artist/

painter, notoriously flighty and disorganized. By all rights, their marriage should never have lasted.

But somehow it did. They loved each other as passionately as they fought, so they found ways to compromise, to strike a balance that allowed them to be who they were without driving each other crazy and to create a peaceful home for their four kids.

That dichotomy of personalities lived on in Morse. She had her father's sense of order and organization to the hilt, but hated math. She had her mother's love of creative expression, but did nothing creative to express herself.

So she bounced around aimlessly, trying to find herself, and traveling the world while she did it, taking on odd jobs and dozens of liberal causes along the way, before becoming an artist's agent, then an art gallery owner, and finally the proprietor of Poop.

I wanted to ask her how she'd become fascinated with excrement, if for no other reason than to remind Monk why he'd been sickened by her to start with, but he interrupted me.

"Have you ever been married?"

"Twice," she said. "Maybe three times."

"Maybe?"

"I'm not sure if the second marriage was

actually legal," she said. "We took our vows in a tribal ceremony in Africa while I was in the Peace Corps."

"Why didn't the marriages last?" I asked, hoping to pry some deep, dark, disturbing truth from her that was deeper, darker, and more disturbing than her Monkish secret life.

She shrugged. "Why do any relationships fail? For me, it was never anything dramatic like betrayals or addictions tearing us apart. The splits were amicable. I suppose it was more about the compromises you have to make, whether it's too many or too few, and not being able to achieve that balance."

"Balance is everything," Monk said.

"What about you?" she asked Monk. "Have you ever been married?"

"Once," he said and he told her about it.

And as he did, I realized that the differences between him and Trudy, a newspaper reporter, were almost as big, perhaps even bigger, than the ones between Morse's parents. And yet I have no doubt that Monk's marriage to Trudy would have endured if she hadn't been taken from him by a murderer.

"She sounds like an amazing woman," Morse said.

"She was," Monk said.

"I'm impressed that you two were able to find that rare and perfect balance," she said.

"I believe that's love," Monk said.

"I believe you're right," she said.

We left at about ten p.m.

That's not true — we left at *exactly* ten p.m. Monk announced at 9:50 that perhaps we should be going, and I'm sure he and Morse then carefully timed their parting pleasantries so we'd be outside the door by 9:59.

"What a great night," Monk said as we walked to the car. "And what a beautiful home."

"It was creepy," I said. "Nobody lives that way."

"I do," he said.

"I rest my case," I said. "There is something seriously wrong with that woman."

"You didn't think so before."

"You did," I said.

"But now that I've had the chance to get to know her better, I see that she's a woman of startling intelligence and complexity."

"She's nuts," I said. "Quite possibly a psychopath."

"Ellen's abiding sense of balance, of natural symmetry, is inspiring, and her at-

273

tention to cleanliness and order is extraordinary."

"It's scary strange. I bet her husbands ran away screaming, if they aren't buried in her backyard. What do you bet they're in her compost heap?"

"You liked her fine when you thought she was simply a purveyor of poop products," he said. "But now that you've learned it's perhaps her only flaw, one born out of her deep and abiding dedication to maintaining the balance and order of the universe, you hate her."

"She served me a cup of hot crap the other night," I said. "And in some ways I think she served us another one tonight."

"You've had a long day, you subdued two robbers — it's no wonder you're feeling cynical," Monk said. "Everything will look better in the morning."

He stopped and the sound of hammering drew him over to the Goldmans' driveway. I joined him. We looked at the garage in the backyard. The lights were on and we could hear Joel Goldman working inside.

"The funeral is tomorrow," Monk said.

"No wonder he's working so hard," I said.

"He should be getting some sleep."

"Maybe he can't sleep. Or he's afraid of what he'll dream about."

"After Trudy was killed, I looked forward to my dreams, because there she was still alive and we were together. The hard part wasn't sleeping. It was waking up."

"It was like losing him all over again," I said, and saw Monk looking at me strangely. "I meant *her.* I meant — oh hell, you know what I meant. And you wonder why he's working?"

I turned and walked back to the car. Monk lingered for a moment longer, then joined me.

Sharona prepared waffles for the two of us the next morning for breakfast, which only added to Monk's obvious good mood.

"I knew you liked waffles," Sharona said. "But I had no idea they'd make you this happy."

"I'm not happy," Monk said, using an eyedropper to fill one of his waffle squares with maple syrup. "I am, however, significantly less miserable."

"So, what's put you in such good cheer?" Sharona set a plate of waffles in front of me and said, "And you in such a lousy mood?"

"You didn't tell us that Ellen Morse has an obsessive-compulsive disorder," I said.

"There's nothing wrong with being neat and clean," Monk said.

"I didn't know she had one," Sharona said. "But so what if she does? It's not like it's something new for you."

"But she hid it so well," I said. "Which makes me wonder what else she's hiding."

"Her poop collection," Monk said. "Thank God."

"So you resent her because she has obsessive-compulsive tendencies," Sharona said, "that she controls so effectively that you were totally unaware of them until she invited you into her home."

"It was creepy," I said.

"It was impressive," Monk said. "You two could learn some valuable lessons from her."

"Sounds to me like you could, too, Adrian," Sharona said, then pointed her spatula at me. "And you, of all people, should hope that he does. Imagine how great it would be if Adrian achieved the same balance that Ellen has."

"She's got amazing balance," Monk said in a far-off, dreamy way.

"Oh my God, Adrian!" Sharona said.

Monk jerked, startled. "What? Did I get syrup on my shirt?" He started patting himself down and searching his body for a stain.

"You're attracted to Ellen Morse," Sharona said.

276

He looked up again. "I admire her sense of order, that's all."

Sharona pointed her spatula at me again. "And you're jealous."

"Suspicious," I said. "What if it's all just an elaborate act?"

"To do what?" Sharona said. "Steal his millions?"

"Get him to like her despite her occupation," I said.

Disher came in, wearing his uniform. "And that's a bad thing?"

"It is if she's only doing it to humiliate him," I said.

"Don't be ridiculous," Monk said. "I was born humiliated."

Sharona handed Disher a mug of coffee. He kissed her on the cheek and sat down at the table. "Why would Ellen want to do that?"

"To get back at Mr. Monk for treating her like crap."

"But she likes crap," Disher said with a grin.

Monk shook his head. "Her lifestyle is genuine. You can't achieve what she has in her home if it isn't something you truly believe in and that comes naturally to you. There are too many tiny details to keep track of and get right."

"Adrian's right, Natalie. Could you do it?" Sharona asked. "Even after all your years with him?"

"I'd like to see her try," Monk said. "God knows I have been begging her to."

They both had a point. But if the way Ellen Morse lived wasn't an elaborate ruse staged for Monk's benefit, that meant she was a pathologically organized person with a raging dung fetish, which was not my idea of a mentally healthy person.

Then again, Monk certainly had his quirks and phobias, enough for just about everybody but me, Stottlemeyer, Sharona, and Disher to write him off as a lunatic.

So why did I care if Ellen Morse was a little nutty, too?

It sure as hell wasn't jealousy.

Yes, I loved Monk, but not in a romantic way.

Maybe I was just being overprotective. I was worried that Monk might get his fragile heart broken.

Or maybe it wasn't that at all.

Maybe it was my ego. I was pissed off because, despite all of my so-called detecting skills, I'd totally missed Ellen Morse's true nature.

But so had Monk.

At least he had an excuse for missing it —

278

he was too distracted by her creepy fascination with excrement to notice anything else. And maybe I was so distracted trying to keep him under control that I didn't see the signs, either.

Or maybe we were both so jet-lagged and caught up in the cases we were investigating that we wouldn't have noticed a walrus if it had walked past us playing drums and singing Neil Diamond's greatest hits.

"Did you ask Ellen my question?" Disher asked.

"Sorry, Chief, we didn't get the chance," I said.

"Poop never came up?"

"It did," Monk said. "She made an interesting and surprisingly valid argument for not just disposing of it as toxic waste."

"So now you're ready to buy a set of poop candles," Disher said, "or maybe drink a glass of dung tea?"

"Hell no," Monk said, pushing his plate aside, his appetite gone. "But I can see, and almost accept to some small degree, her point of view."

"Holy crap!" Sharona said.

"I wouldn't go so far as to venerate it," Monk said. "But perhaps it could have some uses that aren't entirely repugnant."

She came over and crouched down beside

Monk so that she was eye to eye with him. "Adrian, did you really just say that you're contemplating changing your attitude, even slightly, about one of your core beliefs?"

"I'm not an unreasonable person," Monk said.

She shook her head and gave him a kiss on the cheek. "I never thought I'd see this day."

Neither did I.

And that's when I realized that I was jealous of Ellen Morse, but not because Monk was attracted to her.

It was because Ellen Morse was the one who'd achieved this milestone with Monk.

And not me.

Chapter Twenty-Three:
Mr. Monk
and the Knockoff

Our first call on patrol that morning was to investigate a trespassing and disturbing the peace complaint at Homeby's Home of Big Screen on Springfield Avenue.

The storefront windows of Homeby's were full of enormous high-definition TVs playing a continuous loop of scenes from the latest big-budget superhero movies, shots of waterfalls and tropical beaches, and highlights from recent sporting events.

An earnest young man with a Disney park employee haircut and wearing a blue Homeby's polo shirt and khaki slacks met us at the door as we came in. Even though we weren't customers, he still flashed us the Homeby's "We're so glad to serve you" smile that's the cornerstone of the store's advertisements.

"Thank you for coming, Officers. I am at the end of my rope."

"I can tell from your smile," I said. "And

you are?"

"Ken," he said. "Store manager."

"So what's going on?"

"Come in and I'll show you."

There were TVs of all shapes and sizes mounted on the walls or set up in little living room displays, complete with furniture, throughout the vast sales floor. There were streamers and banners across the ceiling, pointing out special bargains and new products, and several blue-shirted salesmen roamed around, talking to customers.

"I don't see any disturbance," I said.

"Are you blind, Natalie? The place has been vandalized. All the TVs are mixed up together, a mishmash of sizes and brands. It's chaos." Monk turned to Ken. "Did you catch the felon who broke in and did this?"

Ken looked confused. "No one broke in. We offer a wide assortment of brands and this is how we always display them."

"I see," Monk said to Ken. "Are you a diagnosed schizophrenic?"

"No, I'm not," Ken said.

"You are now," Monk said.

"How can you say that to me?" Ken said.

"You reported a trespasser and a disturbance of the peace," Monk said. "But now you're saying there was no break-in and the disturbance is intentional. You don't need the police, you need a psychiatrist."

"I called you because of him." Ken pointed to a prematurely balding man in a T-shirt, cargo shorts, and flip-flops, sitting on a couch wearing 3-D glasses and watching *Alice in Wonderland* on a big-screen TV.

"He looks peaceful to me," I said.

"That's the problem," Ken said.

"I'm missing something here," I said.

"Ken's schizophrenic," Monk said.

"His name is Miles Lippe. He has come in every day for the last week and spends hours watching television," Ken said. "He just makes himself right at home and refuses to leave when we ask him to. I warned him that I'd call the police the next time he did it and now I have."

"Is he causing any trouble?" I asked.

"This is a place of business, not his personal screening room," Ken said. "If he wants a TV, he's welcome to buy one. Until then, I want him out of here."

Monk and I headed over to the guy.

"Excuse me, Mr. Lippe," I said. "We'd like to have a word with you."

"Could you move over, please, Officer? You're blocking Johnny Depp."

"That's why we're here," I said. "The manager would like you to watch TV at home."

"I would if I had a TV, but I don't," Lippe said. "That's why I'm shopping for one."

Monk looked at the TV and cocked his head to one side.

"It's 3-D," I said. "You need special glasses to see the picture clearly."

"You aren't shopping," Ken said to Lippe. "You've been lazing around here for days."

"I've been researching," Lippe said. "A new TV is a big-ticket item, especially if you're talking about a Triax Pro a9600. It's four grand. So I've got to ask myself, is 3-D really worth the extra money? Is the technology here to stay? But if I go with a standard high-def TV, which brand do I get? And what screen size? These are tough questions I'm struggling with here."

"You're not struggling, you're sitting around all day in the store watching TV and eating Cheetos," Ken said. "You even bring in your own DVDs."

Monk squinted at the brand name on the front of the TV. It was an even number preceded by the first letter of the alphabet, so I didn't think he'd have much to object to.

"That's because you won't let me take the sets home to try out," Lippe said. "So I'm forced to re-create the home viewing experience here as closely as possible. How else can I possibly choose?"

"It makes sense to me," Monk said.

"But he's practically moved in," Ken said.

"Have you had any complaints from customers or salespeople?" Lippe asked. "Have I intruded in your business or been a nuisance in any way?"

"So what are you saying?" Ken said. "That we should just let everybody hang out here as long as they want and use our store as their personal screening room?"

"Maybe you'd sell more TVs," Lippe said.

"Maybe we should provide food and drinks, too," Ken said.

"Now you're talking," Lippe said.

Ken looked at me. "He's an unemployed loser who is taking advantage of us. We have the right to refuse service to anyone and we're refusing him."

Monk pointed to the TV. "Are all the a9600s just like this one?"

"Of course," Ken said, shifting instantly into salesman mode, Homeby's smile and all. "Each one is an active 3-D marvel that provides stunning 1080p HD clarity to both eyes."

"As well as full wireless connectivity," Lippe said. "Want to check your e-mail?"

Ken's smile evaporated and he turned to

Lippe. "You've been surfing the Net here, too?"

"I'm exploring all the features," Lippe said. "As an informed consumer should."

"What I was asking is," Monk said, "do all the a9600s have a lowercase 'a' in front of the '9600'?"

The question managed to shift Ken's and Lippe's attention to Monk. For the first time, they shared something in common: They were both baffled by Monk's seemingly idiotic question.

"Yes," Lippe said, "I believe they do."

"Not that it makes any difference," Ken said.

Monk rolled his shoulders. "It does to me."

I sighed and turned to Lippe. "Okay, Mr. Lippe, here's the deal. You can stay for one hour each day, spending no more than five minutes in front of any one set, for another week. By then, you should have been able to sample every TV in the store. If you haven't bought a TV by then, you'll have to leave and you won't be permitted back into this store for a year."

"That sounds very arbitrary to me," Lippe said.

"Consider yourself lucky that I'm not throwing you out right now," I said.

"Why aren't you?" Ken asked.

"Because his argument has some validity," I said. "It's a big decision and you have a huge selection."

"That's in total disarray," Monk added. "Perhaps if you organized the store in a coherent manner, it wouldn't take people forever to find the television set that they want and they wouldn't need rest and provisions to fortify them during their search."

Monk headed for the door.

"Is he joking?" Ken asked.

"No, and neither am I." I turned and wagged my finger at Lippe. "Your five minutes in front of this TV set are up. Move along."

As Lippe gathered up his Cheetos and ambled over to the next TV, I followed Monk out the door. I was quite pleased with myself and my Solomon-like solution to the problem.

But when I stepped outside, I found Monk standing outside a jewelry store, staring at the window display of diamonds and Rolexes.

"Looking for an engagement ring for Ellen already?" I asked.

"Don't be ridiculous," Monk said. "Could you do me a favor? Please call the dispatcher and ask her how many times drunken birds crashing into Mr. Prosser's window have set off his alarm."

"Okay," I said. "But why?"

"Indulge me," Monk said.

"What do you think I've been doing day in and day out for years now?" I said, but I did as he asked. I posed Monk's question to the dispatcher using the handset clipped to my shoulder. We both heard the reply.

"Never," the dispatcher said. "But those birds set off alarms all over his neighborhood."

"Why not his?" I asked. "He's been hit by them, too."

"Because Mr. Prosser doesn't have an alarm," she said, using a tone in her voice that suggested, rather strongly, that she was stating the obvious.

And I guess she was, because now that I thought about it, I couldn't recall seeing an alarm control pad on the wall in his entry hall, not that it mattered.

At least not to me. It apparently did to Monk, because the next thing I knew, he was insisting that we pay Mr. Prosser a visit.

I had no idea why we were seeing Prosser again but, like I said before, I was used to indulging Monk's whims. And it's not like we had anything else to do.

Prosser answered his door dressed Miami casual with his hair wet, leading me to wonder if he kept a water bottle around all day to spritz himself or if he just took a lot of showers.

"Back again so soon?" he asked.

"I'm interested in a Triax Pro a9600 flat-screen TV," Monk said. "And you mentioned you could give us a deal."

"So I did," Prosser said. "Come on in."

He led us to his family room. Monk went up and examined the TV, his back to us. Prosser smiled with pride.

"She's a beauty," Prosser said. "The pinnacle of television technology."

Monk rolled his shoulders and turned around to face us again. I could see the change in his demeanor even if Prosser couldn't. He didn't know Monk as well as I did. As Sherlock Holmes might have said, the game was now afoot. I just didn't know what the hell the game was this time.

"This TV costs four thousand dollars at Homeby's," Monk said. "Can you give us a better price?"

"How does twenty-five hundred sound to you?" Prosser said.

"Incredible," Monk said. "How can you offer such a great price?"

"Low overhead," he said.

"Meaning you don't have the cost of the big store, the sales team, or their security," Monk said.

"I run a mail-order business out of my home," Prosser said. "And supply product to some area merchants."

"And yet, with so much expensive equipment in your home, you don't have an alarm system," Monk said.

"I just never got around to it," Prosser said. "But there's really no point, with the birds setting off alarms all the time. Nobody takes the alarms on this block seriously, not even you guys."

"Besides, you wouldn't report a burglary even if you had one," Monk said. "Because the last thing you want is police officers paying too much attention to what you are selling."

"I have a valid business license for this address," Prosser said. "There's nothing illegal about selling items from my home."

"But it is illegal to sell bootleg electronics," Monk said, "The Triax TV model numbers all have lowercase letters but yours has a capital 'A.' These TVs are as fake as the Rolex on your wrist and the Louis Vuitton bag in the entry hall, which is why you didn't report that you were burglarized the other day. Because everything that was stolen was illegal goods that it's a crime for you to be selling."

Now I understood why Monk was so interested in the model number of the TV at Homeby's and why he was checking out the watches at the jewelry store next door.

Prosser took a step back from me, as if he'd just realized I had leprosy.

"I had no idea my TVs were fake," he said. "I am shocked and, to be honest, outraged. I will get to the bottom of this right away and report what I learn to the proper authorities. But I can assure you that I wasn't burglarized."

I spoke up. "So maybe you can explain why we have an evidence room full of fake TVs with your fingerprints all over them."

It was a lie, of course, and it provoked a revealing reaction from Prosser.

He bolted like a rabbit for the back door of the kitchen. I took out my baton and Frisbee'd it at him the way I saw Heather Locklear do it a thousand times on the opening credits of *T.J. Hooker* when I was growing up.

It worked.

The baton hit Prosser behind the knees and sent him flying face-first into the counter.

I ran up, pinned him down, and cuffed his

hands behind his back while Monk read him his rights.

When Monk was done, I sat Prosser up and shoved a dish towel against his nose to stem the bleeding.

"You know what this means, Mr. Monk."

Monk nodded. "That Lindero and Woodlake didn't kill Pamela Goldman. They were busy robbing Prosser at the time of the murder."

"So who killed her?"

"My guess would be her husband," Monk said.

"But he's got an ironclad alibi."

"All the more reason to suspect him," Monk said. "I'd be much more likely to consider his innocence if he had no alibi at all."

"You do realize that defies common sense."

"Not mine," Monk said.

CHAPTER TWENTY-FOUR: MR. MONK REVIEWS THE EVIDENCE

Nobody except Officers Lindero and Woodlake was happy about Monk's discovery. It was another embarrassment for the Summit Police Department and acting mayor Disher. Sure, they'd arrested the two dirty cops who were responsible for a string of residential burglaries, but now Disher would have to concede to the media that those cops had been wrongly charged with murder. It didn't make the police look very bright.

But the bigger problem was that there was still a murderer on the loose who'd killed a woman in her own home. A lot of women in Summit were going to be afraid to be home alone until the murderer was caught.

"The good news is that we've got one of the best homicide detectives in the country on the case," Disher said as the three of us gathered in his office.

"And you, too, Chief," I said.

"I was talking about me," Disher said. "But having someone of Monk's reputation on board is an additional asset, practically speaking as well as from a PR perspective."

"We wouldn't want to forget the PR perspective," I said.

"Now that I'm acting mayor, I've got to think about how it's all going to play on the eleven o'clock news," Disher said. "Because that's what they are watching in Trenton. The state could still come in and take over."

"We can't worry about that," I said.

"I can," Disher said.

"The best thing we can do is to not worry about what anybody else thinks and just concentrate on doing our jobs," I said. "To that end, let's go over what we know about Pamela Goldman's murder."

"Wait, maybe Monk has solved it already," Disher said, then turned to Monk. "Have you?"

"No, not yet," Monk said. "But I think the husband probably did it."

"He couldn't have," Disher said.

"That's the main reason why Monk thinks he did," I said.

"He might have arranged for someone else to do it," Disher said, "but he couldn't have done it himself."

Then Disher proceeded to review all the

facts we knew about the sequence of events leading up to Pamela Goldman's murder.

She had an eleven thirty a.m. appointment at the local beauty salon. She set the alarm when she departed at eleven, then deactivated it thirty seconds later, perhaps to retrieve something that she forgot, then neglected to reset it again when she left the house a second time.

When she got to the beauty parlor, she discovered that her appointment had inadvertently been canceled and that there were no openings, so she returned home, where she apparently surprised an intruder, who hit her over the head with a rolling pin as she walked into her kitchen.

Disher then went over what we knew about her husband's movements during that same period.

That morning, Joel took the 7:16 a.m. train from Summit into Penn Station, then walked to his office at 475 Park Avenue South, where he hosted a live, interactive video webinar at ten a.m. that lasted an hour.

According to Joel's secretary, after that he remained in the office all day working on his next book. He left the office early, taking the 5:17 train out of Penn Station, arrived in Summit at six p.m., and walked home with his next-door neighbor, Ellen Morse, whom he ran into on the street.

Disher's initial theory was that one of the day laborers that Joel had picked up before to work on his garage remodel might have come back to the house to burglarize it and Pamela walked in on him.

But Disher never had a chance to pursue that line of inquiry because the MO of the crime fit the string of burglaries that Lindero and Woodlake committed — and they were arrested for the crimes within a few hours of Pamela's body being discovered. It was assumed, wrongly we now knew, that Lindero and Woodlake killed her when she returned home unexpectedly and caught them in the act.

"I think we've got to track down the day laborers who were helping Goldman convert his garage into a home office," Disher said.

Monk tipped his head from side to side, as if he had a stiff neck. But he was actually trying to work the kinks out of his thinking on the mystery.

"I'm not convinced that Joel didn't kill his wife," he said.

"He might have had an accomplice kill her for him, but he couldn't have murdered her himself," Disher said. "Goldman was doing a live Web broadcast from his Manhattan office that morning. You can see it for yourself. It's archived on his Web site."

Disher went to his computer and called up Goldman's Web site, where there were screencaps of the dozens of video webinars that Goldman had done, arranged in chronological order. All of the webinars were shot at his desk, against the backdrop of a bookcase full of the books that he had written and paisley wallpaper as green as the quick cash he promised his followers. Disher clicked the most recent webinar and played it.

Goldman started talking energetically and with confidence about some investing strategies. I'd tell you what he said but, to be honest, I didn't understand a word of it. He might as well have been speaking in Japanese.

He hadn't spent any of his wealth on the video. The production values were strictly bare-bones efforts. He didn't have a fancy set, there were no snazzy graphics, and the only sound track was the street noise of a police siren passing by outside.

"How do we know this wasn't recorded in advance?" Monk asked.

"Because it was interactive," Disher said. "People were asking him questions in real time, participating either by video, instant messaging, or voice calls, from all over the world. I'll show you."

Disher scanned ahead and some viewers with video-chat capability showed up in pixilated, jerky windows in the corner of the screen while texts from people with questions crawled across the bottom of the frame. Goldman responded to each one individually.

"This doesn't prove anything. The program was over at eleven a.m. but Pamela Goldman wasn't killed until around eleven forty-five," Monk said. "Joel could have come home after the program and killed her."

"Not unless he had a transporter beam," Disher said. "There's no way he could have gone door-to-door from his office on Park Avenue to his house in Summit in forty minutes."

"How do we know for certain that he was in midtown Manhattan?" Monk asked.

"Well, his secretary vouches for him and we have security camera footage of him getting on the Manhattan-bound train in Summit at 7:16 a.m. and of him returning to Summit at six p.m."

Disher hit a few keys on his computer and the two pieces of security camera footage came up on his screen. In one window we saw Goldman getting on the train with the parade of other business commuters holding their coffee cups, briefcases, and newspapers. And in the other window we saw Goldman arriving in Summit and getting off the train in the late afternoon.

"How do we know his secretary isn't lying and that he didn't just get off at the next station instead?"

"Because that's his office in the Web video," Disher said, tapping his screen.

"You can do amazing things with special effects now," I said. "Goldman could have been standing in front of a green screen somewhere in the next town and had his image superimposed over footage of his office."

"That's true, but there's a simple way to find out," Disher said. "You two can go into Manhattan and pull the security camera footage from Penn Station. In the meantime, I'll have this webinar checked out by an expert to see if any video compositing was done. But I guarantee you that Penn Station will have Goldman on their security cameras coming and going and that he was in his office when the webinar was shot."

I had a feeling he was right.

We could have driven into the city in a

patrol car, but I didn't know my way around or the procedure for going through the tollbooths in a police vehicle. It just seemed easier and more convenient to take the train. Besides, that was the method that Joel Goldman used, so it made sense to replicate his movements.

We stayed in our uniforms and Disher called ahead to Penn Station security to let them know that we were coming so that they could queue up the surveillance footage to the proper train arrival and departure.

Taking us off patrol in the middle of our shift meant that Disher had to bring the officers for the next shift in early to cover for us. I wasn't looking forward to their glower of resentment the next time we saw them.

The ride on the New Jersey transit train into Penn Station was fast, smooth, and uneventful. We traveled in silence, alone with our thoughts. But as we got closer to the station, I could sense Monk tensing up even more than I could see it.

"It's going to be all right, Mr. Monk," I said.

"There's going to be a lot of people in there, pushing and shoving and breathing and sneezing and sweating," he said. "It's a good thing I have pepper spray."

"You aren't going to use it," I said. "Or your gun or your Taser. You won't need any of it. You'll have plenty of space around you."

"I've been to New York once before," he said. "It's choked with people."

"But last time you weren't in a police uniform," I said. "Trust me, people will keep their distance."

I was right. When we emerged from the train, a path seemed to naturally open up in front of us, and as we moved through the crowd on the platform, it was as if we were walking in an invisible bubble.

Monk relaxed a bit, but not entirely.

Although he wasn't in danger of bumping into anyone, he could still see all the grime on the floors and smell the thick odors of fast-food grease, human sweat, coffee, chlorinated cleansers, train exhaust, and stale air that built up in the windowless subterranean warren.

A very pale, short-haired woman in a dark, masculine suit, and wearing an earpiece with a cord that disappeared under her jacket, approached us. There was a photo ID clipped to her lapel and I could see the bulge in her jacket created by the gun holstered on her belt. There was no question that she was some kind of law enforcement agent.

"Officers Monk and Teeger?" she asked in a monotone.

"That's us," I said. "What gave us away?"

She frowned, clearly not appreciating my humor. "I'm Agent Lisa McCracken, Homeland Security. Come with me."

We followed alongside her as she moved quickly and with determination through the crowd.

"We're investigating a murder," I said. "It has nothing to do with terrorism."

"But our surveillance matrix does," she said.

I had no idea what a surveillance matrix was, but I nodded like I did. She led us to an unmarked, knobless door between two Doric columns, and swiped a key card into a reader that I hadn't even noticed was there. I heard the door unlatch internally, she shoved her shoulder against it, and it opened.

McCracken led us down a long, empty hallway to another door with another key card reader. This time, the door opened into a very dark room filled with dozens of flat-screens showing different angles of Penn Station. Agents with headsets monitored the activity and spoke in low tones, presumably to agents throughout the station.

"This way," McCracken said, moving to an unoccupied workstation with a bank of four monitors, all showing multiple angles of a New Jersey transit train. She sat down and tapped a few keys on a very slim keyboard. "We pulled Joel Goldman's photo from the Department of Motor Vehicles database. Using facial recognition software, we scanned the faces of passengers arriving at Penn Station on the train from Summit at 7:53 a.m. to see if he was among them."

The image on the monitors zoomed in on one face in the crowd, which we saw from multiple angles.

It was Joel Goldman.

"So that's what a surveillance matrix is," I said.

"One part of it," she said. "I inputted this target manually, but the matrix automatically and continually searches for known terrorists among the hundreds of thousands of people who go in and out of Penn Station every day. Picking Goldman out of the crowd and following his movements was easy."

The cameras continued to track him as he made his way through the station up to Thirty-fourth Street.

"Do you know where he was heading?"

she asked.

"Sure," I said. "He told us he went to his office at 475 Park Avenue."

"Let's see if he did." She typed on her keyboard. "Since 9/11, we've added thousands of closed circuit television cameras. We've got 'em at most of the major intersections in Manhattan, the train and bus stations, and all the freeway tollbooths into and out of the city. We've also got 'em at all the bridges, museums, tunnels, tourist attractions, landmarks, government offices, and the UN, of course. We don't have the city covered as extensively as London is yet, due to budgetary constraints and public privacy restrictions, but we're getting there."

The screens showed us Joel Goldman, in an almost animated sequence of still images, emerging from Penn Station on Thirty-fourth Street, then getting caught up in the flow of people on the sidewalk heading to the corner of Sixth Avenue. The cameras picked him up again two blocks south and tracked him as he made his way east, capturing him at the intersections of Broadway and Thirty-second, Fifth Avenue and Thirty-second, Madison Avenue and Thirty-second, and finally Park Avenue and Thirty-second.

"Joel Goldman definitely came into the

city when he said he did." McCracken typed some more. "And here he is getting on the 5:17 train back to Summit. So he left when he said he did, too."

Once again he appeared on-screen, from multiple angles, stepping onto the train.

"I can backtrack and see if he came to Penn Station from Park Avenue," she said.

"That won't be necessary." I turned to Monk. "It's obvious that his alibi holds."

Monk nodded and sighed. "So there's no question anymore."

"That he's innocent," I said.

"That he killed his wife," Monk said.

CHAPTER TWENTY-FIVE:
MR. MONK IN THE BIG APPLE

We walked Goldman's route to his office on Park Avenue and Thirty-second Street. The skyscraper-lined streets were teeming with people and clogged with cars. Even I felt a little claustrophobic, despite the invisible bubble around us that continued to give us breathing room.

I found the enormity of the city and the density of people and vehicles powerful and exciting. The monumental towers and the long streets that seemed to stretch out into infinity conveyed a strength, a confidence, and a certainty of purpose that was emboldening. And all the movement around us generated a kinetic energy that was as catchy as a musical beat.

It was no wonder New Yorkers felt like their city was the center of the universe. San Francisco exuded character and charm but New York radiated power.

The city didn't have the same effect on

Monk. I'm sure he felt many of the same things that I did, but he didn't like it. It was too much like physical contact, even if there wasn't actually any.

He withdrew into himself, lowering his head, holding his arms tight against his sides and hunching his shoulders, as if he were walking into a strong, icy wind.

Goldman's office was in a tall, imposing building. Luckily for us, he was on the fourth floor and not the twentieth, since Monk was afraid of elevators.

We took the stairs. Because Goldman's business was basically a one-man operation, he shared the floor with an insurance agency, a literary agent, and several accountants.

We walked into a waiting area, the secretary's desk serving as the gateway to the conference room and two closed office doors behind her. The space was decorated with green paisley wallpaper and furnished with heavy wooden pieces, all of which combined to evoke the Dickensian feel of an old, established bank or law firm, only without ink-stained wretches scratching on mounds of yellowed paper with quills.

Instead, we were met by an artificially blond woman in her thirties wearing a tight red V-neck bandage minidress with cap sleeves that hugged all of her zaftig curves and shoved her bosom into her chin. She reminded me of a canister of Poppin' Fresh dough that had just popped.

"May I help you, Officers?" she asked, getting up from behind her desk to greet us, which was no easy feat in a dress like that.

"We're with the Summit police," I asked. "Are you Joel Goldman's secretary?"

"Trina Fishbeck," she said. "I spoke to your chief of police on the phone the other day."

"Yes, we know," I said. "He sent us here just to confirm a few details face-to-face before we close the file. It's standard procedure. He could have been talking to anyone on the phone."

"I understand," she said. "Ask away."

"How long have you worked for Mr. Goldman?"

"A year and a half," she said.

"What do your duties entail?"

"Besides the usual secretarial duties, I stay on top of his book deadlines, arrange his travel, coordinate his schedule. I also answer fan letters, send out review copies of his books, that sort of thing."

"I'm surprised you're not at the funeral this morning," Monk said.

"Only Mrs. Goldman's immediate family

was invited," she said. "Mr. Goldman, her parents, and her brother and sister."

"What was Mrs. Goldman like?" I asked.

"I didn't really know her. I only saw her when she came into the city for shopping or dinner with her husband. She seemed very nice to me. Was there something specific that you needed?"

"We understand that Mr. Goldman did a live broadcast from his office at nine a.m. on the day his wife was killed," Monk said.

"No, that's not correct," she said. "It was at ten and ended at eleven. He does one every month. I'm the producer and director."

She bobbed a little bit with pride.

"What's that involve?" Monk asked.

"Well, there's only one Web camera, so I just make sure that he's nicely framed, leaving enough room for the chat feed at the bottom of the screen and space at the upper edges for the video. My biggest responsibility is selecting the questions and integrating them into the show."

"May we see where it was shot?" Monk asked.

"Of course," she said. She turned and opened one of the doors behind her. "This is his make-believe office, the one we use for the webinars. It's what they call a practical set in the movie business. His real office is the room next door. It has a big window that looks out on Park Avenue."

I immediately recognized the desk, the paisley-papered wall, and the bookcase. There were lights, the kind used for taking pictures or movies, positioned at either end of the desk and a tiny Web camera mounted on a tripod in front of it, a cable running from it to a desktop computer in the far corner. On another desk there were three screens, two of which faced Goldman's desk.

"That's where I sit during the show," she said, gesturing to the corner desk. "I send him text messages on the screen, letting him know what questions have come in, whether they are live video, voice calls, or e-mails. The other monitor shows him the live feed that's going out on the Net."

"Who needs a television network anymore to be a star?" I said. "All you need is a broadband connection, a computer, and a YouTube account and you can be Oprah Winfrey."

"That's exactly the way Mr. Goldman looks at it," she said. "He calls it *sniper*casting, aiming for a specific target audience and striking a direct hit with your full message rather than *broad*casting and splattering everyone indiscriminately with message shrapnel."

Monk walked around the room, tilting his head, framing the scene between his outstretched hands.

"Looks like he wants to be a director," she said.

"You said the show ended at eleven," I said. "What did Mr. Goldman do after that?"

"He went back in his office to proof the galleys of his next book."

"You were here the whole time?" Monk asked.

"Yes, I was, right outside this door."

"What did you two do for lunch?"

"We had salads," she said.

"Did you go out for them or were they delivered?"

"They were leftovers from the day before that we had in our refrigerator," she said. "What does what we ate have to do with anything?"

"We're confirming that he didn't leave the office around lunchtime."

"He was in the office until five and then he went home."

"Why so early?" I asked.

"He always does that on webinar days, since he has to come in earlier than usual.

On most days, he doesn't come in until ten a.m."

Monk turned to me. "We're done here."

I smiled at Trina. "Thank you for all of your help."

"If there's anything more that I can do, please don't hesitate to ask," she said. "Do you need a parking validation?"

"We took the train," I said, then pointed to my badge. "But this is all the validation we need."

We walked out and headed for the stairs in silence. The interview with Trina Fishbeck had been a waste of time and we both knew it. We'd learned nothing we hadn't known already.

As we made our way back to Penn Station, a blue and white NYPD police car roared past, the siren making that distinctive rapid wail that sounded like the *Enterprise* firing its lasers. I wished the Summit police cars could do that instead of just their loud, sustained wail.

There was something thrilling about seeing and hearing one of those NYPD patrol cars. They were as much a part of New York as the Empire State Building, the subway, and corner hot dog vendors.

And that's when it suddenly hit me.

I was in New York City!

Of course, I knew that. I'd felt it walking from Penn Station to Goldman's office. And yet it wasn't until that moment that it really sank in.

I looked around anew, breathing in the sights and sounds of the Big Apple, reinforcing that I was really, truly there.

It seemed foolish not to take advantage of the rare opportunity and go see Times Square, walk through Central Park, and stroll through Greenwich Village.

But then I remembered I was a cop on duty and that I was with Adrian Monk, two situations that severely limited my possibilities.

Visiting New York for fun would have to wait until I had a day off, if I even got one, before going back to San Francisco.

So I settled for grabbing a hot dog from the first vendor I came across.

This, naturally, horrified Monk.

But I managed to shut out his whining and complaining about what I was doing, so successfully in fact that I can't even recount it here for the record.

I slathered the hot dog with cheese, mustard, ketchup, and onions and ate it as I walked, well aware that I was messing up my face and making Monk hyperventilate, and I didn't care.

I was a uniformed police officer eating a hot dog in New York City.

That's what mattered.

If someone had told me a week earlier that this would be happening to me, I never would have believed it.

It was an experience I wanted to savor and remember.

And feeling the mustard on my cheek, and tasting the hot dog in my mouth, made it real.

Listening to Monk's complaints would have just made it annoying. I could experience that at home.

CHAPTER TWENTY-SIX:
MR. MONK AND THE PUZZLE

We were early for the train, so I stopped by a shop that sold food, novelties, and periodicals in Penn Station to get the *New York Post* and something to drink for the ride back to Summit.

On those rare occasions when I visited New York, I always grabbed the *Post*. I loved its snarky, sensationalistic headlines and admired how it managed to accurately and thoroughly report the news but with the colorful, scandalous attitude of a sleazy tabloid, which put it in sharp contrast to the more staid and stuffy *New York Times*.

The *Post*'s story on the ongoing problems in Summit perfectly epitomized that precarious editorial balance. It got all the facts right, but the tone was undeniably snide and smirking, pointing out that there was so much government corruption in Summit that pretty soon every city employee would be behind bars and recently transplanted

San Franciscan Randy Disher would be the only one left to do every job.

At least the article recognized that none of the town's woes were Disher's fault. But I wondered how charitable the media would be once word got out today that Lindero and Woodlake, while guilty of burglary, were innocent of murder and that a killer was still on the loose.

Browsing through the *Post* reminded me of how dull it was living in a one-newspaper town. I used to enjoy reading the original old evening edition of the *San Francisco Examiner*, which cast itself as the mischievous-bad-boy alternative to the snooty and musty morning-edition *San Francisco Chronicle*, with which it reluctantly shared publishing facilities and a joint Sunday edition.

Then again, I liked sneaking peeks at the *National Enquirer* to see what celebs it was outing as "flabulous" with unflattering bathing suit pictures in any given week. It made me feel better about my own losing battle with age and cellulite.

I went up to the counter with the newspaper, along with a can of Diet Coke and a Milky Way bar to clear my palate.

Monk joined me and set a bottle of Fiji water and a Rubik's Cube on the counter beside my stuff. I glanced at him.

"I'm not your mother," I said. "You can buy your own drinks and games."

"My wallet burned in the fire," Monk said. "I have no cash."

I'd forgotten about that.

"Okay, this is my treat, but don't get used to it. I can't afford to support us both."

"Welcome to my world," Monk said.

I handed my credit card to the cashier, an unshaven African-American guy with a head as black and shiny as a bowling ball, and he rang up the purchases.

"Do you have a gift box for the Rubik's Cube?" Monk asked him.

The cashier reached under the counter and handed Monk a wrinkled plastic bag with a grocery store logo on it.

"That's not a box," Monk said.

"It's all I've got," he said.

"It's not even a fresh bag," Monk said. "It's used."

"I'm conserving our natural resources," he said. "I'm going green."

"Then shouldn't you be offering customers paper bags?" Monk asked.

The cashier reached under the counter again, pulled out a stuffed brown-bag-lunch bag, emptied out a sandwich, a hard-boiled egg, and an apple onto the counter, and handed the empty bag to Monk. "Happy now?"

"Never mind," Monk said. He picked up the cube and the water and walked out.

I took the plastic bag, dropped my candy bar and newspaper into it, and thanked the cashier for his help.

We headed for the Dover Line track and our train to Summit. I gestured to the cube in Monk's hand.

"There's something different about that Rubik's Cube," I said.

"This one is corrected," he said.

"Corrected?"

"The original Rubik's Cube has six individually rotating faces made up of nine squares, divided into three rows of three, each square painted in one of six colors. When those rows are properly aligned, it creates a cube with six faces, each with a different solid color."

"I've seen a Rubik's Cube before," I said. "What's wrong with it?"

"It's all threes," Monk said, "which makes it repulsive."

"And yet they've sold tens of millions of them around the world."

"This one is a vast improvement," Monk said and held up his cube. "It's called Rubik's Revenge, though a better name would have been Rubik's Correction."

"That doesn't have quite the same zing as 'revenge,' " I said. "So what makes this superior to the original?"

"This one has six faces made up of sixteen squares, divided into four rows of four, which adds up to fifty-six squares, eight corners, and twenty-four edges displaying two colors each. All even numbers."

"Not all," I said. "There are eight corners that show three different colors."

He stopped abruptly, turned around, and marched back the way we had come. I hurried after him.

"Where are you going?" I asked.

"To return this," he said. "I'm not going to give Ellen Morse a defective product."

I stepped in front of him, cutting him off.

"It's not a defect, it's an odd number inherent in every single one of those puzzles and Ellen Morse isn't going to care. She's going to love it."

"Because she adores crap," Monk said.

"Because it's sweet that you thought of her." I looked past Monk to the ARRIVALS AND DEPARTURES screen. "We don't have time to return it anyway. Our train is here."

He reluctantly turned back and we got on the train. On the ride to Summit, he scrambled the cube and solved the puzzle

319

twice. I read my *New York Post* and tried not to show my irritation. I could spend my entire life working on that cube and never solve it.

When we walked out of the train station, instead of heading left on Springfield Avenue toward police headquarters, Monk took a right, in the direction of Ellen Morse's store.

Monk shielded his face with his hand, as if Poop were shining a bright light at us, and turned his back to the storefront when we got there.

He handed me the Rubik's Cube. "Could you please go in and give this to her with my compliments?"

"No," I said. "You do it."

"I can't go in there," he said.

"You were in there before and came out unscathed."

"I'm scathed," Monk said.

"I don't see any scathing."

"It's emotional and psychological at the moment, but only because the physical effects haven't metastasized yet."

"But you're willing to send me in there."

"You seem to have a natural immunity," he said, "perhaps gained from long-term exposure."

320

"So you're saying that I lead an unsanitary, disgusting life."

"My God, you're finally getting the message. How many years has it taken?" Monk said. "Perhaps now you can begin the road to recovery."

"Gee, thanks. Since you're being so kind to me, I'll compromise. I'll go in and ask her if she'll come out and chat with you."

"Okay," Monk said. "But ask her to wash her hands first."

I didn't bother to respond to that. I went into the store just as a woman was coming out, carrying some dung-paper greeting cards. I wondered if she was sending them to friend or foe.

Morse smiled when she saw me. "Hello, Natalie. Where's Adrian?"

"He's on the sidewalk, a safe distance away. He'd like to talk with you but he hasn't bought into your circle-of-poop philosophy enough yet to overcome his revulsion of everything in this store."

"That's okay. I didn't expect him to change completely overnight," she said. "But I was encouraged by his willingness to keep an open mind on the matter."

"I was shocked," I said.

"I think you underestimate him."

"I think I underestimated you."

"May I ask you a question?"

"Sure," I said.

She took a deep breath and came closer to me. "Did I say or do something to offend you last night?"

I wasn't quite sure how to answer that question, besides knowing that I didn't want to tell her the truth. So I took the easy way out.

"Oh no. I'm sorry if I came across that way," I said. "I was just jet-lagged, frustrated, and angry at the world. It was nothing personal. I had a wonderful time."

"That's good to hear, because I was afraid that maybe you thought I was making moves on your man and resented me for it."

"My man?" I laughed. "Whatever gave you that idea? There's no romance whatsoever between us. He's my boss and my friend and that's as far as it goes."

"You don't want it to go further?"

"Hell no," I said.

"I'm surprised you're so vehement about it," she said. "Is it because he already has someone special?"

"Nope, there's no one else," I said. "He's just not my type."

"That's a shame," she said, but without

much conviction. "He's really a remarkable man."

"Well, Mr. Remarkable is waiting outside to talk with you," I said. "If we keep him waiting much longer, he might start painting lines on the sidewalk to keep people walking on the proper sides."

"That's not a bad idea," she said.

I wasn't sure if she was joking or not, because she made the comment as she was headed for the door. But it was obvious that she was attracted to Monk. I was very curious to see how he would respond. He wasn't accustomed to women being interested in him and, to be honest, neither was I, though I had tried to set him up with a crime scene cleaner once. That didn't work out so well.

When we got outside, we found Monk helping a man parallel park his Range Rover. Monk had his tape measure out and was standing between the huge car and the MINI Cooper behind it.

"Two and three-quarters inches more," Monk said. The man turned off the ignition and put the car in PARK. Monk knocked on the window. "You aren't done yet."

The driver got out and locked the car with his key fob remote. He was in his fifties and looked like he'd just come from the golf course.

"Thanks for your help, Officer, but it's fine," the man said.

"You've still got two and three-quarters inches to go," Monk said.

"I don't think so," the man said, stepping onto the sidewalk in front of us.

"It says so right here." Monk held up the tape measure. "Your car is unevenly parked."

"It's fine," the man said and strode into the Buttercup Pantry café.

Monk took out his ticket book.

"You're not honestly going to ticket him," I said.

"He's parked haphazardly," Monk said.

"Let's let him off with a warning," I said.

"Why?"

"Because Ellen is here to talk with you and we've got to get back to the station."

Monk seemed to notice Morse for the first time and immediately got flustered. He put his ticket book back.

"I'm so sorry, Ms. Morse," Monk said. "I got caught up in my duty."

"It's quite all right," she said. "But if you don't start calling me Ellen, I'm going to be hurt."

"I have something for you." Monk stepped over to the café and picked up the Rubik's Cube that he'd set down on one of the outdoor tables. "I got this for you in New York City."

He presented it to her in both hands, like it was a rare and fragile object. She took it from him with the same grace.

"Is this a Rubik's Cube?" she asked.

"I hear that some people find the puzzle challenging," Monk said.

"But you don't," she said.

"I just like looking at it. I find all those squares soothing and thought you might, too."

"Thank you, Adrian," she said.

"I need to be honest with you," he said. "There's a defect."

"Eight corners with three colored faces," Morse said.

Monk gave me a nasty look, then turned back to her. "I'm ashamed to say I've never noticed that until today."

"But you have such an incredible eye for detail," she said.

"I suppose that I get lost in the beauty and simplicity of the squares and it blinds me to everything else," Monk said. "I won't mind if you throw it out."

"Never," Morse said. "I will treasure it."

"You don't mind the defect?" Monk asked.

"I'm touched by the gift but even more by the sentiment that came with it," she said and kissed Monk on the cheek. "I'd better get back. There's no one minding the store."

And we all know how attractive ossified poop is to shoplifters, I thought.

Morse smiled and walked back to the store. Monk stood still, eyes wide, and stared at her as she went.

"Why did she do that?" he said.

"Because you told her that you think that she's beautiful despite whatever faults she may have."

"No, I didn't," he said.

"Yes, you did," I said and walked past him on my way to the police station.

Men are such idiots, I thought. But then I realized from the look on Monk's face that this time I had actually said what I was thinking out loud.

Chapter Twenty-Seven: Mr. Monk as It Happened

We found Disher in his office, looking weary and frustrated as he sorted through a mountain of paperwork.

"How did it go in the city?" he asked.

"We met an agent from Homeland Security," I replied. "She used some slick facial recognition software and had no trouble finding Joel Goldman on surveillance camera footage arriving at and departing from Penn Station when he said he did."

"So Goldman may end up being responsible for the murder," Disher said, "but we've proven without a doubt that he didn't commit it himself."

"I wouldn't say that," Monk said.

"I would," Disher said. "I had a tech-savvy buddy in the crime lab in Frisco look at the webinar. He says the video hasn't been touched. Joel Goldman was at his desk, in front of that wall, looking into that camera."

"That doesn't mean he didn't do it,"

Monk said.

"A man can't be in two places at once, Monk. And I can tell you for certain that he doesn't have a twin brother."

"You checked?" I said.

"Of course I did. How do you think I became the chief of police? I also had Officers DeSoto and Corbin talk to Goldman's neighbors to see if they saw anything going on that morning. Turns out one of 'em saw a beat-up, rusted-out brown van parked on the corner by Goldman's house around noon and a couple of guys in painter's overalls and caps hurrying out of the backyard."

"That's a good lead," I said. "Did the neighbor get a look at their faces?"

Disher shook his head. "He was a couple of houses down, he wasn't wearing his glasses, and his view was from a second-story window through the branches of a tree."

"So his testimony won't be worth anything as far as identifying the guys," I said.

"No, it won't, but it does put us firmly on the trail of a couple of day laborers," Disher said. "Or I should say, *day killers.*"

"Go ahead," I said. "You're the chief."

"I don't think so," Monk said.

"What's wrong with the day killers?"

Disher said. "Do you have a better name?"

"I don't think Goldman hired anybody to kill his wife. It would have left him too vulnerable to blackmail."

"Who said he hired the day killers?" Disher said. "I haven't ruled out the burglary-gone-bad theory."

"I have," Monk said.

"Why?" Disher asked.

"Because nothing was stolen," he said.

"Maybe because she walked in on them before they could steal anything and then they were too spooked after they killed her to continue with their burgling."

"I don't think so," Monk said.

"Well, I do, and I'm the chief. Tomorrow you two will start talking to the day laborers who hang out around Home Depot. Maybe one of them will know who drives a rusted-out brown van. Now get out of here, you're off duty."

I motioned to the papers on his desk. "What is all that?"

"Invoices from all the contractors the city owes money to. After I've sorted through and prioritized all of them, I've got to go over the former city attorney's draft of a cell phone tower ordinance."

"It must be a thrill wielding such power," I said.

"It sure is," Disher said. "I'm fighting sleep every second. It's a good thing I have a Taser."

I changed out of my uniform and waited for Monk in the lobby. Evie waved me over to the counter.

"I've got a question for you," she said. "When was the last time you were out on a shooting range?"

I shrugged. It had to be more than a decade.

"A couple of years," I said. It was relatively close to the truth.

She frowned and shook her head. "That's not going to cut it. You need to sharpen your skills if you're going to be carrying a weapon on the street. I'm off in a few minutes. Why don't you come with me to the range? I'll even let you try out some of my guns."

"That's a very nice offer, but it's been a hectic few days and I was looking forward to a quiet, relaxing evening."

"There's nothing more relaxing than firing off a few hundred rounds."

"A few hundred?"

"Haven't you ever fired an automatic weapon?"

"Nope," I said.

"You don't know what you're missing.

You'll sleep like a baby afterward," she said. "More important, you need to know, down to your bones, that you can handle yourself in a shoot-out with some deranged, acid-tripping, communist."

She had a point. So when Monk came out, I told him I was going to the shooting range with Evie and that either he could come along with us or I could drop him off at Sharona's first.

He rolled his shoulders. "That won't be necessary. You can go ahead without me."

"How are you going to get back to the house?"

"I'll work something out," he said.

I was uncomfortable leaving him on his own like that, but before I could argue with him, he spoke up again.

"I'm a grown man, Natalie, and a police officer. I think I'm capable of being on my own. Besides, I think we could both use a little break from each other, don't you?"

He was right, though I was surprised he was the one who said it and not me.

"Okay," I said and turned to Evie. "I'm ready when you are."

She jerked her head toward the back door. "Go get your Glock and a box of shells, and I'll meet you in the parking lot."

Evie drove a massive old Buick with a gun locker in the trunk — and there were enough weapons in it to overthrow a small country.

She took me to a training range that was like an amusement park for cops and other law enforcement and security professionals.

There was a fake city street, much like you'd find on a Hollywood backlot, with painted characters that popped out from behind windows, cars, and doors.

The figures were all ridiculously cartoonish caricatures, whether they were gunmen and bank robbers or little old ladies and children. I knew from experience that real criminals were seldom kind enough to dress in ways that instantly identified their evil character and violent intent.

But it was great fun walking down that street, gun at my side, doling out hot lead to the bad guys and, inadvertently, to a nun, a doctor, and a schoolteacher, though I'm pretty sure they harbored criminal intent.

Evie walked the same course, pulverizing the cutouts and nearly entire building facades with her massive weapons. I half expected her to bring out a rocket launcher for some target practice.

On the range, and later just shooting stationary targets at various distances, I was surprised how quickly I loosened up.

I guess shooting a gun is, to use a cliché, like riding a bike. It involves a lot of muscle memory. My reflexes weren't particularly great, but I held the gun steady and my aim was still good.

Aim didn't mean so much to Evie. She relied on firepower over precision. Rather than shoot a bad guy between the eyes, she preferred to blow his head clean off, and maybe even his shoulders, too.

And she was right. It was astonishing to me how relaxing it all was, despite the noise, concentration, and startling recoil of the weapons. I guess it's because shooting things allows you to work out all your pent-up aggression and frustration. Nothing relieves tension quite like blasting something to bits. Boys seem to be born knowing that, but it's knowledge that has to be acquired by girls.

But going to the shooting range with Evie was also a sad experience for me. The last time I'd been to one was with my late husband and I couldn't help thinking of him.

He's often in my thoughts, of course, but

this time the pain had a sharper edge. Maybe it was because it had been so long since I'd relived this particular shared experience.

Sadness is its own kind of tension and I blasted my way through that, too.

After using enough ammo to repel a commie invasion, we stopped at Evie's favorite diner, a place that served massive steaks and was frequented by truckers, all of whom seemed to know her and treat her like one of their own.

All in all, it was a fun night and I was grateful to Evie for inviting me.

The only one in the house when I got back was Sharona. She made me a cup of tea and we sat down at the kitchen table together.

"Where is everyone?" I asked.

"Randy is still at the office. I'm lucky he even manages to come home to sleep with all the work he's got now."

"And Mr. Monk?"

She shrugged. "I haven't seen or heard from him since this morning."

I glanced at my watch. It was after ten p.m. Sharona shook her head and smiled at me over her mug of tea.

"What?" I said. "I'm worried about him, that's all."

"He's not a kid, Natalie. And from what

I've seen, he's more capable now of taking care of himself than he's ever been since the day I met him."

"He's still got his problems," I said.

"Don't we all," she said. "But Adrian seems to have a grip on most of his now. He hasn't called his shrink once since he got here."

I hadn't noticed that until she mentioned it. Yet another milestone reached on this trip.

"A lot has certainly changed for Mr. Monk in the last year or so, especially since he finally solved Trudy's murder. He says his life is more balanced now. Even his brother, Ambrose, has made some significant changes in his life. He's got an assistant of his own now. She lives with him."

"How live-in is she?"

"Same bed live-in," I said.

"Wow. How has Adrian handled that?"

"Not well," I said. "It doesn't help that Yuki's tattooed and an ex-con. Of course, that was before he met Ellen Morse. If he can accept a woman who sells poop for a living, maybe he'll be more open-minded about Yuki, too."

"With all this change going on, do you ever worry that Adrian may stop needing an assistant?"

"It never occurred to me," I said.

"At least now you know you've got other options if that day comes."

"I wasn't looking for a backup plan."

"Well, you've obviously been looking for something," Sharona said. "And I think you've finally found it. You seem to like being a cop."

"It's only been two days and the reality of it hasn't sunk in yet, especially since I'm away from home. It feels more like a role-playing game than reality."

"Even in the mini-mart?"

"Especially then," I said. "I don't know how I'll feel about all this when I get back to San Francisco."

"Who says you have to go back?"

I was about to press Sharona on what she meant by that when Monk came in the front door.

"Where have you been?" I asked.

"I had dinner with Ellen," he said, trying very hard to be matter-of-fact about it and failing.

"You were alone with a woman?" Sharona said.

"I'm alone with Natalie all the time," Monk said.

"It's not the same thing and you know it, Adrian. This was a date."

"It was a meal," Monk said. "Not a date."

"How was it arranged?"

"I happened to run into Ellen on the street as she happened to be walking home and since we happened to be in front of a restaurant when our paths intersected, we decided to dine together."

"That's a lot of happenings," I said. "So what happened over dinner?"

"She talked about her time among the savages in Africa and I talked about my time among the savages in San Francisco."

"What time was that?" Sharona asked.

"From the day I moved out of our family home in Tewksbury to the moment that I was drugged and put on a plane to New Jersey."

"Then you should be grateful that I rescued you," Sharona said.

"Where do things stand now between you and Ellen?" I asked.

"She's a fine woman, but it's hard to ignore the elephant in the room."

"You mean the elephant droppings," Sharona said.

Monk cringed. "I wish I could convince her to give up her crusade to legitimize excrement."

"Wouldn't it be easier if you just accepted it?" I said. "Or agreed to disagree? Compromise is part of any successful relationship."

"We don't have a relationship," Monk said. "It was just dinner."

"No, it wasn't. You didn't just run into her by accident, you planned it. You made sure you were walking in front of the restaurant at the same time that she'd be passing it on her way home. It's already a relationship, Mr. Monk. The only question is what kind it's going to be and if it's going to last."

He rolled his shoulders and tipped his head from side to side. "She spends her day in a room full of poop."

"And her nights alone in her perfect home," I said.

"With her collection of poop," he said.

"Maybe that's only because she hasn't found the right man yet," Sharona said.

"It's not going to happen with all of that poop around," he said.

"Maybe it already has," Sharona said and winked at me.

Monk yawned theatrically and looked at his watch. "Oh my, will you look at the time. I have to go to bed."

"Nice dodge," Sharona said. "But you aren't fooling anyone."

His fake yawn, though, was enough to provoke a real one from me. It's amazing how contagious yawns are.

"Yeah, but we do have an early shift in the

338

morning and a tough boss," I said. "We wouldn't want to get reprimanded for tardiness on our third day on the job."

"If he ever reprimands you, let me know," Sharona said. "And I'll reprimand him."

CHAPTER TWENTY-EIGHT:
MR. MONK IS TRASHED

When I came into the kitchen the next morning, Monk was already up and dressed, sitting at the table, hunched over an iPad. Disher sat beside him, showing him how to use the device while Sharona made waffles again.

"Surfing the Web, Mr. Monk?" I asked, taking the seat on the other side of him.

"No, I'm on the Internets," he said.

"It's the same thing," I said. "Surfing is another way of saying 'looking around.'"

"I know what I want to look at," he said. "Joel Goldman's seminar."

"You can look at it a thousand times and it's not going to change anything," Disher said.

"We're missing something," Monk said. "I kept seeing the video again and again in my head last night."

"So what do you need to see it again for?" Sharona asked, bringing a plate of waffles

340

over and setting it in the center of the table.

"Because I'm not recognizing something that I've seen or my subconscious wouldn't be harassing me."

"Okay, I've got you on the site," Disher said, bringing up the Web page with the screencaps from all of Goldman's seminars. "The iPad works with a touch screen. All you've got to do is touch the screencap you want with your finger and it will play the video."

"What's a screencap?" Monk asked.

"It's a still image taken from the video that you want to watch," Disher said. "In this case, it also doubles as a button to start the playback."

Disher tapped the screencap from Joel Goldman's most recent video and it began to play.

"If you want to pause the video, fast-forward, or do any other playback functions, just tap the bottom of the screen and the controls will come up."

Goldman started talking about interest rates, derivatives, and mortgage-backed securities, and some brilliant way to manipulate all of them to become rich enough to live on his street in Summit.

Monk peered intently at the screen. "Are those smudges?"

"It's on the screen," Disher said. "Not the video."

"So your screen is thick with finger grease," Monk said.

"It doesn't matter," Disher said.

"Of course it does. You know what those smudges are? Billions of virulent germs, transforming your iPad into an electronic petri dish of disease. When was the last time you cleaned it?"

"I don't know," Disher said.

"It's disgusting." Monk took a Wet One out of his pocket, tore open the packet, and started to clean the screen with the tissue.

"Wait, wait," Disher said. "Don't!"

But Monk was already wiping, his touch causing multiple screens, each with a different Goldman video, to pop up, one on top of the other, like overlapping sheets of paper.

"You'll thank me later," Monk said, wrapping the Wet One in a napkin and handing it to Sharona. "We've saved lives today."

"It's just like old times." Sharona frowned and tossed the wipe into the trash. "I'd forgotten the thrill."

The smudges were gone, but now a different video occupied the screen, and a cacophony of Goldmans was coming out of the iPad's speakers.

342

"It's a touch screen, Monk. Your wiping clicked open every video on the page," Disher said. "Now I have to close all of these windows to get you back to the original video."

Disher reached for the iPad but Monk grabbed his wrist.

"Not yet," Monk said, staring at the video.

"But you're watching the wrong video," Disher said. "That's not the one from the day of the murder. Can't you see? He's not even wearing the same shirt. That's a major fail for a guy with your eye for detail."

"Let me see the next one," Monk said.

Disher closed the window and the one underneath appeared. "That's not it, either. Visually, they're all the same, except for what he's wearing. Nothing else changes."

Monk scrutinized the video, getting his face so close to the screen that the tip of his nose almost touched it. "Okay, now let me see the broadcast from the day of the murder."

"I can't with your face in the way," Disher said. "Unless you'd like to tap that tiny X with your nose."

"Don't be ridiculous." Monk leaned back and allowed Disher to tap the various screens closed until he got back to the right one.

"This is it," Disher said. "Knock yourself out."

Disher dug into his waffles while Sharona and I continued to watch Monk, who rolled his shoulders, tipped his head from side to side, and smiled.

Sharona smiled, too. And so did I. For Adrian Monk, in that brief moment, the entire universe was in perfect balance and everything fit where it was supposed to.

But Disher missed it all. He was too wrapped up in devouring his breakfast.

"Whenever you're not rolling on dispatcher calls today," Disher said, "I want you two out talking to the day laborers around the Home Depot."

"That won't be necessary," Monk said.

Disher looked up. "Why not?"

"Because Adrian already solved the murder," Sharona said.

"He did? When?"

"Just now," Sharona said.

"So who killed Pamela Goldman?"

"Her husband did," Monk said.

Disher dropped his fork on his plate and took a deep, calming breath. "We've been over this already a dozen times. The video has been analyzed by experts. There's no trickery involved. Joel Goldman was in his office, doing a live broadcast minutes before the murder."

"Yes, he was," Monk said.

"This video proves that."

"Absolutely and irrefutably."

"So the video proves he couldn't have killed her," Disher said.

"No," Monk said. "It proves that he *did*."

Disher rubbed his brow. "One of us here is losing his mind and I don't think it's me."

I knew the feeling. But I also knew — from long, painful, and repeated experience — that I had to surrender and roll with it, that everything would become clear once Monk got around to giving us all the details. I also knew that he would take his sweet time. He enjoyed our confusion.

"Look at this and tell me what you see." Monk tapped the screen, brought up the controls, and hit pause on the playback.

We all gathered around him and looked at the screen and the still image. Goldman was behind his desk, pointing into the camera to underscore some point he was making. Behind him were the bookcase and the paisley wallpaper.

"I see Joel Goldman in his office doing a live webinar and interacting with people from all over the world," Disher said. "What do you see?"

"I see Joel Goldman in his office doing a

live webinar and interacting with people from all over the world," Monk said. "But I also see something else."

"What?"

"The wallpaper," Monk said. "It's green with a paisley pattern that's repeated every twenty-one inches on a twenty-and-a-half-inch-wide roll."

"I see it, too, only without the exact measurements. So what?"

"There are inevitably going to be seams when the wallpaper is applied and it's imperative that the installer makes sure the patterns line up whenever possible."

"Okay, if you say so, but what does any of that have to with the murder?"

"The seams and the patterns on his wallpaper line up in the other videos shot in his New York office," Monk said, "but not in this one."

"But you just agreed with me that this was shot in his office," Disher said.

"It was," Monk said. "In the office he re-created in his backyard in Summit."

There was a long moment of stunned silence as all the pieces of the puzzle fell into place for me, Sharona, and Disher.

"I'll be damned," Disher said. "He built a movie set."

"It was staged, just like the open house in

San Francisco," Monk said to me.

"And just like the photo of the killer's office on the wall of Five Star Realty," I said.

"We were fools not to see it again," Monk said.

I hadn't seen it the first time, so I didn't think I had to be too hard on myself for missing it this time, too.

Disher shook his head in confusion. "What are you two talking about?"

"Here's what happened," Monk said. "Joel went into New York by train that morning and walked to his office on Park Avenue merely to establish his alibi."

"Goldman knew he was on camera the whole time," I said.

"He certainly hoped that he was," Monk said. "That's really why he went into the city so early, to give himself plenty of time to drive back home disguised as a day laborer and sneak into his backyard office, where he broadcast his show from ten to eleven a.m. without his wife being aware of it."

"But his secretary, Trina Fishbeck, had to be," I said. "She lied about him being in Manhattan."

"I wouldn't be surprised if Goldman and his secretary were having an extramarital sex affair," Monk said, glancing at me. "Like that couple we met here the other day."

"It's hardly unusual for people in Summit to be having affairs," Sharona said. "There's a reason they call this a bedroom community."

"So Goldman's secretary must have been the other day laborer that the neighbor saw," I said.

"And probably the one who called and canceled Pamela Goldman's hairdresser appointment," Disher said, "setting the stage for the theory that she surprised some burglars in her home and they killed her."

I picked it up again from there. "That means when Pamela left for her hairdresser appointment, it was Joel who went into the house immediately afterward and turned off the alarm."

"That's right," Disher said. "He did that so it would look like she forgot something, came back in, then neglected to reset her alarm again when she left."

Monk nodded. "You are both correct. Goldman then waited for her to come back and struck her with the rolling pin. After the murder, Goldman and his mistress drove back to Manhattan. He stayed in his office until five and then took the train home to complete his carefully constructed alibi."

348

"And the next morning the arrogant bastard was back in the garage, dismantling the set, right in front of us," I said. "How are we going to prove any of this?"

"We'll get a search warrant for his home office and the Dumpster," Monk said. "We're bound to find remnants of the wallpaper and the matching furniture."

Disher shook his head. "It'll never happen. No judge is going to give us search warrants on the basis of mismatched wallpaper in a video."

"There's more than that," Monk said. "There's also the siren."

"What siren?" Disher asked.

"The one you can hear in the video. It's not from an NYPD police car. What you're hearing is Natalie's siren as we responded to the McAfee burglary," Monk said. "The sirens are distinctly different in the rapidity of the wails and the pitch. And if you compare the time code on the webinar with the Summit police dispatcher's log, you'll see that they match up exactly."

"That's still not going to be enough," Disher said.

"What kind of judges do you have here?" Monk said.

"Ones that require solid evidence before issuing warrants," Disher said. "That doesn't mean I won't try, but I'm telling you wallpaper and siren aren't going to cut it."

"So Goldman gets away with murder?" Sharona said.

"I didn't say that," Disher said. "There's another way we can get him."

"What's that?" Sharona asked.

"We wait for the Dumpster to get picked up by the garbage company. The moment the Dumpster leaves his driveway, it's fair game for a search," he said. "But if the Dumpster goes much farther than that, say all the way to the dump, we'll have a hard time linking him conclusively to the trash in court."

I got up. "Then what are we waiting for?"

We piled into Disher's car and sped over to Goldman's place so we could keep our eye on the Dumpster. Our plan was to call the trash company to come get it and then watch it until the truck got there.

But when we arrived, the Dumpster was gone and Joel Goldman was outside, sweeping his driveway. He smiled when he saw us.

Disher pulled over to the curb and rolled down his window.

"Good morning, Chief," Goldman said,

ambling over. "I'm glad you stopped by. I was going to call you today. I was very upset that I had to read in the paper that the murder charges were dropped against those two police officers rather than hearing about it directly from you."

"How soon after reading the paper did you call the trash company to pick up the Dumpster?" Disher asked.

"What does my trash have to do with anything?"

Monk leaned forward and looked Goldman in the eye. "Because you wanted to dispose of the evidence that you re-created your Manhattan office in your backyard."

Goldman shrugged. "I told you that I was moving my office from Manhattan to my home. There's nothing unusual about me wanting to have the same familiar décor in the new one. Nor would there be anything felonious about it if I changed my mind, say a day or so ago, and decided to go for a different look."

"It is if you're trying to establish a fraudulent alibi for murder," Monk said.

"Prove it." Goldman smiled and went back to sweeping.

Disher sped off, radioed the dispatcher, asked her to find out the current location of the trash truck that had picked up the

Dumpster at Goldman's place.

The response came back two minutes later.

The truck was just leaving the dump.

CHAPTER TWENTY-NINE:
MR. MONK
AND THE WEAK LINK

We convened in Disher's office to scream profanities, kick desks and, in Monk's case, pace sullenly back and forth.

"He knows we know that he killed his wife and he doesn't care," I said. "It's a good thing that you were driving, because I would have run him down."

"This isn't over yet," Disher said. "To drive from Manhattan to Summit and back again, he had to pass through at least two tollbooths. We know roughly when he had to go through them, so we'll get him either with the debits on his E-Zpass card or, if he didn't use one, with video footage from the tollbooths."

"Joel Goldman is cunning," Monk said. "He would have been careful not to use an E-Zpass or let himself be filmed going through the tollbooths, even in disguise."

"But would he have been as careful about his secretary?" Disher said. "Somebody had

353

to drive that van."

"And I bet that Homeland Security's surveillance matrix includes the tollbooths through New Jersey and into, and out of, Manhattan," I said and turned to Disher. "Call Agent Lisa McCracken at the Penn Station security office. Maybe she'll do us another favor and have her supercomputers scan the tollbooth videos for Goldman and Trina."

Disher started dialing and Monk kept pacing.

"Relax, Mr. Monk, we're going to get him," I said. "His secretary is the weak link."

"You don't think that he's already thought of that?"

The dire implications of that simple, and obvious, statement stopped me cold, and Disher, too.

Disher had McCracken on the line, but he interrupted the call to give us an order.

"Get suited up and park your patrol car in front of Joel Goldman's house," he said. "Don't let the man out of your sight."

We got to Goldman's house ten minutes later. He wasn't in the driveway anymore and there was no sign of activity in the house.

"I've got a bad feeling about this," Monk

said. "He's been one step ahead of us from the start."

"He's panicked now," I said. "He's going to start making mistakes on top of the ones he's made already."

"He didn't seem panicked to me," Monk said. "He seemed pretty satisfied with himself."

"He won't be when we put him in handcuffs."

Monk got out of the car and by the time I caught up with him, he was already at Goldman's front door, ringing the bell.

"What are you doing, Mr. Monk?"

"The chief said not to let Joel Goldman out of our sight. Well, I can't see him, can you?"

"Do you think he's just going to invite us in for tea?"

"No, I don't."

Monk stepped off the porch, walked over to the living room window, and peered inside.

"Don't be so impatient," I said. "He could be in the bathroom."

Monk drew his gun and fired two shots into the window, shattering it and setting off car alarms up and down the street.

"Congratulations, Mr. Monk. You just gave him all the evidence he needs to question your competence in court and to undermine any case we manage to put together against him."

Monk stood still, staring at the broken window. People came out of their houses to see what was going on.

My radio crackled. It was the distraught dispatcher, radioing us about multiple reports of shots fired at our location. I responded, letting her know that everything was under control, that no one was hurt, and that we had no need for backup. I turned to Monk.

"Have you lost your mind?"

"If you were in the bathroom, wouldn't that ruckus have brought you out by now?"

I looked at the broken window. The gunfire had drawn out everybody in the neighborhood except the man who lived in the house Monk had just shot up.

"Damn," I muttered to myself.

I took out my baton, cleared away the remaining shards of broken glass, and climbed into the house. I drew my gun and did a quick search inside.

Monk was right. The house was empty.

I was still in the house a few minutes later when Disher pulled up in his car. But even in my short time inside, I was able to convince myself that Goldman hadn't packed up and fled the country. Everything was very neat and organized except, of course, for the shattered glass all over the living room floor.

"Are you two crazy?" Disher said as he marched toward the broken window, glancing up and down the street at all the people who were out on their lawns. "You've got the whole neighborhood watching. You can't shoot up a suspect's house just because you're angry at him."

"My sentiments exactly," I said. "I told Mr. Monk the same thing."

"If you're so sensible, what the hell are you doing in Goldman's house?" he said. "You don't have a warrant to be in there."

"That's the least of our problems," I said. "Joel Goldman is gone."

"He could be out having breakfast, or shopping at the grocery store, or stopping by Starbucks for a coffee," Disher said. "And when he comes back from wherever he is, we'll be in deep trouble and so will our case against him."

"Do we even have one?" I asked.

"As a matter of fact, we do," Disher said, coming close to the window. "Your friend in Homeland Security came through for us. Trina Fishbeck tried to disguise herself with a hat and sunglasses, but the facial recognition software wasn't fooled. Trina was positively identified on surveillance camera footage going through the cash lines at the New Jersey Turnpike and Lincoln Tunnel tollbooths in a rusted-out brown van the morning of the murder."

"Did we get the license plates?" I asked.

"There was mud caked on them," Disher said. "They were unreadable."

"How convenient," I said. "Was Joel Goldman visible in the surveillance camera footage?"

"No, he was not," Disher said. "But we've got enough leverage on his mistress to make her sing like a contestant on *American Idol*."

"If you can find her," Monk said, always the optimist.

"I called the NYPD," Disher said. "They've sent officers to her apartment and Goldman's office. We'll have her in custody any minute now."

I glanced at the family photos laid out on the living room mantelpiece. Joel and Pamela seemed to be deeply in love. There were pictures of them in each other's arms, with contented smiles on their faces, at their wedding and over the years at the lake, several ski resorts, some tropical beaches, against the backdrop of various European locales.

I wondered if Pamela had any idea that his passion for her had died and that he wanted her to suffer the same fate.

Was it some deep hatred that drove him to kill her or merely greed, an unwillingness to face divorce and having to divide up all the assets they'd accumulated during their marriage? What amount of money did it take to make someone seriously consider committing murder and taking the risks that go along with it, rather than facing even a messy divorce?

"Do you have Goldman's cell phone number?" Monk asked Disher.

"Yes."

"Call him and tell him I just shot up his front window," Monk said.

"You really are crazy," Disher said.

"Maybe I am. But notifying him about what I've done will demonstrate that you are proactive and reasonable."

Disher sighed, took out his phone, and dialed. A cell phone rang inside the house. I followed the sound to the kitchen, where an iPhone lit up on the counter. The caller ID showed Disher's name.

I came back out to the living room and faced Monk and Disher through the shattered window. "Goldman left his phone here, but I don't see his wallet or keys."

"He didn't want you to be able to locate him using his phone," Monk said.

"You think he's on the run?" Disher asked.

"No," Monk said. "I think he's murdering his secretary."

CHAPTER THIRTY:
MR. MONK TO THE RESCUE

Disher posted Evie at Goldman's house to secure the scene until the window could be boarded up, and we went back to the chief's office to wait to hear from the NYPD regarding Trina's whereabouts.

We figured that Goldman must have been using a throwaway cell phone for his non-business-related calls to Trina so that his wife wouldn't find out about the affair or her own impending demise.

It made sense that Goldman would use the same phone to contact Trina now. He wouldn't want anything leading back to him from her on the day she disappeared.

But without any information from the NYPD, there wasn't really anything more we could do except scream profanities, kick desks, and, in Monk's case, pace sullenly back and forth.

We were well into our second round of the morning doing exactly that when

Disher's phone rang.

It was the NYPD. The news wasn't good. Trina Fishbeck wasn't at home and she wasn't at Goldman's office, either.

So Disher used DMV records to find out that Trina drove a blue 2006 Honda Accord and put out an APB for it. But I had a few ideas of my own to track her down.

"Let's ask Lisa McCracken to see if Trina's Honda passed through any tollbooths on the highways out of Manhattan in the last couple of hours. Maybe Mc-Cracken can also see if Trina made any calls on her cell phone during that time and pinpoint the nearest cellular tower the signal bounced off of to give us a clue where she's headed."

Disher gave me a look. "Someone has been watching a lot of *Law & Order*."

"The real challenge is turning on your TV in the afternoon and finding a program that's not *Law & Order*."

Disher made the call and pleaded with McCracken to do two more little favors for him. When he was done, he hung up the phone, sat back in his chair, and sighed.

"I owe that woman so much now that I might as well just quit my job and become her indentured servant for life."

"Look at the bright side, Chief," I said.

"What resources could the Summit police force possibly have to offer that Homeland Security would want?"

"She might demand that I pay off my debt to her with my body."

"You think you're that hot?"

"I know I'm that hot," Disher said.

"Speaking of which," Monk said, "if Joel Goldman lured Trina out to meet him, it was surely on the pretext of a romantic rendezvous."

"So they're meeting at a hotel somewhere," I said.

Monk shook his head. "He won't take her to a hotel. There's too high a risk that they will be seen together. He'll take her somewhere remote, but not so much so that she finds it suspicious."

"It could be anywhere," Disher said.

The phone rang. It was McCracken.

I turned to Monk. "She's almost as fast at detective work as you."

"Her detecting is primarily done by computers."

"Do I sense a little defensiveness?"

"She's an efficient keyboard-and-mouse detective," Monk said. "You, of all people, should know the difference between what she does and what we do."

"We?" I said.

"We," he said.

Disher quickly scrawled some notes on his blotter.

"Thank you so much, Agent McCracken. I owe you big-time," he said, and hung up. "Trina Fishbeck left Manhattan for New Jersey over an hour ago along Interstate Eighty."

"How did McCracken get that information so fast?" I asked.

"We made it easy for her by being timely and precise. We were asking her surveillance matrix to scan activity regarding a specific person over the last few hours along key geographical checkpoints. It would have been a different story if we were talking about days." Disher got up and went to the map on the wall. "Trina made and received calls that puts her in the general area of Denville."

He tapped an area about twenty-five miles northwest of Summit. Monk and I stepped up on either side of Disher and looked at the map.

"What's out there?" Monk asked.

"A good chunk of the state of New Jersey," Disher said. "Forests, rock quarries, gravel pits, and other good places for disposing of bodies."

But I saw something else, too. Lots of little

patches of blue dotting the area.

"And there are a lot of lakes," I said.

"How does that help us?" Disher asked.

"When we first met Goldman, on the night of the murder, he mentioned that he'd built a cabin at Spirit Lake," I said. "Where's that in relation to Denville?"

"How do I know? I'm new here," Disher said. "I have no idea."

"You knew about the rock quarries and gravel pits out there," I said.

"Only because I watched *The Sopranos*," he said.

Monk looked at the key on the side of the map, found Spirit Lake on it, and then found the grid where the lake was located.

"The lake is only a few miles north of Denville," Monk said.

"You two start heading out there," Disher said. "I'll find out where Goldman's cabin is and be right behind you."

The lake was thirty minutes away from Summit if you obeyed the speed limit, which I assumed Joel Goldman had done. The last thing you want to happen on your way to a murder is to get stopped for a speeding ticket.

But we could go as fast as we wanted without any worries, though judging by the

365

look of terror Monk had on his face as I drove pedal-to-the-floor, I don't know if he would agree with me about that.

Even though Goldman had a big head start on us, I was determined to make up the difference by hitting the siren and driving like Michael Schumacher up 287 to I-80.

By the time we reached the turnoff on I-80 that led to Spirit Lake, Disher was right behind us. He'd alerted the local police that we were coming and requested backup, but they were busy dealing with a report of a kid with a gun in their local high school, which was on lockdown until they found him.

So we were on our own.

We turned off our sirens as we left the major streets and transitioned to the narrow, unpaved roads that wound through the thick woods to the mobile homes and hunting and fishing cabins that dotted the area around tiny, undeveloped lakes.

I finally came across a rusted mailbox pocked with pellet holes that had the address Disher had given us over the radio.

I slowed way down as we bumped and bounced along the rutted road until we reached a small clearing surrounded by towering pines. In the center was a wood-planked cabin, an outhouse, and a storage shed.

A blue Honda Accord was parked out front, right beside a rust-eaten, salt-corroded brown van.

We were definitely in the right spot. But were we too late to save Trina Fishbeck?

We parked our patrol cars side by side and took out our guns as we emerged from our vehicles. Monk didn't look very comfortable holding his weapon. He probably would have preferred to be wielding a can of Lysol instead.

Disher made some very military-looking, rapid hand signals that I interpreted to mean: be quiet, I see you, you see me, there's something in your hair, you two go here, I'll go there, circle here, circle there, and your zipper is open. Or he could have been saying something entirely different. I had no idea what he was trying to say.

So he went to the front door, Monk went around back, and I headed toward the outhouse and shed.

I kicked open the door of the outhouse and was hit by a smell so awful I almost gagged. I quickly moved to the shed, nudged open the door with the toe of my shoe, and saw that it was filled with rusted tools and cobwebs.

That's when I heard the digging.

I looked over my shoulder to signal Monk and Disher to follow me, but I didn't see them. They were probably in the house.

I took a deep breath and moved slowly through the trees in the direction of the sound. A bead of sweat rolled between my shoulder blades, tickling my skin as I crept along cautiously, trying not to crunch too many twigs and leaves under my feet so I wouldn't announce my presence.

The trees were thick and it was hard to see very far ahead. But the sound was getting louder, though less frequent. Whoever was digging was either nearly finished or getting tired.

I came through some trees and caught a glimpse of a mud-caked and sweaty Trina Fishbeck standing in a shallow grave, shoveling out dirt as Joel stood over her. His back was to me and he was aiming a shotgun at Trina. Her shoulders were heaving, as much from her sobs as the strain of digging.

"That's deep enough," Joel said.

I took a quick, desperate glance over my shoulder. If Disher and Monk were back there somewhere, I couldn't see them. I was alone.

"I can't believe you're doing this to me,"

she said, her voice cracking as she struggled to speak through her sobs. "I loved you."

"So did Pamela," Joel said. "But you can blame Adrian Monk for this. Somehow he figured it all out. If that hadn't happened, we'd be in bed right now."

"We still could be," she said.

"You'd sleep with me even after I made you dig your own grave?"

"I'm a very forgiving person," she said.

"I'll remember that about you," he said and raised the shotgun.

I planted my feet firmly on the ground and took aim. "Don't move, Goldman."

"Who do we have here?" he said, without lowering his weapon.

"Summit Police. Drop the weapon and put your hands on your head."

"Oh, it's you, the make-believe cop."

I felt a pang of anxiety in the pit of my stomach because he'd said pretty much what I was feeling at that exact moment.

"My badge is real and so is the gun I've got aimed at you."

I wasn't sure who I was trying harder to convince, him or myself.

"Yes, but I don't think you've got the balls to fire it. So here's what's going to happen. I'm going to shoot you and then I'm going to shoot her and then I'll bury you both."

"I'm not alone, Goldman."

"I'm even less afraid of Monk than I am of you," he said and whirled around toward me.

I heard the gunshot and saw him tumble backward into the grave, the shotgun flying out of his hands, before I even realized that I'd fired my weapon.

Perhaps that's because Trina's scream was even louder than the gunshot.

She scrambled out of the grave and ran into the trees, nearly colliding with Disher and Monk as they came out.

I marched up to the narrow grave and peered down into it. Joel Goldman was wedged faceup in the middle of it, his body bent at the waist so that his legs were sticking up over the edge. He was conscious and moaning in pain, pressing his hand against a big, bloody wound in his right shoulder.

I was so relieved that Goldman was alive that I almost cried. But instead I kept my gun leveled on him and forced myself to look him right in the eye when I spoke.

"Are you afraid of me now?"

He nodded, gritting his teeth against the tremendous pain. I nodded, too.

"Then I guess we've both learned something today," I said. "You're under arrest."

Monk stepped up beside me. "Are you okay?"

I thought about it for a moment so that I was sure of the answer myself.

"Yes," I said, "I am."

CHAPTER THIRTY-ONE:
MR. MONK
MAKES A BIG DECISION

Our next two weeks, compared to our first few days, were relatively uneventful.

I didn't have any regrets or go into much soul-searching about my actions at Spirit Lake and didn't suffer any stress over it, either. I really was okay with shooting Joel Goldman. I don't know how I would have felt, though, if I'd killed him.

Monk and I continued patrolling Summit, New Jersey, on the day shift, dealing mostly with traffic violations, a few drunk-and-disorderly calls, and we arrested a serial shoplifter. No major crimes or murders were committed, much to my relief.

When we weren't working, I honed my shooting skills at the firing range with Evie, who I gradually grew to like quite a bit, much to my astonishment and probably to hers as well.

But that wasn't nearly the most surprising relationship that developed in Summit over those weeks. That honor would have to go to Adrian Monk and Ellen Morse.

Monk spent almost all of his free time with her. Although he still wouldn't set foot in Poop, he had no qualms about being in her house, where they worked together on assembling a ten-thousand-piece jigsaw puzzle of George Chambers's painting of the 1916 naval bombardment of Algiers by the British and Dutch fleets.

They probably completed the whole puzzle together in an hour and just kept repeating the process every night, but that's a guess on my part.

Beyond telling us about the puzzle, and praising her culinary talent, organizing prowess, and exemplary sanitary habits (with the exception of her business, of course), Monk didn't talk much about their time together, despite frequent and persistent interrogations by me and Sharona.

Things might have continued along indefinitely like that if not for the call I got from Captain Stottlemeyer on my cell phone one night at Sharona's house.

"How's it going out there?" he asked.

"Randy's got the city government running more or less smoothly and crime is at a bare minimum," I said. "The scandal is still in the news every day, but he's not part of the story anymore. The powers-that-be in Trenton, and the people in town, seem to have faith in his stewardship."

"Great. So, when are you planning to come back? Monk has a pay-or-play consulting contract with us. The payroll department wants to know if we're suspending it and, if so, for how long. I'm kind of curious about that myself."

We'd been so caught up in the flow of things, we hadn't given any thought to our return. But now that Stottlemeyer had brought it up, I started thinking about how nice it would be to sleep in my own bed instead of on Disher's couch.

"Let me talk to Mr. Monk and Randy about it and I'll get right back to you."

"I'd appreciate that. But from what I hear, you seem pretty comfortable wearing the badge and uniform. Are you thinking of a career change?"

"Are you offering me a job?"

"The department is always on the lookout for qualified men and women who are willing to serve. But I couldn't fast-track you the way Randy did. You'd probably have to go through the academy training program. Law enforcement here in the big city is a whole lot tougher than it is out in Summit."

"I'm well aware of that," I said.

"I'm just reminding you, that's all. You've got a good thing going now. You might want to think twice before you walk away from it."

"What thing are you referring to?" I said. "My job here or my job with Mr. Monk?"

"I'll be waiting for your call. Give my best to everyone."

And then he hung up, pointedly avoiding my question. But his comment made me think of something Sharona had said to me one night two weeks ago.

Who says you have to go back?

I thought about the questions he'd raised and wondered why I hadn't been thinking about them myself. Stottlemeyer was right. I was enjoying my new job. But was it something I wanted to make permanent?

But then I started to think about my life in San Francisco. Although my daughter was an adult now, and on her own, she was only across the bay in Berkeley, close enough for me to still see her often. How much longer would that last?

And I still lived in the home that Mitch and I bought together. Next to Julie, it was the one thing I had left that we had all shared together. Was I willing to walk away from it and make a clean break from my past?

That still left open the possibility of being a cop in San Francisco. Was that something I really wanted? Wasn't I already a de facto homicide detective? How important was it to me to wear a badge and carry a gun? And did I want the responsibilities, and dangers, that came with it? And did I want to be a cop if I wasn't partnered with Monk?

Those were big questions to consider and I hadn't even talked to Monk or Disher yet.

So I went into the kitchen, where everyone was gathered around the table, watching Monk cutting a pan of fresh brownies into squares using a compass, a tape measure, string, a knife, and a spatula.

Strings were stretched taut across the pan in evenly spaced horizontal and vertical rows and taped to the edges. Monk was preparing to cut, using the strings as his guide.

"That was Captain Stottlemeyer," I said. "He's wondering when we're coming back."

Disher leaned back in his seat. "He's been on me for a couple of days about that, but I've been stalling him."

"Are you still having trouble finding two candidates to replace us?" Monk asked as he cut into the brownies with the precision and concentration of a coronary surgeon performing a quadruple bypass.

"I've found a few good candidates. But to be honest, I've been putting off a decision because I figured the longer I waited, the more likely it was that you two would consider staying."

"Both of us?" I said.

"Absolutely, though I'm making the offer to each of you individually. You don't have to both agree to it."

I sat down.

Monk stopped cutting the brownies and sat down, too.

This was a big decision.

"I've spent my entire life in the Bay Area," Monk said.

"Maybe that's reason enough to make a change," Sharona said. "You could have a new life here, Adrian, one that's slower and less stressful, and Ellen could be a part of it. We all could. You'd be among family."

"But Ambrose is there," Monk said.

"He's got a motor home now," Sharona said. "He can come out and visit. In fact, you being here would be a strong motivation to get him to leave the house, hit the open road, and see the country."

Monk shifted from side to side in his seat as he mulled it all over.

Disher looked at me. "What about you, Natalie? What do you have holding you in

San Francisco?"

"Mr. Monk, for one thing."

"Okay, let's say he decided to come here, or at least gave you his blessing to leave, then what have you got back there?"

"Memories," I said.

"Me, too," Monk said.

"You can bring your memories with you wherever you go," Sharona said. "You don't need your homes for that."

She had made a good point.

I looked at Monk.

He looked at me.

"What do you think, Mr. Monk?"

He thought about it for a long moment, rolled his shoulders, and then came to a decision. . . .

ABOUT THE AUTHOR

Lee Goldberg has written episodes for the USA Network television series *Monk,* as well as many other programs. He is a two-time Edgar® Award nominee and the author of the acclaimed *Diagnosis Murder* novels, based on the TV series for which he was a writer and executive producer. His previous *Monk* novels are available in paperback, including *Mr. Monk and the Two Assistants,* which won the Scribe Award for Best Novel from the International Association of Media Tie-In Writers.

The employees of Thorndike Press hope you have enjoyed this Large Print book. All our Thorndike, Wheeler, and Kennebec Large Print titles are designed for easy reading, and all our books are made to last. Other Thorndike Press Large Print books are available at your library, through selected bookstores, or directly from us.

For information about titles, please call:
  (800) 223-1244

or visit our Web site at:
  http://gale.cengage.com/thorndike

To share your comments, please write:
  Publisher
  Thorndike Press
  10 Water St., Suite 310
  Waterville, ME 04901